A Costly Affair

Caroline Rebisz

No part of this book may be reproduced, scanned or distributed in any printed or electronic form without permission in writing from the author. Please do not participate or encourage piracy of any copyrighted material in violation of the author's rights.

Any trademarks, service marks, or names featured are assumed to be the property of their respective owners and are only used for reference. There is no endorsement, implied or otherwise, if any terms are used.

A Costly Affair is a work of fiction. Any similarities to persons living or dead, places or locations are purely coincidental. The author holds all rights to this work and it is illegal to reproduce any part of this novel without the author's expressed consent.

Copyright © 2021 Caroline Rebisz

All rights reserved.

ISBN: 979-8-5266-6970-2

DEDICATION

For my family Alan, Danuta and Beth who inspire and support my writing.

CONTENTS

Acknowledgements

1	Chapter One	Pg 1
2	Chapter Two	Pg 8
3	Chapter Three	Pg 17
4	Chapter Four	Pg 22
5	Chapter Five	Pg 30
6	Chapter Six	Pg 36
7	Chapter Seven	Pg 42
8	Chapter Eight	Pg 46
9	Chapter Nine	Pg 50
10	Chapter Ten	Pg 54
11	Chapter Eleven	Pg 60
12	Chapter Twelve	Pg 65
13	Chapter Thirteen	Pg 69
14	Chapter Fourteen	Pg 72
15	Chapter Fifteen	Pg 79
16	Chapter Sixteen	Pg 83
17	Chapter Seventeen	Pg 88
18	Chapter Eighteen	Pg 94
19	Chapter Nineteen	Pg 98
20	Chapter Twenty	Pg 102
21	Chapter Twenty-One	Pg 107

22	Chapter Twenty-Two	Pg 111
23	Chapter Twenty-Three	Pg 116
24	Chapter Twenty Four	Pg 119
25	Chapter Twenty-Five	Pg 123
26	Chapter Twenty-Six	Pg 128
27	Chapter Twenty-Seven	Pg 132
28	Chapter Twenty-Eight	Pg 135
29	Chapter Twenty-Nine	Pg 139
30	Chapter Thirty	Pg 145
31	Chapter Thirty-One	Pg 151
32	Chapter Thirty-Two	Pg 157
33	Chapter Thirty-Three	Pg 163
34	Chapter Thirty-Four	Pg 167
35	Chapter Thirty-Five	Pg 170
36	Chapter Thirty-Six	Pg 173
37	Chapter Thirty-Seven	Pg 178
38	Chapter Thirty-Eight	Pg 183
39	Chapter Thirty-Nine	Pg 186
40	Chapter Forty	Pg 192
41	Chapter Forty-One	Pg 196
42	Chapter Forty-Two	Pg 204
43	Chapter Forty-Three	Pg 208
44	Chapter Forty-Four	Pg 214

45	Chapter Forty-Five	Pg 223
46	Chapter Forty-Six	Pg 226
47	Chapter Forty-Seven	Pg 228
48	Chapter Forty-Eight	Pg 231
49	Chapter Forty-Nine	Pg 239
50	Chapter Fifty	Pg 247
51	Chapter Fifty-One	Pg 250
52	Chapter Fifty-Two	Pg 255
53	Chapter Fifty-Three	Pg 260
54	Chapter Fifty-Four	Pg 263

ACKNOWLEDGMENTS

Thank you to my family for indulging my passion for writing. They patiently listen to my stories and progress reports. My long suffering husband, Alan and my daughters Danuta and Beth who encourage me and humour me. My mother, Pamela, who hopefully will not read this book or at least skip over the naughty bits. My love of reading was developed at her knee.

A special thank you to my friend Helen Mudge who kindly agreed to proof-read my document. Your attention to detail has been invaluable and hopefully saved my blushes.

PART ONE – THE AFFAIR

CHAPTER ONE

"Excuse me. Is anyone sitting here?" Those few simple words would change the course of my life. Irrevocably.

The voice was deep and strong with a hint of a Northern accent. Frustratingly, my concentration was broken. With a sigh, I raised my gaze from the laptop. I made eye contact with the unknown perpetrator. Fixing him with a glare may do the trick. Hopefully, my look of irritation would put him off and send him on his way. I was desperate to have the table to myself for the entirety of the journey. Greedy I know, but a mountain of emails needed my attention this morning.

Wow. I wasn't ready for the vision in front of me.

Or the consequences this chance meeting would have on my life.

The man was Adonis in the flesh.

Over six feet tall, with the frame and devilish good looks of a Greek god. His chestnut-coloured hair was closely cropped; his face neatly framed by a stubbly beard. A broad smile lit up his face, which was chiselled within an inch of its life. Resembling a typical City gent, he was immaculately turned out, in a well fitted suit with a fashionable overcoat hanging over his arm. The other arm held, what looked like, an expensive Maxwell Scott briefcase. My eyes rested on the case, instantly envious and thinking of my own battered and well-used receptacle.

It was those eyes that did it for me. Deep brown pools of desire which seemed to bore into my soul, ensnaring me instantly. Some sort of bumbling idiot took me over as I scrabbled to move my papers around to make space for my new companion.

"Sorry, yes. No… I mean no. There's no-one sitting there." I'm struggling to string a coherent sentence together. What the hell is wrong with me? I'm the definition of uber confident, not this poor excuse for a woman behaving like she has never seen an attractive bloke before.

The Adonis took his seat after carefully placing his overcoat and jacket in the overhead storage. I couldn't help but check out his firm buttocks as he reached up overhead. His body was lean and tight, like a panther, as he stretched to reach the top shelf. His shirt was pristine white and fitted his torso like a second skin.

I really must stop staring at him like this, I admonished myself. He will think I'm some sort of pervert. Surely he is used to the stares, with a body like that. Just don't let him catch me looking. So embarrassing.

And so not me.

Get a grip woman, I thought to myself as I tried to take control of my senses. I played for time by plugging in my laptop charger whilst slowing down my breathing. To say I was shocked at my reaction is an understatement. I'm used to working with good-looking men, but this beautiful specimen had certainly unsettled me. At work I've built a reputation as the ice queen. That fact certainly didn't bother me and, to be fair, I tended to encourage the perception. It helps to keep a sensible distance when you head up the Human Resources department and share a bed with the Chief Executive of the company.

Let me set the scene for you.

I was on the 7.07 a.m. train from London Euston to Manchester Piccadilly. We had just stopped at Milton Keynes where my handsome companion joined the train. I'm on my way to an overnight conference of UK HR Directors. A fun-packed event which will involve numerous boring presentations then dinner followed by copious amounts of wine. One of the perks of the job or the downside of the role, depending on where you stand on the copious amounts of wine stance.

Having got my breathing under control, it seemed a good time to take another look. As I raised my eyes, I could see that my companion was looking straight at me. Shit. Straight at me without even lowering his gaze as my eyes connected with his. The confidence of this man was shocking. Isn't it normal practice to look away when caught staring, not just continue brazenly?

"Hi there," he smiled. "Dave. Dave Roberts."

He offered his hand across the table. Those eyes smiled at me, along with his twitching lips which seemed to be stifling a grin. God, I hope he hasn't noticed the obvious impact he is having on me.

I cleared my throat, frantically swallowing down the saliva which filled my mouth. "Hello. I'm Madeline Saville. Nice to meet you." I took his hand which was warm to the touch. His hands were soft and fingers well groomed. Fancy noticing the state of his nails at this point. "Have you got enough room there? Sorry, there never seems to be enough room on these trains." I made an exaggerated move to pull my laptop nearer to my side of the table, making space.

"Nice to meet you, Madeline. Don't worry I have plenty of room. I'm not as committed as you," he grinned as he continued. "I don't plan to do any work this morning. Just a quick shifty at the paper and hopefully enjoy the company of a beautiful lady."

I swear he winked at me. How crass.

But I'm flattered.

Why?

The alarm bells should have been ringing at this comment, but my inner vanity came rushing to the fore. It was so obviously 'un-PC' but I literally giggled as I soaked up the compliment.

This is just not me.

I am an extraordinarily sensible woman. I'm director of Human Resources for a large financial institution, so fully compliant when dealing with the opposite sex. Especially an attractive member of the opposite sex, who knows it too. Some would say I am boringly predictable. That's my job and I'm extremely proud of my expertise in the area of employment law. I don't usually fall for the flattery of charmers.

Well, I didn't, until Dave Roberts came crashing into my life.

Thankfully, my blushes were spared by the arrival of the first-class carriage hostess offering breakfast and drinks. My usual start to the day included yogurt and muesli with fresh orange juice. I had no intention of doing anything different today, although I was suitably jealous watching Dave tuck into a full English. The smell was amazing. I can't remember the last time I had treated myself to a greasy carb-heavy breakfast. It just wasn't the sort of thing my new family did. The smell reminded me of my own working-class roots prior to meeting Charles.

I took great delight in watching Dave enjoying his food. He ate with precision movements, piling a piece of sausage, mushroom and egg on his fork and expertly negotiating its way into his mouth without any spillage. He had tucked his tie into his shirt front, with the napkin tucked gently into his collar. It shouldn't have been a good look, but Dave carried it off. There was something seductive in the way he ate, whilst casting glances in my direction.

Every time I looked at him, he was looking at me. We were making conversation with our eyes. Dancing around each other without words.

I finished my yogurt and was sipping my cappuccino as the hostess returned to clear away the remnants. It was fascinating to watch Dave's indifference to the young girl serving us. She was an attractive young lady with a bubbly personality. It was clear she was flirting with Dave. I noticed that her top button had miraculously come undone since she first served his breakfast. He didn't seem to notice the attention. Perhaps he is just used to women going silly around him, I thought, as I watched the poor girl trying her hardest to get his attention.

Once she had given up and left us in peace, Dave retrieved his newspaper, The Times, of course, from the seat beside him and started to flick through. I took that as my cue to get back to my emails. I'm usually on top of things at work, thanks to my brilliant PA, Stacey.

She is the most amazing asset to my work life. Every morning she would review my inbox and organise the numerous items into those that needed my personal attention and those which she could action on my behalf. I had got into the habit of only reviewing my electronic work once in the morning and before I left work at the end of the day, as I was confident that anything urgent would be flagged by Stacey, often with comments for action or a suggested reply. My PA was keen to progress and grabbed hold of opportunities with both hands, keen to grow her experience. All of which was to my advantage. Unfortunately for me, Stacey was taking a few days off to coincide with this conference. Her boyfriend was taking her to Rome for a romantic long weekend, which she fully deserved. I had been piling the pressure on her recently, so the time was right for her to recharge her batteries.

"So, Madeline, if you don't mind me asking, are you going all the way?" There was a pregnant pause before he continued. "To Manchester that is?" Dave folded his paper and placed it back in his briefcase. O-M-G even his conversation is seductive in a 'Carry-On movie' manner.

I looked up from my keyboard in mid stroke, "I am. Yes. I have a conference to go to, hence the early start. You?"

"Small world. I am at a conference in Manchester for the next two days. Recruitment and Employment strategy for the 21st Century." Dave pulled his conference pack from his briefcase as he spoke.

"Seriously? Wow, small world. I'm going to the exact same one. At the Pendulum Hotel."

I certainly don't believe in fate, but it was more than weird to find we were both going to the same event. I had got to know so many of my peer group from across the country over the last five years and had never come across Dave at any of these sessions. The events were usually a great opportunity to catch up with old friends and share challenges and experiences. It was strange, but true, that these same colleagues only met up once a year, but naturally fell back into friendships which were all too quickly forgotten at the end of day two.

Dave had been leafing through his paperwork and suddenly came to an abrupt stop. He glanced back up at me as the penny dropped. "M Saville, keynote speaker. Recruiting Attitude above Skill. Main conference hall at 11am today. So that's you then? I didn't make the connection. Crikey your photo on the agenda pack doesn't do you justice at all."

Dave laughed as he pointed at the aged photo which had been used over a number of years at the annual conference. It wasn't the most flattering of photos and, if I remember rightly, it had been taken after a fairly heavy night.

"Well yes. I really should update that photo, but I guess you get complacent as I know most of the key attendees. Interestingly I don't think we have met before, have we? Have you been to this conference before Dave?" I too had pulled out my paperwork and was quickly scanning the attendees to try and work out who Dave must work for.

"No, it's my first time," Dave responded. He must have spotted my intentions and continued. "I have recently taken on a new role at South Western Bank, heading up their Head Office HR function. My boss thought it would be a great idea to attend this conference as a networking opportunity. And of course, to see what best practice ideas I could bring back and employ. We are a fairly new organisation so we are trying to pull the best disciplines from other companies. Actually, I'm in the process of creating my team to be based in Bristol so I am keen to make some connections too."

"Oh, that sounds really exciting. The chance to pick and develop your own team is amazing. In most new jobs you end up having to take on a team and try to shape it into your own which is so tough. Changing habits can take so much longer than recruiting the best fit to your team don't you think?"

I had joined Saville Financial Planning Ltd straight from university and had been grateful for the chance to put my learning into practise. My meteoric rise to head of HR had taken a great deal of hard work and a huge slice of luck. The malicious amongst you may say that marrying the boss must have helped, but I hold firm that my ability got me to where I am. Marrying Charles was just a by-product of working so closely together.

"I'm really excited about the role. I only received my appointment contract three weeks ago so it's all new and interesting at the moment. And of course, I need to up sticks and move down to Bristol in the near future. I don't want to be doing the commute across country for too long," sighed Dave.

I couldn't help checking out his ring finger before I asked the personal question you should never ask someone who has been blatantly flirting with you; unless you want to take it further, of course. "Are you married then Dave? Does that mean uprooting your family?"

"No not me. Free as a bird," he smiled and if I'm not mistaken winked at me again. "Divorced two years ago, so happily single and no kids to worry about. It does make it so much easier when work takes you to new places."

"True. Well, I think you will find a few delegates come from the South West so may be useful contacts. Let me make some introductions for you over lunch later. Come and find me after my slot and I will see what I can do for you." I already knew of a couple of acquaintances that would be ripe for a conversation and were looking for fresh challenges.

"Thank you, Madeline. That's very kind of you. I owe you a drink for that. Perhaps we can catch up over a glass of wine later?" His eyes captured me in his piercing gaze as if to seal the deal.

"I'd like that, Dave. Catch you in the bar tonight."

How was I to know that this innocent conversation was the start of a dangerous series of events which would send my perfect family into a spiral of chaos and hurt? This man would bring me to my knees. His revenge would have far reaching consequences.

He would destroy all that I held sacred.

One chance meeting. Or was it?

If I had known what was to come, would I have stopped it?

Could I have stopped it?

Hindsight is a wonderful tool but one that wasn't available to me as I sat on that train enjoying the company of Dave Roberts. Unknown to me then, I had embarked on a journey that there was no coming back from.

CHAPTER TWO

I swiped the key card and put my shoulder to the door, balancing overnight bag, briefcase, and coffee cup.

Dropping my bags on the black leather sofa, I looked around the executive suite, a reward for speaking at the conference. Most of the delegates would be in the standard doubles so I knew I was being treated to the space and extra comfort. The hotel was a firm favourite for the annual conference as, whilst it wasn't the plushest in Manchester, it was great value for money and had catered extremely well for our group over the last few years. I have got to know the manager and many of the staff over the years which also helped in terms of the upgrade.

The room was dominated by a comfortable looking king-size bed, flat screen TV on the facing wall, with both sofa and desk area so I could do some work before the sessions started again tomorrow morning. An ornate flower display added a welcoming touch to the room. I glanced longingly at the plunge bath, wishing I had the time to kick back and relax in bubble-infused water. Unfortunately, time was against me. I had less than an hour to change for dinner.

As I drained the last dregs of coffee, my thoughts were interrupted by the shrill of my 'evening breeze' ring tone. I'm not the most adventurous when it comes to my mobile phone so had opted for the least offensive ring tone I could find. I hated listening to those dreadful individuals who had crazy outlandish ringers that must have seemed funny when they set them up, but when it goes off in the midst of a meeting, is bone crushingly embarrassing.

Swiping right, I answered the call. "Good afternoon, Madeline Saville speaking."

"Darling, it's Charles. How are you? Has your day been successful?" My husband was clearly still in the office as my call record showed an unknown number.

"Charles. Are you not home yet?" I sighed. "You promised you wouldn't be late tonight as Jessica is going out. Don't you remember?"

Jessica is our live-in nanny who cared for our two children, Sophie and James.

"Don't panic darling. It's all under control. Gerald is picking me up in five minutes and will have me home before Jessica needs to leave. I've checked in with her and she's happy to hold on until I get there. Now tell me how did your presentation go?"

One of the perks of Charles's job was the use of the company chauffeur, which meant that he didn't have to struggle into the office in Fenchurch Street on the underground from our home in Richmond. I personally enjoyed the trip on the District line each morning rather than arrive at work with Charles in the Bentley. However, I'm not adverse to taking advantage of his perk after a long, tough day in the office.

"It went really well, thank you Charles. I had some really interesting questions in the open forum afterwards too. I hope you don't mind though, darling, but I'm really pushed for time. I've only just checked into my room. I got chatting with Geraldine Spencer after the close. You know what Gerry is like once she gets going. I just couldn't get away and now I need to shower and get ready for dinner."

"Alright Madeline. I understand how it is. Well, you have a lovely evening. What sort of time do you think you will be home tomorrow? Shall I order takeout for when you are back?"

Charles was lost in the kitchen. No that's a lie. He was an expert with the wine fridge but he relied on his wives, both me and his first wife, Catherine, to keep his belly fed.

"My train gets into Euston at 7pm so I should be home by 8pm at the latest. I'll text you and let you know how it's going. Takeout will be lovely thanks. Can you give the kids a big kiss from their mummy when you get home? I seriously don't have time to ring home now. Sorry. Goodbye Charles."

I didn't wait for my husband to respond before cutting the line. Dropping my mobile on the bed, I reached round the back of my neck to grab my zip pull. The tight-fitting blue dress fell to the floor as I slipped out of my Jimmy Choo shoes. Underwear joined my dress on the carpet as I headed for the shower.

Standing under the hot, streaming water I reflected on the day.

I had enjoyed the trip up to Manchester. Having Dave's company helped the long train trip fly past. He was a good companion and once we had got past that initial flirting, we had a constructive conversation about all things work related. Other than my nosey question about his marital status, we had steered clear of any personal discussion. We had shared a taxi to the venue and then went our separate ways; me to the speakers' lounge for a full briefing, and he to the general delegate area. I had seen him at lunchtime when I had arranged to introduce him to a couple of contacts.

It was strange but I felt a bit jealous that they had then gone off to lunch together leaving me behind.

My presentation was textbook. I enjoy sharing my knowledge with others and had never been fazed by the thought of standing on stage in front of my peer group. Not blowing my own trumpet but I'm not a bad presenter. As a speaker, my table was right at the front of the conference room. Tonight, the tables for dinner were mixed up again so I looked forward to meeting some new colleagues over food. The bar would be open until midnight, so tomorrow's session was shorter, starting at 10am and finishing by 3pm.

I'm certainly glad not to be scheduled into day 2. It was always a tough gig to present during the graveyard shift when the delegates were struggling with various degrees of hangover. Not that I'm saying we are not totally professional at these annual conferences but let's face it, it happens.

Within the hour I had managed to dry and style my hair and redo my make-up. Tonight, I was wearing a navy Mao silk dress from Reiss. The style fell flatteringly from my full bust in ripples with a silk belt pinching in, emphasising my slim waist. I had struggled into lace hold-up stockings. A suspender belt would not work with the style of dress, but I do dislike hold-ups. You spend the night either worrying if you might find your stockings round your ankles or losing the blood supply to your legs. I believe the latter might be the case tonight. My sapphire necklace and matching earrings finished the look, a wedding present from Charles to match my

Princess Diana style engagement ring.

I made my grand entrance to the bar moments later.

A number of male delegates gave me appreciative glances, which was flattering. For some reason there was one set of eyes I wanted to see watching me. Scanning the room, I saw him. He was leaning against the bar, deep in conversation with Jerry Hill from Barclays. As I watched, his eyes left Jerry's face. We made eye contact across the room.

I felt butterflies fighting for space in my stomach. It's crazy. I feel like a schoolgirl with her first crush. I'm a married woman. This really shouldn't be happening to me but for some reason I just can't seem to help myself. It's that part of your head that tells you the hotplate on a cooker is burning hot, but it still takes seconds for your brain to tell you to move your hand away.

Pain is inevitable. As I would find out soon enough.

I knew this was so wrong but for some reason I just couldn't stop myself falling.

Wandering over towards the bar I'm trying to act cool. Smiling at Jerry, I joined the two men.

"Madeline, lovely to see you again. Can I get you a drink?"

Dave gently placed his hand on my shoulder as he spoke. The touch is too familiar. As if we have known each other for years; not five minutes.

I should be offended.

I'm not.

"Thank you, Dave. A G&T would be lovely." I smiled as I turned slightly away from Dave. "How have you enjoyed today Jerry?"

Regaining control, I engaged Jerry in a professional conversation about the format of this year's event. Dave listened in, making appropriate comments during breaks in the discussion. To the outsider there was nothing untoward. We were three colleagues discussing our day, over a drink.

The reality was an undercurrent of two people fizzling with sexual attraction, trying their hardest to hide it.

At dinner I was surprisingly relieved to find that Dave wasn't on my table. I should have been disappointed, but it did allow me to enjoy the evening and relax amongst friends. The hotel had lived up to its usual high standards with an excellent three-course meal.

We were finally finished and relaxing over coffee and chocolates when Dave wandered over to my table. Waiting for a break in the conversation, he took a seat beside me.

"Madeline, I was wondering if I could impose on you," he started. "You mentioned that we could have a catch-up tonight so was hoping I could steal you away." He smiled apologetically at my fellow table companions.

"Of course. I did promise. My apologies all." I glanced around the table acknowledging my friends. "Thank you for your delightful company tonight." A chorus of voices reciprocated and a number of glasses were raised in appreciation of a night well spent.

Picking up my clutch bag, I got to my feet and took Dave's outstretched arm. Together we wandered back into the bar area and found a secluded booth where we could talk with an element of privacy. Within moments the barman had taken our orders.

"I've missed your company today, Madeline. Everyone seems to want a piece of you so I feel pretty epic to have you to myself now." Dave swirled his whiskey in his hand as he fixed his deep brown eyes on me.

"Are you flirting with me?" I whispered as I caressed my brandy.

"I think I am. Do you mind? No, don't answer that one," laughed Dave. "I don't want to be devastated by your answer. I couldn't help noticing the bling on your left hand. I guess that means some chap has got there first."

I glanced down at my rings, turning my hand back and forth as the diamonds winked in the subdued lightning. I should have stopped the conversation at that point but, like a moth to a flame, I was destined to get burnt.

"Very observant of you. Yes, I am married. To Charles. For the last seven years." I looked at him, confident that he would back away at this point.

"Are you happy?"

What a question to ask. We'd only just met. Surely this was way too personal a question.

Was I happy?

I guess if I was to find a word to describe our marriage it would be content.

I met Charles through work. He was my boss and during my first couple of years with the company we had become good friends. Charles was single, having been divorced from Catherine some years before. He was over twenty years my senior so this whole relationship thing should never have worked. But it had. I liked him. He was good company. He had position and power and could give me the finer things in life.

I swallowed as I looked across the table at Dave. "I don't know. If I'm happy that is. Does that sound really bad?"

Looking intently into my eyes, he took my hand under the table discreetly. "It doesn't sound bad, Madeline, but it does sound sad. You are the most beautiful woman I have met in such a long time. Beautiful and successful, both incredibly sexy attributes. You should be appreciated; worshipped. Not just exist in a marriage. Oh god, sorry. That's bang out of order. Not my place to say."

Inside, those butterflies had returned. I can't remember the last time I felt so attracted to someone, especially someone who, to all intents and purposes, was a stranger. It just felt so exciting. I never flirted but for some reason I was falling for his game.

I don't know if there was a point during this evening when I could have backed away gracefully and none of this would have happened. Knowing what I know now, I should have run a mile.

Fast.

"I really can't complain," I continued softly, conscious that I didn't want anyone overhearing. "I have a lovely house, a comfortable lifestyle and two adorable children whom I wouldn't be without. Most women would kill to get what I have."

"But when was the last time you had fun? Did something impetuous? Got your blood racing?" As Dave spoke, he stroked his fingers in circles around my palm. It was an intimate act, but one which I couldn't pull away from. It had a mesmerising effect on me. I was trapped in his stare. I was the proverbial rabbit in the headlights.

"You are a bad man, Dave Roberts. You don't know anything about me really." If I was sensible, I would have admonished him but to my surprise my voice came out gravelly and almost sexy. "Shall we have another drink?" I raised my hand to catch the attention of the waiter.

That movement broke the intimacy. We both seemed to step back from the brink.

For a while, at least.

For the following hour we relaxed in each other's company and spoke like friends. The flirting departed as quickly as it had invaded our thoughts. I enjoyed Dave's company. He had a brilliant sense of humour which had me in stitches. He had the ability to mimic others and his observations on many of our fellow delegates were clever and amusing. Time passed at speed. I had a couple more brandies which, after wine with dinner, were going to my head. I didn't feel drunk, but I was relaxing more than I would normally in company. I would have loved to slip off my shoes and tuck my feet up under me. Luckily, my natural reservations stopped me.

I glanced at my watch and spotted that it was fast approaching midnight. If I was going to stand a chance of working in the morning, then my bed was the next priority.

"Dave, I have had the most amazing evening. Thank you. You are such good company. Just what I needed. But now I need my bed. Do you mind?" I was gathering my phone and clutch bag together as I spoke.

"Madeline, let me walk you back to your room. I don't want you wandering around this hotel on your own," Dave smiled as he offered his arm.

I didn't need him to walk me to my room. We were on completely different floors. My behaviour was sending signals to him. Signals he wasn't going to ignore. I have to take some responsibility for what was about to happen. It wasn't just him.

We continued chatting as we rode the lift to the executive floor. Fumbling for my key card I opened the door. Somehow, I was through the door with Dave following me. Not a word was spoken.

As I turned to face him, Dave cupped my face in his hands and stared deeply into my eyes. Slowly he lowered his lips to mine and kissed me. Gently caressing my lips with his, I could feel his stubble on my cheeks. He forced my lips apart and the kiss progressed to deep passionate tongue caresses. His arms moved around my waist as I lifted my arms to touch his shoulders. Passion grew as we kissed. I was lost in desire, feeling emotions I don't think I knew existed.

Dave's fingers worked at the silk belt holding my wraparound dress together. Freeing the belt, the fabric shimmered to the ground leaving me exposed. Our lips parted as Dave drunk in my body.

I didn't feel embarrassed. Under his intense gaze, I felt incredibly sexy.

"Oh Maddy, you are exquisite," he panted in my neck as his hands fumbled to remove my bra. Inwardly I was relieved that I always insisted on quality matching underwear. How embarrassing it would be if I had my granny knickers on. When my mum warned me about always having matching underwear on, this was obviously not the sort of situation she was referring to.

I pulled at his tie, whilst he struggled out of his jacket. With nimble fingers I worked on his shirt, pulling it off his torso. His chest was hairless and tanned golden. Running my fingers across his abdomen, I found his trouser belt and continue to explore.

We made our way across to the bed, falling together. Rolling me over him, Dave positioned me on top. He took my breasts in his hands, working his fingers around my full nipples then dragged me down to his mouth.

I was lost.

And so it began.

Could I have stopped it all then?

Not a chance.

CHAPTER THREE

Daylight streamed through a gap in the curtains.

Struggling to open my eyes, I rolled onto my side. Fumbling for my mobile, I press the screen looking for the time. 8am. Oh god I feel dreadful. My head is banging with the aftereffects of those brandies. As I slowly start to regain consciousness, I realise I'm naked. Touching my body, I can feel soreness around my nipples.

My body feels different.

I reek of sex.

It's not unpleasant although I can feel myself blushing with embarrassment. As I explore my body further, I feel the soreness. I ache down below but in a very nice way.

Last night comes back to me in a rush of emotions. We made love for hours. I can't remember the last time I didn't have to fake it. I'm not saying Charles does not try to please me, but we have got used to a conventional love life and the excitement died years ago.

Last night took me to heights I could only have imagined.

Dave was an amazing and considerate lover who had taken his pleasure only once I had been spent. He had worshiped at the temple of my body. My body which has come alive, at last. It made me realise I have been sleeping through my marriage for years.

What have I done?

Sitting upright in bed, guilt slaps me in the face. Clutching the bedcovers to my chest I try to examine how I feel. I'm ashamed of myself to have spent the night with another man. I have been unfaithful to Charles. How do I face him with that knowledge? I am so bloody selfish. I am so lucky to have a great life. Why am I throwing it away for a night of passion?

Oh, but it was an amazing night.

I feel a sense of completeness as a woman. God, I'm one hell of a sexy woman. It was fun. It was exciting. No-one ever need know about it. It's my secret. I feel liberated. Why should I feel guilty? I wouldn't hurt Charles and what he doesn't know about, can't hurt him.

Breaking through my thoughts, I heard water running. Flinging my legs over the bedside, I made my way towards the bathroom. The shower cubicle was steamed up and I could hear the sound of the water slapping on the glass walls. With a confidence I never knew I had, I opened the door and step inside.

Dave turned to face me with a beaming smile. "Hello beautiful. I didn't want to wake you. You looked so peaceful." As he spoke, he took me into his tender embrace.

We kissed.

Drinking deeply of each other we ignored our morning breath. Making love in a shower was another first. We soaped each other into a lather. Touching each other intimately, like lovers who had known each other's bodies for all time. Turning me to face the wall, Dave took me quickly.

We came together.

Rinsing ourselves we finally made it out of the cubicle and took our time drying each other with warm fluffy towels.

I can't believe this other woman, waking up with a strange man in her room. Confident in her nakedness despite knowing so little about this man. It just felt normal despite it being nothing like Madeline Saville's normal. I am quite prudish. As a couple, Charles and I didn't walk around naked, we made love in the dark in the missionary position. Last night I had learnt new things about my body, what it could do and what it had been yearning for all my adult life.

I have been reawakened.

Finally, I managed to make us coffee and we sat on the bed, draped in towels, to drink. We were both gasping for refreshment after a night of heavy alcohol and lovemaking. The complimentary biscuits were our only sustenance but enough for now.

"I had the most amazing night, Maddy." Dave took my hand and stared deeply into my eyes. "I don't want this to be a one-off. I really like you and I want to see you again."

My head was spinning with the reality of what he was suggesting. I hadn't even thought about what comes next. My head was still all over the place with guilty pleasure.

I should have said no.

Let him down gently and chalk it up to a moment of madness. Or a night of madness. And, of course, not forgetting that wonderful shower of madness.

I know what I should have done.

But I didn't.

"I would like to see you again, Dave. I enjoyed last night so much." I blushed as I thought about the things we had done together as strangers. "And this morning."

The elephant in the room was trumpeting in my ears. I tried to ignore it, but it was like a sledgehammer to my brain.

"It's not going to be easy though. I am married and I'm not going to hurt my husband. You must understand that." I took Dave's hand in mine, emphasising how difficult this was for me. "I can't promise you anything, Dave. But I can't just walk away from you either. So, can we take it one step at a time?"

His eyes didn't waver from my face as he nodded in agreement. "I will take whatever time I can get with you, Maddy. I know it's going to be difficult but if we both want this, we will find a way."

With his right hand he tucked my wet hair behind my ear lobe, kissing me seductively on the neck. A phone rang, breaking the moment. It was mine. Reaching across the bed, I fumbled to find it in the covers, letting the towel drop as I stretched. I could see it was our home number.

"Hi Madeline. It's Jessica. I hope you don't mind me calling but it's the children."

My heart jumped in panic. It was unusual for Jessica to call during the working day. "What's up Jessica? Has something happened?"

Dave looked at me with concern, hearing the worry in my voice. He mouthed "Everything ok?"

"Sorry Madeline. Nothing to worry about. It's just that Sophie wanted to talk to you. She was a bit upset that you didn't call last night so I had promised we would try you in the morning. Can I put her on?"

"Of course, Jessica. Hello darling. Are you being a good girl?"

My voice lightened as my precious girl took the line. Sophie is four going on fourteen. She came into the world in a rush and has continued ever since. She knows she can wind me and her father around her little finger. She's not spoilt but definitely understands how to be at the centre of everyone's attention. Sophie knows what she wants and Sophie usually gets it.

"Hello mummy. Are you coming home today, mummy? I miss you and James is being naughty. He keeps crying and pulling my hair. I don't like it, mummy. Please come home," her little voice pleaded down the phone, tugging at my heartstrings.

"Sophie sweetie, mummy has to work today but I will be home tonight. We can do something special at the weekend. Do you fancy the zoo? We can go and see the animals."

Bribing my daughter with a fun weekend was not great parenting, but needs must when balancing the demands of a hard-working executive and a mother. Then, if you add in mistress, that adds another level of guilt entirely.

Without shame, I giggled as Dave's hand worked its way up my leg finding my heat. It was so inappropriate but exhilarating at the same time.

"Promise mummy. Can we really go to the zoo? Wow that's fab. Jessie, mummy says we are going to the zoo." I could hear Jessica in the background as I persuaded my daughter to hand the phone back to her nanny.

"Jessica, I should be back home by about 8pm tonight so if you could just set expectations with the children. I will try and be back before they are asleep, but I can't guarantee that. If I take the children to the zoo tomorrow, then you are more than welcome to come with us or you can have the day off. Up to you."

"Ok Madeline. Leave it with me. Once I get the children settled this morning, I will strip the beds and get the sheets in the washing machine. Saves a bit of time for tomorrow. Have a great day and see you later."

Jessica is a godsend. She is a qualified nanny and had been with us for four years. Despite me employing a cleaner, Jessica helped out around the house and was very much part of the family. She had recently met another nanny, Bella. Over recent weeks they had been inseparable whenever they had free time. I wouldn't be surprised if Bella joined us at the zoo tomorrow.

Dropping the phone back on the bed, I turned back to Dave. "We have about an hour before the conference starts again. What shall we do then?"

"I can think of something," Dave groaned as he took me in his arms.

CHAPTER FOUR

Walking up the path to our front door, I see the lights blazing through the kitchen window.

Charles created a shadow as he strolled across to the island, depositing plates and cutlery. A shining image of the haven which is my home. Normal life resuming within the confines of our family nest. He glanced up, catching my eye as he heard the gate latch snap shut. He smiled, raising a hand in greeting.

My loving husband.

The man I have just betrayed.

Fishing in my bag for front door keys, I made my way into the hallway. Kicking off my shoes, I struggled out of my raincoat. It was a nightmare trying to find a space on the London Underground shaped coat rack. It was brimming over with an assortment of jackets and coats. I drop my overnight bag at the bottom of the staircase and draped the handle of my Mulberry handbag over the ornate pommel, standing proud at the end of the handrail.

I'm buying time before I have to face him.

My poor husband.

Employing a further delaying tactic, I shouted a greeting to Charles before running up the stairs. It was late and, in my heart, I know the children will be asleep but I was determined to catch them if I could. Tiptoeing across the spacious landing, I crept up to Sophie's door. Her nightlight was sending a warm protective glow, exposing the darkest corners of the room and reassuring my little darling that there were no such things as monsters.

Sophie lay on her front with her thumb in her mouth. Her sweaty hair stuck to her rosy face, relaxed in sleep. I could see the concentration dance its way across her brow as she sucked, with the other hand twirling a clump of hair around her middle finger. She had her favourite Lion King pyjamas on. Sophie loves animals and has been obsessed with lions since watching the film, hence her desire to visit the zoo at the weekend. Leaning over carefully, I kissed my little girl on the forehead, pushing her fringe away from her face. She snuffled but didn't wake.

James was asleep too. Still a baby at three years old, he enjoys a large cot. A toddler cot, almost full-sized with built in cupboards at one end and vertical safety bars ensuring he couldn't fall out in his sleep. James lay on his front also, with his little bottom stuck up in the air. My younger child wasn't fully potty trained so wore night-time pants which saved his bedding from a nightly wetting. He had wriggled around causing his covers to be bundled around his feet. Gently I pulled the duvet out from under his pyjamas and tucked him back under, stroking his forehead.

I was upset to have missed the children's night rituals.

The scope of my job resulted in me missing so many of those first steps and activities. It was tough but the inevitable price of success. I realise I am extremely fortunate in so many ways; having the opportunity to hold down a rewarding career and having the security of back up support. Jessica is my rock when it came to the children. She loves them, making sure they knew they were surrounded with affection, safety, and suitable role models. Over the years I had grown to value Jessica not only as a member of staff but as a friend; indeed, an integral part of our family unit. I honestly could not imagine my life without her in it.

As I paused on the landing a wave of guilt washed over me. I'm just so lucky to have the most adorable children. I live in this beautiful house which welcomes you in and protects you in a loving embrace. I have a husband who is good to me. He treats me as his equal. He values my thoughts and opinions. He puts me on a pedestal as his model wife. It's not being immodest to reveal that, in fact, he tells all our friends how lucky he is to have me as his wife.

The perfect wife has well and truly fallen off her pedestal and her golden crown is smashed to smithereens on the rocky ground of deceit.

Will Charles be able to see my cheating shame? Am I changed beyond recognition? Is there a moment when someone you love can look deep into your soul and see you for the wretch you are? At the height of infidelity, there is no reminder of what you could lose. That would be the perfect passion killer. Where was that little voice in my head last night?

I know I must face my husband. My delaying tactics are failing.

Inwardly pulling my spine straighter, I walk back into the kitchen to face the music. Charles is perched on one of our bar stools placed around the kitchen island. His face lights up as he sees me and moves towards me taking me into his embrace.

"Darling, good to have you home."

Charles kissed me gently on the cheek as he let go of me. It was the briefest of embraces, so different to the passion experienced over recent days. The hug spoke of safeness and normality. My rock to cling to after the buffeting of lovemaking last night.

Charles turned sixty at his last birthday, although his little ways make him seem so much older than the twenty-four-year age gap between us. My husband had lost much of his hair years ago and regularly shaved the top of his dome leaving a small ring of greying hairs surrounding his head, which resolutely remained in defiance. I fell for his kindly face; a face you would trust which was perfect for his profession. People want to trust the person who manages their fortunes and I guess my husband had learnt over the years to develop his image as the archetypal bank manager. He was always immaculately turned out. His suits were custom made and he would not leave the house without his matching tie and handkerchief combo.

"Charles, so good to be home. I missed you and the children. How have they been?"

Had I missed Charles? I don't know about that, but I certainly had missed Sophie and James.

Does that sound dreadful?

Don't answer that. I feel a bitch already. I don't need you to confirm that to me.

"They have been fine as far as I know. They were excited to have you back tonight and a bit disappointed they couldn't stay up for you. Jessica had a job trying to get them down."

Charles left the childrearing to me and Jessica. His second family was still too young to hold his full attention. My stepdaughter Amelia, however, was finally at an age where her father found his offspring interesting. Charles enjoyed the company of Amelia who, at 26, had a natural curiosity for life and was developing a drive and ambition which her father loved. It wasn't anything to do with favouritism. Just the fact that Charles doesn't really do small children. They amuse him but can't capture his imagination like his older daughter.

"I ordered in Thai. Is that alright with you Madeline?"

"Lovely. Thank you. I'd kill for a glass of wine too if you have a bottle open."

We shared our meal seated at the island which was the centre point of our expertly designed kitchen. The room had taken days of research and the support of a wonderful designer who had listened to how I used the space. The design was ergonomically planned to flow with the movements I would make during food preparation, even through to the location of sink and dishwasher. The colour scheme was classy white with black granite worktops.

Off to the side was a large utility room which housed washing machine and dryer with ample room for the ironing board. Not that I made use of that room. I had a wonderful Spanish lady, called Manuella, who visited twice weekly to clean the house, wash and iron all our clothes. She also dealt with our dry cleaning and generally kept the house running for me. Alongside Jessica, I honestly don't know how I would have coped without Manni.

The feast was excellent. Charles had ordered a couple of mains, including a green curry and beef stir fry, which we shared with noodles and some sweet chilli beans. All washed down with an excellent bottle of Chardonnay. As we ate, I filled my husband in with the details of the conference, obviously omitting a large part of the more personal detail.

Charles listened intently to my feedback on the event. My husband is a good listener, another quality I valued. All too often in business, I have come across powerful and important leaders who like the sound of their own voices to the detriment to others' views. Our team at Saville's look up to Charles as a great leader of the business. He communicates a clear strategy for our direction of travel and, more importantly, sets the standard for the culture and behaviours he expects his staff to display.

Our company culture was the principal reason I had chosen the subject of recruiting for attitude as my keynote speech this week. Charles and the executive team, of which I was a part, believe that we can train our staff to do the job, but you really cannot train people to have the right values and behaviours. You either have them or you don't. It has made our recruitment process more dynamic than the normal financial services interview process and I have really enjoyed playing a part in this groundbreaking approach.

Right values and behaviours! Seriously, I should have listened to my own preaching, considering my behaviour last night.

Once we finished our dinner, we decided to take our wine through to the snug rather than the formal lounge. The snug very much lives up to its name. We have two large sofas facing each other, divided by a chic glass coffee table which is laden down with books and magazines. We have a huge wide screen TV on the wall and music system underneath. The sofas are covered with faux fur throws and large cushions in myriad colours. This room is out of bounds for the children unless supervised, as is the formal lounge. This is our space for the adults when we entertain and for chilling out when it's just the two of us.

Charles sorts out the music as I flop back into the cushions. Ella Fitzgerald's sultry tones fill the room with warmth as 'Dream a Little Dream of Me' washes over me. I had never listened to any jazz before I got together with Charles. He has taught me to value the eclectic tastes in music which his wide selection of vintage LPs gives us. Relaxing into the folds of the sofa, Charles thumbs through The Times as he winds down from a busy day.

My phone pings disturbing the mood. I quickly turn the sound off to avoid annoying my husband. I take a quick glance at the screen to see the name Davina displayed. I smile. One of my new deceitful behaviours was to enter my lover's phone number into my phone in disguise. Charles would not dream of nosing at my personal phone, but I would hate for him to start doing so if he became suspicious.

I open the message. 'Hi Maddy, hope you got home ok. Missing you already D x.'

Glancing up to see if Charles was watching I type my response. 'I'm home. Thanks. Miss you too. M x.' I delete the text from Dave and my response immediately.

Shameful how quickly we learn deception tactics.

Within seconds a follow up text pings into my box. 'Have a lovely weekend and hopefully catch-up next week. D x.'

Keen to close off the conversation before Charles notices, I respond purely with a kiss and again delete the messages. I pick up my work laptop and start to shift through my emails. I had managed to clear a number on the train back to London as Dave had been booked on a different train to me. It was a shame not to spend more time with him, but the upside was that I was able to get ahead before the weekend. I was determined to spend time with the children this weekend. A mixture of work commitment guilt and my own shocking behaviour guilt.

"Oh Charles, I don't know whether Jessica told you, but I promised Sophie a trip to the zoo this weekend. Did you want to come? We're planning to go tomorrow."

Charles looked up at me over the rims of his glasses. I find his habit of doing so quite endearing. The children loved it, especially Sophie who would laugh as her Pappa cast an eye from over his glasses.

"I don't think so Madeline. If you don't mind. I was going to meet Jeremy for a round of golf." Charles tried to play weekly to keep his handicap up. It was a huge asset in business and many a future deal or business relationship was cemented over a drink at the 19th hole.

I'm not unhappy with my husband's decision. The children were often more subdued when their father was around. He is generally serious and that behaviour had an impact on family dynamics. When the children were with me, we are much more relaxed and even silly. It gives me the chance to let my hair down and play the role of a young mother rather than the busy executive.

Regular as clockwork at 10.30pm, we both put down our reading material and commenced our nightly routine. Charles would check all the doors and set the night-time alarm system. I rinsed the wine glasses and turned off the lights across the kitchen. Together we made our way up the staircase with our relevant reading material. Charles always reads before lights out each night. I was exhausted tonight after the events of the last couple of days, so would probably resist the urge to open my latest novel.

Our bedroom was located at the front of the house overlooking the close. Our bed was a super king-size and was piled high with cushions which ended up on the chaise longue at the foot of the bed. Along the far wall we had fitted wardrobes where I hang my suit, discarding my blouse into the wicker washing basket in the ensuite. Standing in my bra and knickers, I took my face off and cleansed. I was fanatical with my nightly routine and invested in anti-wrinkle creams to keep my skin fresh and youthful. I like to think it's paying off.

Our ensuite sported double sinks allowing us to complete our ablutions together. Charles was cleaning his teeth in his boxer shorts. I actually looked him up and down, making a comparison with Dave.

What a bitch! A new wave of guilt washed over me. I certainly could not condone that sort of behaviour.

At home I did not sleep naked. T-shirt and shorts are my normal attire. As I mentioned before, our sex life was routine. Usually Saturday night once a week. The only time that had ever increased was when I was trying desperately hard to conceive James. I had fallen so easily for Sophie and was surprised when the same thing hadn't happened second time around.

As a couple we were creatures of habit; boringly predictable.

As we settled into bed, Charles lent across to my side and kissed me chastely on the cheek.

"Good night darling. Sleep well." He opened his book up dismissing me as he immersed himself in a new James Patterson.

"Night darling."

I reached across to switch off my bedside lamp before pulling the duvet up over my shoulders. I settled into a foetal position. Normally if we went to sleep together Charles would tuck himself around me spoon-like. I can't sleep all cuddled up. Don't know why. Just never have. Once Charles is gently snoring, I would wriggle out of his embrace.

Sleep should have eluded me tonight with my troubled conscience. A lack of sleep last night and the effects of a hangover helped to lull me into slumber the minute my head hit the pillow.

Oblivion was what I needed tonight to ease my guilt.

CHAPTER FIVE

Sophie was jigging up and down on the spot with excitement as I handed over my credit card.

I was juggling paying our entrance fee with keeping a watchful eye over my elder child's enthusiasm for the zoo. Sophie had insisted on wearing her favourite blue jeans, Lion King T-shirt along with pink sandals. Completing her ensemble, she protected her eyes from the spring sunshine with her Minnie Mouse sunglasses we picked up in Disneyland last year.

Our party was swelled with the additional of Bella, Jessica's friend. She had the day off from her nanny job and had chosen a day out with my children, surely a busman's holiday. I secretly believe there is something going on between Jessica and Bella. It's not something I would ever ask my employee as it's certainly not my business. That said, I am extremely happy for Jessica. Bella puts a lovely smile on her face and they clearly have a special bond. You can see it in the exchange of smiles and little looks, especially when they think I'm not watching.

James is settled in his stroller with his wrinkled thumb stuffed into his mouth. My determined daughter had insisted on walking, although I had decided to bring the second stroller along anticipating that her energy will wane as the day goes on. I'm secretly delighted that Jessica and Bella have come along to help out. Two small children and the excitement of seeing their favourite animals made the trip here on the tube stressful enough. Corralling children up and down escalators whilst carrying strollers and bags is a feat at the best of times. Adding their over enthusiasm, on top of that, is guaranteed to make for an interesting journey.

We are through the gates and I bring our party to a stop so we can consult the map. Gorilla Kingdom is straight ahead so would seem the best place to start. Introducing my little monkeys to their distant relatives seems a good idea. The children can hardly contain their excitement as we enter the gorilla house. Most of the huge primates are outside basking in the temperate sunshine. To the children's delight, an enormous female gorilla is hunched near the glass wall cuddling a tiny baby. She seems oblivious to the watching humans as she feeds her infant. The offspring is sitting in the curve of its mother's leg as she squats on a bed of straw. Its little arms are clinging onto its mother's chest as it takes large pulls on her breast. The moment is beautiful to watch, with the similarities with its human cousins so profound. Anyone who says that animals don't show love clearly has not had the benefit of witnessing this example of this bond between mother and child.

James is out of his stroller and pushing his way under adult legs to reach the glass, closely followed by his older sister. I smile as I watch the way children can cut through the crowds with no concern for others. I raise my hand in a pacifying gesture to my fellow adults who have to wriggle aside for my little monkeys. Once they reach their target, both children squash their faces to the glass watching the mother gorilla. I swear she makes eye contact with Sophie before she turns her back to the crowd, ending the fun.

It's amazing how quickly the interest in the gorilla house ends as the nursing mother cuts off her engagement with her audience. We gather the children up and wander around the various monkey enclosures. Sophie has hold of Jessica and Bella's hands and is jumping under their direction. James is a mummy's boy and always seems to find his way to my side when we are out as a family. His face is a picture of concentration as he carefully picks his way around the enclosures, glancing up into the canopy.

"Mummy, why don't the baby monkeys fall from up there? The trees look so high and scary." James's concern is clear to see on his serious face. He is a thinker, my son.

"Don't worry my darling. They learn to hang onto the branches as soon as they are born. Out in the wild a baby monkey needs to know how to get away from danger, especially if they get separated from their mummies." I squeeze my son's hand gently in reassurance. Jessica has also noticed my youngest's tendency to worry and we have been trying to explain things to him to help his childhood anxiety.

"I'm glad I'm not a monkey then mummy." He grins up at me.

"Oh, you are my little monkey, munchkin. Come on then it's nearly time for Good Morning Meerkats. Shall we go and find out what that's all about?"

Sophie had overheard the conversation and quickly dragged Jessica and Bella in her wake as she rushed to catch up with us. "Quick, Jessie. Let's get at the front to see the meerkats," she squealed at the top of her voice.

We had found a bench to perch on as we watched the keepers feeding the mongooses. It was amusing to watch the way they bob up and down and scurry from one vantage point to another as the food was being distributed. Bella had taken a seat next to me as we watched Jessica and the children who were gripped with the view.

As I glanced across the scene in front of me, a movement caught my attention, just out of the corner of my eye. Swiftly I turned my head, straining to work out what had captured my attention. I could have sworn I saw Dave standing at the back of the crowd. My eyes scan the visitors' faces, searching for that familiar visage.

"Are you ok Mrs Saville?" asked Bella. She looked concerned. "You've gone as white as a sheet."

Shaking my head, I mentally cleared my brain of crazy thoughts. There's no way that could be Dave. He's in Milton Keynes. He hasn't got kids. Why in the hell would I imagine him being at the zoo?

"Sorry Bella. No, I'm fine thank you. I just thought I saw someone I know and it gave me a bit of a shock. But it wasn't them. Just my eyes playing tricks." I was keen to shut down the conversation. "Anyway, tell me about your new family. Are they good to you? What are the children like?"

Stretching my jean-clan legs out in front of me, I settled back to learn more about Bella's new placement. The family lived across the park from us in Richmond which was ideal for the girls' budding friendship. Bella seemed delighted that the children were much older than mine so she was able to live out. She had her own flat in Finsbury Park where Jessica spent all of her spare time. Our nanny worked weekdays for us but lived in. Jessica had her own suite at the very top of the house above the children's room, so she was on hand if the children had a problem during the night. Most weekends were family time and whilst Jessica was more than welcome to join us, over recent months she had been spending more time away from the house as she developed her friendship with Bella. Today's trip was clearly a treat for the young women, spending time with the children Jessica loved and sharing that with her new mate.

The sun shone throughout the rest of the morning as we watched the lions laze in a heap on their raised platform. Occasionally a lioness would raise her head to survey the crowd, only to flop back into repose. The big cats were plagued by flying bugs which appeared to hover around their eyes. I had felt their frustration as I beat a horsefly off my arm. The damn insect had drawn blood. Tell me what purpose does a fly serve? None whatsoever.

The children loved the Farmyard. Despite the exotic excitement of monkeys, lions and giraffes, the biggest squeal of the morning was for the pigs. Sophie and James spent time in the petting area, giggling at the hairy-faced goat and stroking the fleeces of the baby lambs.

Finally, we made our way to The Terrace for lunch. Both children were tucking into a bowl of pasta supervised by Jessica. It gave me the chance to kick back and indulge in an avocado salad washed down with a chilled Chardonnay. After a long morning of excitable children, it was wonderful to sip on the nectar and watch Sophie and James set about their meal. They both chattered non-stop about their favourite sights and sounds whilst gobbling at their pasta. I really should have told them off for talking with their mouths full, but I was enjoying their sheer delight. Charles definitely would have got involved in supervising their table manners. Another reason I enjoy spending time with the children alone.

The terrace was a sun trap with views across the various enclosures. I tipped my sunglasses from my head to shield my eyes as I observed the other diners. The open-air area was crammed with families and the noise of myriad conversations became trapped under the sun awning, magnifying its volume. Just inside the patio doors there was a small bar area which was home to a small collection of fathers. I know I'm being stereotypical, but I guess they are the fathers. Men wouldn't come to the zoo just for a drink, would they?

My heart began to race as my eyes were drawn to a familiar face. Surely I wasn't mistaken again? That is definitely Dave. As quickly as I saw him, he melted into the crowd propping up the bar.

Grabbing Jessica's attention, I gasped, "Keep an eye on the children a minute would you. I just need to visit the loo."

Jumping from my seat, I was in the bar area in seconds. Excusing myself, I gently pushed my way through the crowd of drinkers as I worked my way from one end of the bar to the other. No sign of Dave. I scanned the crowd in desperation, trying to confirm what my eyes had surely shown me.

I must have looked a confused mess as the barman leaned across the sticky bar and touched my arm. "Excuse me madam, are you ok?"

Blinking back to reality I smiled back at the young man. "Yes sorry," I said. "I thought I saw a friend at the bar but I think I must have missed him."

"There was a gentleman just here a minute ago. He seemed in a rush to leave. Went towards the gents, I think." The barman pointed in the direction of the furthest corridor as he spoke.

"Thank you," I cried as I headed swiftly in his pointed direction. The corridor was long and tight and felt quite claustrophobic. At the end it widened into a lobby which had three doors indicating the toilets and emergency exit. Now what to do, I thought? I can't just walk into the men's room, can I? Perhaps I could just hang around a few minutes to see if anyone emerges.

As I was pondering what to do, a man wandered down the corridor towards me. Plucking up the courage to make an idiot of myself, I asked him if he would check if there was anyone in the men's toilet. I guess he assumed I had lost my son or partner and he politely obliged. The toilet was empty. The only option would have been the emergency exit and surely that would have set off some sort of alarm. The confusion was frustrating me.

"Crazy woman," I muttered as I made my way back to join the family.

My mind must have been playing tricks on me. There is no way a single man without kids would be at the zoo just because he knew I was coming today.

Or was there?

Was he some sort of stalker watching my every move?

Tracking my movements.

Watching me.

Crazy.

My mind is surely just playing games.

CHAPTER SIX

"Hi Madeline," Amelia breezed into the kitchen, enveloping me in her distinctive Gucci perfume.

She pulled me into a strong embrace and deposited a smacking kiss on both cheeks. Amelia was Charles's daughter from his first marriage. At 26 she was closer in age to me than I was to her father. Her resemblance to her father is striking. Luckily, she had been blessed with his best features. Her face was full and round with naturally plump lips.

Her father would have been disgusted if she had ever adopted that dreadful fashion faux pas of over plumped lips which seemed to be flying around the children of many of Charles's peer group. I hate the look. In fact, I hate all types of plastic surgery. Grow old gracefully is my mantra. Although that is easy to say when you are young and in your prime.

Her dark chestnut hair fell in waves to her shoulders, framing her face. Amelia was as tall as me so we fitted naturally into our familiar cuddle. She worked hard on her figure, attending the gym every morning before work. Unfortunately, she shared her father's ability to pile the extra pounds on and I had always admired her dedication to keeping that in check. She also had a confident fashion style, a feature of her privileged upbringing. She wore a beautiful Ted Baker dress, a favourite of mine. Sleeveless, the dress was cut at her waist then flowed to her knees with a lace underskirt. The colour suited her skin tone with a cream background offset with large blush rose flowers.

"Amelia, darling. So lovely to see you. That dress is gorgeous. I love it and it suits you so well," I squeezed her a bit tighter.

I was so very close to my stepdaughter. There had never been any ill feeling between us. I don't think I had ever been seen as the archetypal wicked stepmother. From our first meeting I was determined to build a relationship with Charles's daughter which would complement her mother's and not compete with it. I treated her as the adult she was, and she treated me as the woman her father loved. It worked.

"Thanks Madeline. Can I help with lunch?"

It was Sunday.

Charles loved his roasts, so it was a family tradition to eat together each week. Amelia normally joined us when she wasn't at her mother's in Tunbridge Wells. She had a flat share arrangement in Chelsea with a girl from university, so secretly preferred to come to us on a Sunday as it meant she still managed her lie in. No need to face the train journey out to the Kent countryside after a busy Saturday night clubbing.

"Don't worry Amelia. It's all under control. I was just putting the potatoes on so we have a bit of time to chat. Fancy a glass of wine?" I opened the chilled wine rack to select a bottle of Chardonnay, pouring two large glasses. "Your father is in the day room with the children. Shall we join them?"

Charles was attempting to read The Sunday Times while keeping a watchful eye over Sophie and James. The children were doing a puzzle we had picked up at London Zoo the day before. I had challenged them to find all the animals we had seen and show Daddy. As we joined the rest of the family, Amelia was launched on by Sophie and James who jumped up and down trying to get her attention first. She fell to the sofa as I extracted the glass from her fingers. Both children climbed onto her lap, bombarding her with facts about their trip to the zoo. Amelia could only listen and smile as they chattered. I looked across at Charles and winked, knowing that our work was done for the next hour. Big sister Amelia was the most important person for the children now.

I picked up The Sunday Times magazine and started to flick. The day room was our main family reception room at the back of the house. A huge corner sofa, in burnt orange fabric, dominated the space and surrounded a large low level wooden coffee table. The table was covered in magazines and newspapers along with the remains of morning coffee, cups and cafetière. The large screen TV was set off in the corner of the room with a couple of footstools in front. The children were allowed to use the day room for CBeebies. When the adults wanted to watch TV, we mainly used the snug. Our formal living room didn't have a TV as we used that room for entertaining.

The children weren't allowed in either of those two rooms without a parent in tow. It may sound harsh, but we needed our own space. Children fitted into Charles's life and not the other way round. Whilst he adored all his offspring, he had certain standards. I was comfortable compromising to suit his views. I don't think the children were bothered that certain rooms were out of bounds and it certainly hadn't done Amelia any harm.

Bi-fold doors opened up to the garden patio. We were lucky to have a south-facing garden with the sun shining across the lawns and flower beds all day. I had come to enjoy pottering around in the garden. I can't say I have a natural flare for gardening; but I try. We do have a lovely chap, Fred, who comes in once a week to cut the grass and tidy around the flower beds. When I'm at home on his day, which isn't often, I do try to pick his brains on horticulture and then try and put that into practice. Sat at the bottom of the garden we had a swing which the children loved to use.

Once things had calmed down and the initial excitement of seeing their sister had worn off, the children went back to their puzzle. Charles raised his arm and without a word being spoken, Amelia shuffled over and snuggled into her father's side. I smiled as I watched the two of them together. They had a special relationship.

Charles's first marriage had broken down when Amelia was a teenager. You could probably expect a teenager to go off the rails when their parents split in those formative years. Charles and Catherine had handled the whole affair with gentleness. There was no other party involved. Both of them just got to a point where they no longer loved each other. They had sat down and explained the situation to Amelia without any emotional drama. To follow that up, they had behaved like adults throughout.

Amelia had lived with her mother until going to university but had access to her father whenever she needed it. When Catherine remarried some years ago, her new husband, Roger, fitted neatly into the trio. Amelia was bridesmaid at the wedding and Charles had been a guest. When I came on the scene, it soon became very apparent to me that there was a great deal of mutual respect between Charles and Roger.

Roger was a successful stockbroker and he and Catherine owned an old rectory on the outskirts of Tunbridge Wells. I have been there so many times and have always felt welcomed by the couple. Catherine and Roger do not have children of their own so, understandably, Roger is devoted to Amelia.

I know this probably sounds too good to be true. All too civilised. But it is true. Perhaps it's just a good example of how you can move on to another relationship and not hate your previous partner. The whole situation feels normal to Charles and Catherine and, most importantly, Amelia.

Leaving the rest of the family, I head back to the kitchen to finish lunch. I had a huge joint of rib beef slow cooking. We have a wonderful butcher within walking distance who supplied most of our meat requirements. I do favour the use of local shops at the weekend which I complemented with a weekly online supermarket shop. The vegetables were all prepped and the batter for the Yorkshires was resting as I waited for the fat to reach the right temperature. My Yorkshire pudding recipe came from my grandmother who made the most amazing ones. Charles loved them so I couldn't resist spoiling him rather than using the easier Aunt Bessie option.

I love to cook when I get the time. That predominantly means the weekend. My working day rarely finishes before 7pm so during the week Jessica will see to the children, feeding and bathing them before bed. Charles works similar hours to me and often works on papers in the evening, so we often rely on ready-cooked meals or takeaways. Sometimes Jessica will leave us a dish from the children's supper. She is such a love and I really don't know what I would do without her.

The dining room is at the front of the house with a huge bay window facing the road. Luckily our close in Richmond is not a busy thoroughfare so we don't get disturbed by traffic noise. Whilst we use the large kitchen table for most family meals, Sunday is reserved for the dining room. Our beautiful antique table can seat up to 12 diners, which is brilliant for Christmas entertainment. I picked the table up at a local antique market and whilst it had a bit of wear and tear, a local French polisher restored it to its previous glory. A couple of chairs have been removed to allow the children's highchair and booster seat to come into play.

I should explain that my upbringing was vastly different from Charles's. I don't think I have ever got completely used to the advantages of money.

I grew up on a council estate in Manchester. As an only child, I was the centre of my parents' universe although I was never spoilt; just loved. My dad spent his life working as an engineer in a local car part factory. He was responsible for maintenance of the conveyor belt and machinery. He worked shifts and was a grafter. It was from my dad that I developed a passion for hard work. My mum had a part-time job in one of the big department stores in the city centre. Between them they saved every penny to support me through university. They were so proud of me getting a place at the London School of Economics and even prouder when I qualified with a 1st in Human Resource Management and Economics.

I never underestimated the cost to my parents of my education. They could have retired early; travelled the world; enjoyed time together. But instead, they piled their resources into me. I never got to repay their financial investment. Five years ago, they were killed in a car crash on their way down to London on the M6. They never even got to meet their grandchildren. Life can be so bloody cruel sometimes. They were the centre of my world and I felt bereft when they were gone. Charles was amazing throughout that period. He was my rock to lean on. He sorted out all the formalities, paid for the funeral and was by my side throughout.

Less of my sadness.

The reason for telling you of my background was to explain why I love the benefits money brings my new life. Losing my parents at such a young age has taught me that money is no good to you when you die. Spend it now on the nice things in life. Our home is full of beautiful furniture. I never imagined such wealth as I was growing up in our homely council house. That doesn't make me mercenary. I didn't marry Charles for the life he could offer me.

I love Charles.

Our relationship is complicated. We both value each other's business brains and as a team we are formidable. Charles became my friend first and lover second. We fit together and it works.

You are probably thinking that this is just meaningless words.

This woman who loves her husband and sees themselves as a team has just slept with a complete stranger. Well, I didn't say I was perfect, did I? I have never been unfaithful to Charles before. Oh yes, I have had offers, but have never even been tempted. I can't explain what happened last week. I don't understand it myself.

Yes, I feel guilty, but it's my guilt to bear. It won't make it any easier confessing all, will it?

Oh well. Dinner is ready. Better call the family in and serve up.

Mulling over my recent mistakes can wait for another day.

Today is all about family.

CHAPTER SEVEN

"Good morning team," Charles brought the meeting to order as he spoke forcibly over the sound of numerous conversations around the vast board room table.

All the heads of the business were in attendance for the daily meeting. Charles liked to get his top team together at the start of each day to review results from the previous day and to discuss priorities for the coming day. The audio box was placed in front of Charles so that any of the team away on business or working from home could join by conference call.

I choose to sit much further down the table from Charles to keep our professional distance. It's never been questioned by my peer group, but I like to ensure I don't make it obvious I am the boss's better half. I am sat next to Rupert, the Finance Director and Jimmy, Head of Retail Deals. Jimmy deals with the smaller scale funds for our Retail customers and is a rising star in the firm. We managed to head hunt him from one of our competitors and the huge salary he managed to negotiate is already paying off.

In the last month Jimmy's team has been our highest performer, doubling income for that sector. I was involved in the negotiations to bring Jimmy on board so share some pride in the performance of his team. He drives his team hard, but early feedback indicates that he is fair and his team value his approach. His predecessor was a bit of an old fossil who just hadn't moved with the times. A good result all round.

As Charles started to run through the previous day's results from his laptop, heads went down as everyone followed the charts online. My husband commands an audience. He's not authoritarian but his knowledge and experience instils the kudos of the leader. Each business head chips in to highlight their key pressure points and achievements. The morning meeting is cathartic. It allows us to celebrate the success of the business and generate powerful energy for the day ahead.

My mobile is lying on the table in front of me, in silent mode. My eye is drawn to an incoming call. It's Dave's mobile number. I watch as the icon vanishes to be replaced by a voicemail message. I smile to myself as I anticipate calling him after the meeting.

"Madeline." I am jolted out of my reflection by Jimmy. "I need your support on a prickly issue which I really want to bottom out before it escalates."

"Of course, Jimmy. Is it something you want to share now or shall we get together later?" I am keenly aware that Charles likes to have high level overviews of any staffing issues, even though he trusts me implicitly to ensure the business stays on the right side of employment law.

"High level, I have a member of the team I have concerns about. I don't think it's serious enough for discussion at Board level, but I would really value your input before I take any action." As he spoke, Jimmy was pulling up his online calendar and I could see him organising a meeting invite. I nodded in acknowledgment.

"Right then, if there's no further business, I will call the meeting to a close." Charles stood up and surveyed his top team. "Have a great day guys and let's go make some money."

My office is just down the corridor from the Board room. The sixth floor of the building housed the executive offices. I had chosen one the other end of the floor to Charles's. Again, this is my attempt to keep a professional distance at work. My PA is at her desk as I arrive back.

"Morning Stacey, how was Rome?"

I perch on the side of her desk as she regales me with a summary of their long weekend enjoying the sights and sounds of the historic city. Stacey isn't just my PA; she's also a really close friend. We have spent many a boozy night together talking girlie stuff. I love a good gossip. Well, who doesn't?

Stacey is fiercely loyal to me and is like a dog with a bone when it comes to defending my diary. When I suffer from self-doubt, which I do, she is the one I go to. She has a very level head on her shoulders and is never afraid to give me a straight answer when others may sugar-coat it.

As our conversation draws to a natural close, I wriggle my bottom off her desk, smoothing my skirt wrinkles. Today, I'm wearing a plain pencil skirt and one of my many power shirts. My wardrobe is immense; sorry to boast, but it is. A walk-in closet which I have organised for ease in a rush. Work dresses, suits and shirts huddle together in one side of the room leaving my home clothes opposite. Since I started at Saville's, I have stuck to a strict dress code. No dress down days for me. Perhaps it's an insecurity issue, but I feel more confident when dressed for power. Probably the younger staff think I'm a bit stuffy. They don't know how hard I have worked to get to where I am. It requires sacrifice and if that means creating a bit of an ice maiden image then, I guess, that's my strategy.

"Stacey, can you give me 15 minutes. I need to catch up on a couple of calls. I will give you a shout once I'm done," I called out as I headed for my office, shutting the door behind me.

Dialling my voicemail, I listened in eager anticipation to Dave's message. It was short, sweet, and appropriate if anyone overheard it. I pressed his number as I settled down on my leather chair. It was designed to fit my body shape, supporting my back for those long days at the desk.

"Morning." I spoke softly.

"Morning, you. So glad you phoned me back. I was a bit concerned you might not," replied Dave. I could sense a bit of trepidation in his voice which was surprising.

"Why wouldn't I call," I teased. "Did you miss me this weekend?"

"Desperately." Dave laughed as he appeared to relax. "I had to make do remembering our shower scene. That got me through my desolation."

"Now I know you are taking the piss, young man," I giggled. "Seriously though, did you have a good weekend? Do anything nice?"

"Nothing too special. Met one of my mates for a beer and the rugby. Well, it started as a Saturday afternoon rugby session and ended up in the curry house. Late, and I mean late. Drunk as a skunk."

Well, that blows my theory that it was Dave I saw at the zoo. I knew my eyes were kidding me. There's no way he could be in two places at once.

"How was your weekend, Maddy?"

"Good thanks. The children loved our trip to the zoo. Exhausting after a hard couple of days away, but the weather was good to us. Had a lazy one Sunday. My stepdaughter came for lunch so lots of food and too much wine."

"Nice. Anyway, Maddy, the reason I called is I'm in London tomorrow for a meeting. Any chance of meeting up for lunch or dinner? I can't wait to see you again."

All my instincts are telling me this is wrong. I'm flirting with another man and even considering meeting up again. No, I won't do this. It's just not fair on Charles. It was a mistake, last week. A mistake I should just put behind me and bear its guilt.

"That would be lovely, Dave." I groan mentally. What a stupid bitch. All I had to do was make an excuse. Just let things cool off naturally. "It will have to be lunch if that's ok. I have a window at 1pm if that works for you."

"Perfect. I will book somewhere and text you the details. See you tomorrow Maddy."

Gently I place the mobile down, deep in thought. Despite my instincts, I am quivering with excitement at the thought of seeing Dave again. Just one more time, I think. Have lunch and then let him down gently.

CHAPTER EIGHT

The TV murmured softly in the background.

I flicked through the papers Jimmy had shared with me earlier. It was a simple case of underperformance, but I'm never totally convinced that a member of staff just drops off the scale without a reason. I was reading through Colin's personal file to try and get to know the individual and his circumstances. There must be something more to this case and I wanted to be as prepared as possible before my meeting with him and Jimmy tomorrow.

We are in bed.

Charles and I have an annoying habit of taking work to bed. I had changed into my grey-striped flannel PJs and was propped up on the numerous pillows which live on our bed. Our duvet is covered with papers for both of us. Charles has his glasses wedged on the top of his head as he works through emails on his laptop. It's probably not a good habit to get into. Sleep therapists would hold their heads in horror as we stimulated our brains before rest. It works for us and often we pick each other's brains over a particular problem.

Charles shuts his laptop down and wearily removes his glasses to place them on the bedside table. "I'm getting a bit concerned about Amelia, Madeline."

Charles is clearly wrestling with a problem. I shuffle my papers together as it's clear that any further work tonight is off the cards.

"What's up, Charles? She seemed full of beans on Sunday."

Charles has a close relationship with Amelia and is very perceptive of her mood which probably is unusual for many fathers.

"It's that internship of hers. She loves the work but I'm just a bit concerned that they are taking advantage of her. It's about time she got a proper job. One that pays."

Amelia has been working as an intern at Stylish Magazine for the last couple of years. She only gets expenses which is standard for internships, so Charles supports her with a monthly allowance to keep her in the state she has been used to. She hasn't earned any money since leaving university. Initially she travelled across New Zealand and Australia for 18 months before coming home to try and get an entry into journalism.

I don't resent Charles supporting Amelia. It's just another example of the difference in our upbringing. No one ever gave me a leg up the ladder. I had to work so hard for everything I have.

"Have you tried speaking to her about it, Charles? I guess if she loves the work and you aren't putting any pressure on her to get paid employment, then she doesn't really get pushed outside her comfort zone, does she?"

"I know." Charles groaned, knowing that he was part of the problem. "Perhaps I have been too soft on her. Correction. I know I have been too soft on her, but I do think the magazine has taken advantage of that. If they wanted her so badly they would have offered her a contract by now. I think I am going to have to have a conversation with her, aren't I?"

I reached across the bed divide to take his hand. Amelia is his little angel and it will be hard for my husband to challenge her current thinking. But it needs to happen if she is ever going to have a proper career.

"Yes, you are," I confirm his thoughts. "You need to pick the right moment darling. You know how she gets when she feels she's being backed into a corner. I think you need to try and help her to make the decision. Slowly slowly, catchee monkey ,as they say."

I squeezed his hand in support. Amelia can be as obstinate as her father when she doesn't want to comply.

"As ever your counsel is wise, dearest." Charles reached across to pull me to his side. Gently he kissed the top of my brow as I cuddled into his shoulder. "I don't know what I would do without you, Madeline."

As he switched off the bedside light, we both wriggled our way down the pillows. Reaching behind my back I did my best to discard a number of them, making room. I lay in Charles's arms, enjoying the warmth of his embrace. I can hear the rhythmical beat of his heart vibrating against my cheek as my breathing slows. Charles slowly rubs his thumb across my ribcage, working its way towards my breast. I sense the change in his breathing as his passion builds. He rolls me onto my back as he takes a deep kiss from my lips. His hands push down my PJ bottoms as the kiss deepens. Charles is ready.

Making love is simple and short but certainly not unpleasant. It's the act of two individuals who love each other. There may not be the passion of youth, but a simple expression of care and desire. After, Charles rolls away and is asleep within minutes. Beside him, I lie still letting him reach a deep sleep.

Once I am satisfied he is asleep, I silently leave the bed and head for our bathroom. The harsh light stings my eyes as I adjust from the dark. I stand holding the vanity top as I gaze in the full wall mirror. My lips are swollen from Charles's kisses and my hair is unruly. My PJ top is open and my bottoms have been discarded.

I touch my nipples and they instantly respond. In my mind it's Dave touching me. Reaching down I find my pleasure.

I feel a wave of guilt wash over me.

Why is it that I have to think of my lover to release my pent-up emotion? Why isn't my darling husband enough?

I really don't like the person staring back at me from the bedroom mirror.

One prize bitch.

I feel dirty as I dress and return to bed. Charles has his back to me so I spoon against him clutching his rotund belly with my arm. My breathing moves in time with his. Our bodies working in tandem. My mind is racing as I think about what I am becoming. I don't like the changes in me. I must dump Dave and forget it ever happened.

That's decided then. Yes, I will do it. Tomorrow.

Now to sleep. I wrestle with the covers trying to find a comfortable position.

Sleep will come soon.

I hope.

CHAPTER NINE

I was only a few minutes late as I rushed through the entrance of The Tower Hotel.

Dave had been very considerate choosing a restaurant within walking distance of the office, I thought. Added to that, I am far too vain to be changing into my flatties, so I have staggered the last few steps across the cobbles in my heels. Thank God I achieved that without breaking an ankle. It would have taken some explaining at home.

The Vanity restaurant was ahead as I scanned the periphery for his familiar face. The restaurant was glass fronted and faced Tower Bridge giving a delightful vista. The hustle and bustle of traffic crossing the Thames was silenced within the inner sanctum of the restaurant.

Dave raises his hand to gesture me over and I make my way between the busy tables. Dave is standing as I arrive and reaches across to place a chaste kiss on each cheek. To anyone observing us, we are business colleagues meeting on neutral ground.

It's just us feeling the spark of electricity which fizzles between us as our hands touch.

"I ordered you a glass of Chardonnay, Maddy. Hope that's ok?" Dave smiled as I settled into the chair opposite him, placing my handbag on the chair between us.

"Oh, I really shouldn't at lunchtime," I smiled back.

I was usually so careful not to indulge during the day. The professional in me insists on teetotalism during the working day. Dave has a dreadful way of tempting me to do those things I would never contemplate normally. I pick up my glass, raising a toast to my companion and take a long slug.

"I'm so glad you could make it, Maddy." Dave had a serious look on his face as he cupped it on his propped-up hand. "God, I had forgotten how beautiful you are. I just can't believe my luck. To be sat here with the most stunning woman in this room."

I laughed whilst blushing like a teenage schoolkid. I really can't remember the last time I had flirted with someone or had felt so special at another's compliments. Conversation was stilted at first as the waiter kept interrupting to take our orders. It wasn't until we had our food in front of us that we could really start to catch up.

"Tell me more about the zoo then. Did you have fun?" Dave seemed genuinely interested to hear all about the children and their delight in the vast array of animals.

"Funny thing was I could have sworn I saw you on Saturday." I continued. "I know it's crazy because you told me you were in the pub all afternoon. But you know when you see something out of the corner of your eye. Well, I was sat there and I could have sworn I saw you at the bar."

"Oh, so every guy you see at the bar reminds you of me, eh?" laughed Dave. "Not sure if I should take that as a compliment that you were thinking about me, or an insult that you think I'm some type of alcoholic stalker."

"Take it as a compliment." I giggled. "You must have been on my mind. I was seeing you in all the most unusual places. But please don't think I'm some possessed woman who can't get you off my mind."

"Seeing me in unusual places? I think I like that. Makes me sound mysterious. If I'm honest, I think a trip to the zoo would have been a much better way of spending my day, and I wouldn't have had the hangover from hell on Sunday. I'm getting too old for all day drinking. It just doesn't agree with me next day."

Dave's hand was resting next to mine on the tabletop and he gently stroked the side of my little finger in an amazingly intimate gesture. I could feel shivers running down my back as the sexual tension between us took rein.

"You said you have a stepdaughter. How does that work with your own children, Maddy?" Dave seemed keen to move the conversation away from old age and back to youth. I hadn't a clue how old Dave was. I'm no good at guessing people's ages, but all I do know is that Charles has a fair few years on him.

"Amelia is amazing. I love her to bits. The children adore her and she's very good with them. Amelia is only 10 years younger than me, so our relationship is not really a mother, daughter one. We are friends. She accepted me into her life so easily. I guess she can have a different relationship with me than she can with her mother or father." I smiled as I thought about the special bond I share with Amelia.

"Gosh that means she's still at school," winked Dave. "Seriously though what does she do? Is she part of the firm too?"

"Oh, you smoothie." I accepted the compliment. "No, she doesn't want to work for her father. She's training to be a journalist. Well, to be exact, she's an intern at a women's magazine. Funnily enough we were discussing Amelia last night. She's been an intern for two years now and her father thinks it's about time she got herself a proper job, if you know what I mean."

"True. From an employer's viewpoint, having an intern is great news. Someone to do the hard graft without having to pay them a proper wage. All under the banner of self-development. Actually, that's a thought. A mate of mine works for The Sunday Times magazine. I'm sure he was talking about recruiting the other day. He was after some free advice from yours truly. Did you want me to have a word? Happy to pass on her CV if there is anything going. What do you think?"

"I don't know what to say?" I grinned as I thought about the opportunity which had just fallen into my lap from my lover. This was going to be a difficult one to position with Charles, but if his darling daughter could get a leg up the career ladder, it's got to be worth the risk. "That's amazingly generous of you, Dave. I would love it if you could put in a word."

"Let me drop him a call this afternoon and I'll let you know. Then you can talk to your stepdaughter and get me a copy of her CV. You can thank me later over dinner." Dave's eyes penetrated into me.

"Oh Dave, I really cannot make dinner tonight. I have had to juggle my diary around to get out for an hour."

"OK Maddy. Hear me out. I'm booked into this hotel for the night. If you can't make dinner, tell me you could sneak away for an hour or so after work. I will make it worth your while." He grinned at me as his finger continued to stroke mine.

"You are so terrible," I laughed. "Alright. I don't know how I'm going to organise it but I will try and get back here about 6ish. But honestly, I can only stay for an hour. I will have to make up some serious cover story to get away with it."

It's amazing how quickly we slip into deceit when the chase is on. Work has always come first for me and here I am considering how I can skip out for my own personal gratification. First it's a boozy lunch with my lover, followed by a quickie with him after work. What is happening to me?

Oh yes, I can rationalise it all to myself but this behaviour just goes against everything I hold dear.

It's just not my way.

Or it wasn't.

Until now.

CHAPTER TEN

The District Line was still heaving with people despite it being 7.30pm.

I had managed to get a seat and was staring into space. City workers all around me, with heads buried in some form of reading material. Usually, I would be thumbing my way through The Evening Standard, catching up on the day's news. But tonight, my mind was replaying the events of my latest deception. I'm staggered by how easily I found it to lie to those close to me. I never imagined that I could behave like this. The tangled webs we weave when we practise to deceive. Whoever wrote that passage touched my conscience. They certainly knew what a mess I had got myself into.

Earlier when I got back into the office, I had spun a line to Stacey that I needed a favour. I told her that I was planning a surprise present for Charles and would be telling him I was heading for Oxford Street tonight. I assured her that I couldn't tell him the truth about my shopping trip, could I, and I really wouldn't have time to shop for me and him at the same time. Stacey had happily agreed to pop out and purchase a couple of dresses I had my eye on so that I could take them home with me as evidence of my shopping trip.

It was rare for me to hit the West End after work. I'm usually so busy at work that the last thing I want to do is enjoy retail therapy. My darling husband had taken the lie at face value and agreed to get dinner ready for my return. He really doesn't deserve this betrayal of trust. To rope my PA in on my lies is really not professional either.

What have I become?

Leaving the office just before 6pm, I had headed back to the Tower Hotel and straight to Dave's room. We had spent a wonderful hour reacquainting ourselves with each other's bodies. The passion of those snatched moments was etched across my face as I thought about the things he had done to me.

He is like a drug. One sniff and I'm hooked.

It was so hard to leave, both mentally and physically. Every time I tried to get out of bed and dress, he would find a way to pull me back, driving me along another wave of excitement.

It was only the thought of missing the children's bedtime routine which had forced me to throw my clothes on and run to the Tube. What a mother! Risking being late to kiss them goodnight for my own personal passions.

I look around the tube carriage and wonder whether my travel companions could sense the guilt on my face? They probably just see a businesswoman weary from a hard day in the office. Not a lying cheat who has spent the evening in bed with her lover whilst her poor husband made his way back to the family home.

Who am I kidding? The empty faces opposite me are not bothered at all. This is London. People don't care what you are up to as long as you don't encroach on their space.

I am jolted out of my contemplations as the train pulls to a halt at Richmond. The driver is announcing the termination of the service as I grab my bags and head for the door. Glancing down the train carriages, my stomach jolts. Two carriages down stands Dave.

Or at least it looks like Dave. He's holding the overhead bar as the train pulls into the station. He's not looking at me, but I could swear it's him. I know that profile. Rushing out of the doors, I join the wave of commuters as we are discharged from the station and thin out as we go our separate ways. I'm carried along by the rush while I scan the crowds looking for my lover. What in the hell is he doing in Richmond? It's miles out of his way. I pull over to the side of the human snake and watch the remaining commuters rush out of the exit. Standing there, I have a good view of everyone. There is no Dave or even a Dave lookalike.

God, I am tired. My mind is definitely playing tricks.

I need to get home to my babies. Pulling myself together, I shrug my shoulders and head down the road towards home.

The warming glow of family greets me as I slam shut the front door. Sophie comes running towards me in her rabbit sleepsuit. She squeals with excitement as she jumps into my crouched arms.

"Mummy," she cries. "Daddy said I could wait up for you as I'm such a big girl."

Sophie cannot stay still for a minute and is wriggling in my arms. As I let her go, she is pulling me by the hand towards the stairs.

"Oh darling, you are such a big girl," I agree. "Let me just blow daddy a kiss before we get you up to beddy-byes."

As I pass the kitchen, I can see Charles fussing around the range. We catch eyes and I blow him a kiss as I head off to settle Sophie and place a loving hand on James's sleepy head. Stashing my new dresses in our wardrobe, I take a few minutes to breathe slowly and compose myself. The normality of evening routine calms my racing heart.

The transition from floozie to loving wife is complete.

Charles is serving up the lasagne as I return to the kitchen. A fresh green salad is already positioned in front of our place settings and a glass of wine is poured. I reach for Charles and pull him into my embrace. Resting my head on his shoulder, I squeeze him gently. I feel so safe in his arms. I sigh deeply as I smell his familiar cologne. Reaching up I touch his cheek and kiss his lips lightly.

"I love you so much, Charles," I whisper.

Charles pulls back from me and his eyes seem to penetrate into my soul. "Woah, where did that come from?"

I shrug off the moment as I reach for my wine and take a deep slug. "Oh, just me being soppy." I smile at my husband. "Come on let's eat. I'm starving."

Jessica is an excellent cook and often makes a family dinner for her and the children, leaving portions for Charles and me. We are indeed blessed to have found Jessica; I remind myself yet again. Not only does she care for our children expertly, but she also knows how to feed our appetites. This lasagne is amazing, dripping with tomato-rich sauce.

Charles remains silent as he eats, concentrating on his food. I follow his lead. As we eat, I watch my husband. The concentration on his face is amusing. He divides his food into portions on his plate in a methodical way, piling a piece of lasagne alongside a portion of salad. Once he is comfortable that the correct proportions are balanced on his fork, he raises it to his mouth. There is a structure and a system to the way he eats. That's the same methodology he brings to everything he does. How he works, how he interacts with his children and how he makes love to his wife. It's familiar. It's obvious.

It's boring.

Oh, what a bitch I feel.

This is the man who has given me everything I want. He's the father of my two beautiful children. He gives me safety and security. His support has crafted a career for me which most women would be jealous of.

He does not deserve this.

I need to break out of the downward spiral of guilt and self-pity. This really is not helping. If I choose to deceive then I have to learn to live with this guilt. I need to ensure that I protect Charles and the children from my deceit. They will never know how bad their mother has been. If there is any chance of hurting my family then this will stop immediately.

"Madeline, I heard you were out for lunch today." Charles interrupts my thoughts. "You didn't mention you were going out. Who did you meet?" Charles has never been one to track my activities.

Until now.

Is he suspicious? A stupid mistake found out?

I need to stay calm and casual. "Well, you know me, darling, I don't often take lunch. It was one of the team I met at my conference last week who was in London for some meetings. He wanted to pick up on a couple of points from my presentation." The lies drip from my lips. "I decided to meet for lunch as it would give me the excuse to leave when I needed to. He's a bit of a talker so if I had met in the office it would have busted my diary all day." I laughed with a show of confidence which my belly wasn't agreeing with. My lasagne was sitting heavily in my stomach as the panic brewed inside me.

"Oh OK. Who is he? Which company?" Charles seemed to be watching me intently.

"A guy called David, from South Western Bank. He's just started a new role as Head of Human Resources and is building a new team so was keen to understand more about recruiting values. Actually, I was going to talk to you about him."

"Really? Why's that?"

"We were talking about Amelia actually. He's got a friend who works for The Sunday Times magazine. They are recruiting at the moment and he said he would have a word with his mate. Well, I got a call back later this afternoon. If I could share Amelia's CV, he will pass it on. It's a paying role; not an intern. So, can you get your hands on Amelia's CV for me?"

Charles's face lit up with a huge beaming smile. "Seriously?"

Nicely deflected Madeline, I congratulate myself.

I nodded. "Seriously. It was a really useful meeting to be honest. If we can get Amelia's foot in the door then it's just up to her to win them over. Which I'm sure she can do."

"Madeline, that is brilliant. Thank you. What a stroke of luck. I really appreciate you thinking of her. She's so lucky to have you fighting her corner. What would we do without you?" Charles reached across the breakfast bar and squeezed my hand. "I'll give her a ring shortly and tell her to email it over. I love you, Madeline Saville."

I should be feeling over the moon at Charles's reaction. Winning his recognition is usually so important to me.

But I don't feel great. I feel an absolute shit.

The joy is sucked from the moment.

OK, I am helping Charles and Amelia with the possible chance of her big break, but I'm only able to do this because of my deception. Dave is only helping me help Amelia as he wants more time with me and probably thinks this will sway things in his favour. I'm using this as an excuse to see Dave again. There is a trade-off if Amelia gets the job, but that's not the driving factor.

If only Charles knew. His gratitude is so misplaced.

I'm no hero.

Quite the opposite.

CHAPTER ELEVEN

Spring sunshine dances through the heavy canopy of leaves, leaving a trail of twinkling sparkles across the footpath.

Charles is in his element, in charge of the pushchair which nestles our son into its cushioned softness. James is desperately fighting sleep, trying his hardest to stay alert as he watches the world walk by. Or to be more accurate, children. James has a natural obsession with other children, which some might see as rudeness. He stares and stares. It's all part of developing skills in childhood, but it can look so intimidating. His little face concentrated on what they are doing.

Sophie skips between us holding a hand of each parent. Every few strides Charles and I lift our arms, swinging our daughter from her feet. Her giggles break the silence. Her laughter comes in waves as she swings. Sophie is so different to her baby brother. She is a bundle of noise and laughter to his concentration and silence. I often wonder how we could have created two such different children.

It's a perfect late spring day.

It's a chance for us, as a family, to spend some quality time together. We had just finished a delicious Sunday lunch and decided it would be good to wear off the calories in Richmond Park. The children are excited to visit the playing grounds, especially the swings, which are favourites for both our little ones. Charles delights in pushing Sophie higher and higher as she demands speed. Our darling daughter knows no fear. I know I will be wincing at her devilry as she urges her father to the extremes of safety. My mind will be focusing on the chances of the seat collapsing or even swinging right over the top; all of which is highly unlikely, but a mother's brain is wired that way. At least I don't have to worry so much about James. He will waddle across to the junior swings and will enjoy a gentle sway rather than the enthusiastic excitement of his sister. Again, so different; our children.

"What a beautiful day." Charles breaks the silence between us. "One of those days when you feel glad to be alive."

I smile across at him, understanding his meaning. Our shared work life is so busy and we make numerous sacrifices for our jobs. Those sacrifices, all too often, involve losing time with our young family. It's a price we are willing to pay, but that doesn't make it any easier. Our work ethic brings substantial rewards which allows us the lifestyle, the house, the au pair, and everything you could want in terms of material items. Money can't buy you quality time with your youngsters. We both share a fear that, in the blink of an eye, Sophie and James will be Amelia's age; will be spreading their wings and flying the parental nest.

"Such a lovely day," I respond. "It's been such a relaxing weekend, darling. Tomorrow will be a struggle and if I remember rightly, I have a pig of a week ahead."

"I really appreciate how busy you are at the moment, Madeline. But I had a thought. Do you fancy getting away for a week soon?"

Those words were music to my ears. "Oh yes please, darling. Where did you have in mind? I would love some sun if that's possible."

Charles is not a fan of the sun but will do anything for me. His ideal holiday would be hiking in the Alps in the summer or bombing down those same slopes in the winter. For me, it's all about the heat. My body craves sun. I'm never as happy as when I'm flat out on a sunbed with a good book and a glass of Prosecco.

"I just knew you would say that, Madeline, so I was thinking of asking Jeremy if we could borrow his villa in Portugal. A week of lazing round a pool may be just the tonic you need."

We have stayed at the villa just outside Vilamoura before. It is in the most perfect location for dining out and the villa is a home from home, with all the luxuries you could ask for. The prospect of a week of sunshine has perked me up no end.

"Sounds like heaven, Charles. Why don't we see if Amelia fancies coming with us too?"

Charles is one step ahead of me and informs me that he has already spoken to his daughter about his plans. We continue to discuss our upcoming break as we reach the fenced off children's playground. Sophie is like an elite athlete at the sound of the starter gun. She is out of the blocks in seconds and runs towards the swings.

"Sophie, stop!" I yell.

My daughter has no conception of the swing trajectory and was seconds away from being smacked in the head by the plastic seat. Luckily, the sound of fear in my voice is enough to stop her in her tracks. Rushing over I grab her by the hand, perhaps a bit too forcibly.

"Silly girl. You must never run towards a swing, sweetheart. It could have hit you on the head and that would really hurt." My heart is racing with fear as I stare at my impetuous daughter.

Sophie gazes at me with her big baby-girl eyes. Crushing my anger in an instant with her smile. She has that inbuilt ability to pluck at my heart strings. "Sorry Mummy." She wriggles to escape my hold and rushes over to Charles for him to take over swing duty. All thoughts of danger have been wiped from her mind instantly.

Kids.

James is holding out his arms to me, determined to get out of his buggy. It is so much easier to get him installed into the nursery swing and he doesn't struggle as I secure the safety buckle. Pulling the seat back gradually, I release, watching my son flap his arms and legs in time with the rhythm. As I settle into the flow, I glance around the playground and further out across the parkland. Richmond Park is busy with families taking advantage of the warm sunshine.

My reflections are interrupted suddenly as I spot a familiar face in the crowd.

Dave.

He's way off across the park and even at that distance I can tell it's the spitting image of him. He's with a woman, holding hands as they stroll along the path. The woman is beautiful. Tall, slim with stunning long blond hair which flows behind her as she walks. She struts with confidence. A woman who knows her worth and is prepared to show it.

They look relaxed together as if this is normal behaviour. There is no sign of newness. To the observer they look like a long-standing relationship, comfortable in each other's company. It certainly doesn't look like they are making an effort to impress.

Hey, I cannot be jealous or insist on his monogamy. He's my lover not my boyfriend.

But I am jealous.

Why didn't he tell me he was seeing someone else at the same time as me? He has no reason to keep things from me. I haven't asked for any commitment, but why not be honest? When we first met, he made it clear he wasn't married and I just assumed that meant he wasn't serious with anyone.

And what the hell is he doing in Richmond? It's nowhere near his home. What are the chances of him seeing two women who live in the same area of London?

This is beyond weird.

And if he is, why wouldn't he tell me that. The risk of me and Charles running into him could be embarrassing in the extreme. I was so clear with him that our affair was secret and there is no way Charles must ever find out. Surely he would tell me if he were spending his weekends on my doorstep. That's the least he could do to support me. I'm the one taking risks. Not him.

"You OK darling?" Charles interrupts my thoughts. "You look like you have seen a ghost." My husband reaches over to me and takes my hand.

I shake myself, giving a secret dressing down to my conscience. "I'm OK darling. I think someone just walked over my grave. You know that feeling. Sends shivers down your spine."

I smile reassuringly at Charles as we switch places. Sophie's excitement will soon cure me of my troubled mind.

Next time I see Dave I am going to have it out with him. There has got to be some ground rules in this relationship.

For us both to commit to.

CHAPTER TWELVE

The Ten O'clock News is just starting as the phone rings.

The handset is nearest me so I wearily push myself out of the comfy folds of the sofa. It's an effort. There is no way I'm doing it elegantly. Whoever designed this sofa did not think about how you extract yourself in a hurry. The phone has rung for about five repetitions before I make my way across the room to the Accent table. It was one of my favourite acquisitions this winter. Fashioned in a dark wood, the square top is attached to four slim legs. The table reminds me of one of the monsters from War of the Worlds. It's just unusual and caught my eye when shopping in one of our local boutiques just before Christmas.

The phone connects as I lift the receiver. "Hello," I whisper into the handset, conscious that Charles is engrossed in the news programme.

Silence.

I can tell there is someone on the other end of the line. I can hear the steady low vibration of breathing. It certainly doesn't resemble a dirty phone call, not that I have ever experienced one, to be totally honest. It just sounds like the other person is waiting to speak.

"Hello," I say a bit louder.

Charles looks across at me and grimaces. He mouths "Who is it?"

Putting my palm over the handset, I whisper back. "No idea."

All of a sudden, the receiver goes dead as the other person disconnects. Shrugging my shoulders, I throw myself back on the sofa, instantly forgetting the interruption.

Once the News finishes, we continue our nightly ritual. We are both creatures of habit. Charles will do the checks downstairs whilst I ready our bedroom for the night. Our bedroom has a feature bay window which faces out onto the street. When we first moved in, we considered the bedroom facing the garden as our own but the room at the front of the house was huge, with a substantial ensuite. It made the decision to change our mind a no-brainer. Thankfully, we have never been bothered by noise from the road. Despite us living on the outskirts of London, this is a quiet suburb and not a road which people would use to get to anywhere other than one of our neighbouring houses.

As I untie the heavy curtains from their holdbacks, I glance out of the window. Something catches my eye. A movement in the street. At this time of night any activity is rare.

What caught my eye?

Scanning the space outside our window, I spot something unusual. Just across the road from our house I can see a dark shadow. It appears to be a man. The body shape and size would suggest male. The streetlight is on the blink so it's hard to see any detail, just a shape. The person is standing and appears to be looking towards our house. I think they must have spotted me, watching them. Suddenly the shape moves away at speed down the road and back towards the tube station.

My hackles are up. Whoever that was, they were definitely checking out the house.

We have been reasonably lucky as burglaries are rare in this part of Richmond. I think the criminal world is well aware that most of the houses round here have great security systems in place. We don't always have ours on at night in case one of the children wanders, but perhaps tonight we will.

Charles has just entered the room and spots me staring out the window. "Everything OK, darling?"

"I'm not sure. There was someone out there," I point. "I couldn't really see properly but they were looking at our house. Not any of the others. Really strange. With that phone call earlier and now this, could we put the motion senser on tonight." I was feeling more and more unsettled now as I pieced the two unusual situations together. "They were definitely looking at our house." I'm convincing myself at the same time as my husband.

"Of course, darling. I'm sure it's just a coincidence." Charles pulls me into his embrace. "Don't worry my love, I will protect you."

The thought of my husband battling a dangerous burglar lightens the mood. He is no Arnold Schwarzenegger, but he's my hero tonight.

"Let me just go and have a quick look outside too. Just in case."

"Please be careful." I squeeze Charles's hand as he leaves the bedroom.

Charles heads back downstairs as I continue to peer out of the curtains. Whoever was out there is long gone, but I understand his need to check. It doesn't immediately occur to me that he is taking a risk. But what if the burglar returns and confronts him?

I scan the street trying to locate Charles. He has wandered to the end of the road as it joins the avenue towards the tube. His manner appears casual as if it's his normal behaviour to have a pre-bedtime walk in the dark. If one of the neighbours looks out, they will be confused. Oh well. My knight in shining armour all ready to protect his family from the underbelly of society.

Before I know it, he is back inside. The alarm is set and we can settle down for the night. As we resume our night-time regime, to the outside observer, nothing is different. The concern of a moment ago is forgotten.

As I lay there in the dark though my mind is unsettled. Over the last week there has been a number of weird things which on their own don't raise any red flags. But adding them together, something's not right. It's no coincidence that I have seen Dave or someone who looks like Dave far too often. The zoo, the tube, the park. The instances run through my sleepy brain.

Why would he be following me? Or is he trying to unsettle me? Why?

It's just sex. It's just a bit of fun.

If he's playing games with me then perhaps the time has come to end it all. It's not worth the stress. Yes, the sex is great, but the whole business scares me. There is no way I am taking any risk of Charles finding out.

If there is any chance Charles will find out then this thing is over. No matter how exciting it is.

It's just not worth risking my marriage over.

CHAPTER THIRTEEN

The sex was amazing. As usual.

We fall apart, collapsing on the tangled sheets. It has been the first time we have managed to meet up all week and absence has certainly increased the passion. We are both exhausted from our exploits. It's hard not being able to see each other whenever we want. But perhaps that's why it feels so good. Captured moments of passion, then long hours thinking about it and waiting for a repeat performance.

Getting our breath back, Dave lights a cigarette and hands it over to me. I take a long, deep breath in, enjoying the nicotine hit. I don't smoke. Never have. Never will. Except after sex with Dave Roberts. It just feels right. The rebel in me, who can turn off all emotion for her husband and children, is the same rebel who has a sneaky smoke post-coital. I hand the cigarette back to Dave who sucks hard on it. Making smoke rings with his lips, we continue to enjoy the drug in silence.

Conversation is certainly not our main purpose when we are together. We spend less and less time talking, as our opportunities to catch secret meetings become more difficult. But then let's be honest, we are not together for our scintillating conversation. It's a much baser need. More often than not, I'm getting dressed the minute we have finished so I can skedaddle back home before I'm missed. Today, I have a free pass for a couple of hours. Unusual, but Charles has the children and is out all morning so I'm not under any particular pressure.

Lying beside my lover, I flop my arm across his chest and start to draw circles with my fingers. He groans.

"Maddy, you are insatiable. Give me a chance. There is no way I can perform again so soon," he laughs.

"I'm not after round two," I smile into his chest. "Just fancied touching you."

Out of the corner of my eye I spot his shock. Sex is impersonal between us. It's fast, furious, extremely athletic, and sweaty. Unnecessary acts of affection are definitely absent. I guess that's the rules when conducting a sleazy affair. Not too sure of the protocol myself, I have been guided by Dave throughout our liaison. He has led and I have been his willing apprentice.

Despite his reluctance for conversation, I am determined to push on. My sleepless night at the weekend has been playing on my mind. It's about time I confronted the issue and sort the whole thing out. I'm sure it's nothing, but it needs a voice.

"Have you got a girlfriend, Dave?"

"What?" Dave rolls over, pushing himself up to a seated position. The speed in which he has disentangled from me is an early indication that this conversation is not one he wants to have. I don't care. It has to be now or I will never broach the subject.

"It's just that I thought I saw you in Richmond Park at the weekend with a stunning blond. I don't mind if you are seeing someone. Just interested."

The atmosphere has changed.

You could cut through the mood change with a knife. Dave's body language is screaming out negativity. What the hell is wrong with him? There is no way we are inclusive. I have never set out any rules on either of us or our behaviours. And he hasn't ever tried to insist on any inclusivity rights from me. I can't understand the sudden change in atmosphere.

"Listen Maddy. Why in the hell would I be in Richmond? I'm not that desperate to see you that I have to wander around your manor trying to make you jealous." He laughs but it comes out more like a sneer.

"Who said anything about being jealous?" His attitude is unsettling me. "I just could have sworn it was you. They do say everyone has a doppelganger somewhere in the world. Yours obviously lives in Richmond." I sigh trying to defuse the situation. God knows why he is so pissed with me.

The silence between us stretches as Dave lights up another cigarette.

This time he doesn't offer me a drag but pulls in big, harsh breaths of nicotine. I'm still lying rather awkwardly beside him and self-consciously wrap my arms across my naked breasts. Don't know why, but it feels weird lying exposed like this whilst he tries his hardest to ignore me. Perhaps now is the time to get dressed and get out of here.

Today has been ruined now.

Perhaps I just shouldn't have brought it up. Perhaps I should have kept it all to myself. Especially as he insists it wasn't him. Just my eyes playing games.

Perhaps.

The mood changes instantly. His hand starts to play with the back of my neck, massaging my taunt muscles. Moments later he is biting gently on my shoulders as his hands move around to touch my breasts.

I can't stay angry for long.

Not under this sort of pressure.

"Come on, Maddy. You know there is only one woman for me and she is right here with me now. Show me how much you want me."

He turns me round revealing his desire.

All thoughts of a rival disappear as we fall back on the bed for round two.

This man knows how to manipulate me. He is in charge of what we do. He is in charge of what we talk about.

In my weakness I don't see what's staring me in the face.

Dave Roberts is controlling me and I am walking blinding into danger.

If only I had really seen the true person before falling for his sweet talk. But I wasn't thinking logically at all.

Was I?

CHAPTER FOURTEEN

It's mid-morning and the sun is blazing high in the Algarve vista.

There is not a cloud in the sky as a gentle breeze wafts across my supine body. There is very little shade around the pool area, so I am basking in the heat. As I take in the sun's rays, I watch my family enjoying the early summer fun.

Charles managed to persuade Jeremy to lend us his villa for the week. Not that it required much persuasion. Jeremy is a good friend and very accommodating with his holiday home. Unfortunately, Charles doesn't really do sunbathing, so he is sat at the outside dining area working his way through the paper. Even in Portugal, my husband finds a way to keep abreast of the daily news.

I watch as he picks up a pen to start on The Times crossword. That will keep him occupied for a while. He makes a nod to the weather by sporting tailored shorts and a polo neck shirt. I honestly can't remember the last time I saw Charles in trunks. He doesn't swim, he never learnt, so the pool is out of bounds for him. But he knows how much I love the sun and will do anything to make me happy.

Amelia is lying on the sunbed next to me. She looks amazing in the tiniest bikini which hardly covers her modesty. She has a cracking figure and it is fully exhibited in the tasselled bra top and thong. Her toenails are beautifully manicured, matching my own. We went to the nail bar together last week, at her insistence, as she wanted to treat me.

It was her way of thanking me for getting her the interview at The Sunday Times magazine. Dave had really come up trumps. His mate turned out to be Amelia's new boss. After her interview and pre-prepared presentation, which I had worked hard on with her to refine, she was offered the role two weeks ago. Once we return from Portugal, she will be starting her first paid employment at the grand old age of 26. Charles was so proud that he had decided the week away was a family celebration of his daughter's success.

Sophie is playing quietly in the paddling pool. She has a selection of bowls which she seems to delight in, pouring water back and forth. It's the simplest things which children love to play with. We have erected a sun brolly above her head to protect from the strongest rays. James is asleep, curled on the vast outdoor sofa, watched over by his father. Jessica has the week off and is spending it with Bella. She had been invited to join us at the villa, but she was keen to spend some time with her girlfriend, alone.

I feel totally relaxed and refreshed in the sunshine. We have been here for two days now and my tan is coming along nicely. Being able to just lie in the warm; read a novel, listen to some music, and spending time with my fabulous family, is food for the soul. We have spent our days by the pool and long, lazy evenings around the BBQ. A perfect recipe for holiday fun.

I have been feeling reflective since we arrived.

Getting away from London has made me think about the last two months and given me a sort of reality check. I honestly cannot believe it has been over two months since I started my affair with Dave. Two months on and Charles has no idea about what's been happening. I have been very discreet.

It's hard to congratulate myself on keeping my affair secret from my loving husband. The whole thing is just so wrong. I don't want to hurt him and I will do everything in my power to keep him shielded from my sins. The longer this affair has gone on, the more I have worked to protect Charles from its fallout.

My affair has developed a structure of its own. As part of my subterfuge, I joined a fashionable gym not far from home and have a weekly yoga class on Saturday morning. I have never actually made it to the yoga class. Every Saturday morning I meet Dave at a hotel in Wimbledon. Dave is renting a house in Reading despite working in Bristol. He does the daily commute, allowing him to also travel into London whenever we meet. We are both making sacrifices for our lust.

Our snatched hours together are worth the lies and deceit. Our relationship is not just about sex. We enjoy each other's company and have a laugh together.

Who am I kidding?

Our relationship is about sex.

Long, hard, sweaty, orgasmic sex. I'm not with Dave for his titillating conversation, or his intellectual grasp, or business acumen. I enjoy having sex with him. He does things to my body which Charles has never managed to do. His body is the altar I worship at every Saturday morning. After an hour of amazing sex, I shower and rush back home to carry on my normal weekend activities. I transition from sexy lover to mother and wife in the flick of a light switch.

There is one big elephant in the hotel room or should I say, one which has grown into existence in recent weeks. After a particularly beautiful session last week, Dave rolled onto his back and pulled me to his embrace. Then he said those god-awful words I did not want to hear. "I love you, Maddy."

Shit.

That was not supposed to happen. I don't want him to love me. I just want him to make me feel good.

I don't love him. I love Charles. Dave is just someone who can drive me wild in bed. I don't want commitment.

I don't want his love.

No way.

This changes everything.

Dave expected me to say it back. I could feel it. The tension was dreadful. It was one long unpleasant silence after he said it. I wasn't going to lie to him. I do like him, but I don't love him.

We have spoken again a couple of times since that awkward moment. Dave has been fine with me but I get an unnerving feeling that he is waiting for an answer.

It has become an uncomfortable wedge between us.

Deep down I know what I have to do. I think the holiday has hastened my decision. This relationship has run its course. It's time to draw it to a close.

When I get back from holiday I am going to gently break it off. I really don't want to hurt him but is only fair to let him go, especially as I cannot give him what he wants.

As if he knows I'm thinking of him, my phone pings as a text arrives.

'Hi darling. Hope you are having a lovely time. Can't wait to see your white bits. Missing you xxx'

The irritation I feel as I read his message surprises me.

I am so over this.

I should have stopped it all before we came away, in hindsight. It would have given him time to forget about me whilst I was out of the country. He has got way too clingy. I know that if I don't respond then I will get numerous messages for the next hour or so. Best shut it down for now so it doesn't spoil the rest of my day.

'Weather hot and working on my tan. Can't message more today. Speak when home. M x'

That should do it, I think to myself. To make extra sure I decide to turn my phone off for now. If work needs me then there is always Charles's phone.

"Darling, do you fancy a trip out for lunch?" calls Charles as he folds the paper up neatly. "How about a drive into Vilamoura for a spot of lunch and a stroll around the harbour?"

"That sounds lovely Charles. Let me grab a quick shower first to rinse off the sun cream. Half hour?" I stretch myself out across the sunbed to gently nudge Amelia. "Lunch in Vilamoura, Amelia?"

"Great, especially if Dad's driving," winks my stepdaughter. She knows that Charles has insured her to drive the hire car but Amelia will want a glass of wine when we are out so is happy for her dad to take control. He is such a pushover when it comes to his daughter.

There's a hive of activity as Amelia and I shower and between us we dress the younger children. Within the half hour we are all strapped in the jeep and on our way.

Charles finds a parking space at the entrance to the marina. We have bought buggies for both Sophie and James. With the weather being so hot, it is too much to expect the children to walk. It just gets far too traumatic.

There is the usual hustle and bustle of tourists strolling around the marina and admiring the expensive yachts. There are some really beautiful examples on display. I have never really been interested in sailing, but you cannot help but be impressed by the size of these specimens. The sheer scale of the harbour with the white, slick speedboats lined up in formation is a sight to see. In between are dotted some of the more top of the range yachts. Most of the boats look sadly deserted, but I did notice a number of attractive people lazing on the decks, enjoying the beautiful weather and surroundings.

We haven't made it into Vilamoura before on this holiday, so we enjoy a stroll around the harbour, stopping on occasions to observe a boat manoeuvring its way out of dock. It took expert workmanship to ease one's way between the vastly expensive boats and out to clear water. A bit like working your way through Richmond in our Chelsea tractor on a Saturday afternoon when the streets are heaving with people. I smile at the analogy.

All too soon the pangs of our empty stomachs drive us towards the many restaurants dotted around the marina. Charles is in charge of choosing the establishment and we approve his decision as we settle at a veranda table of the Haven Restaurant. Pristine white cloths adorn the table. They won't stay like that for too long, I think, as the children are wedged into highchairs. James does love to play with his food and despite my attempts to clear up after him, there is usually a trail of destruction behind him. I don't think either of us have really got the handle on managing food time. That's where we are spoilt with Jessica.

We order Portuguese paella to share amongst the adults whilst the children have settled for fish fingers and frites. The paella is stuffed with various types of seafood and it is some time before we all draw breath.

"I am so happy about the new job, Amelia." Charles starts the conversation off. "Are you excited to start?"

Amelia finishes a mouthful and takes a slug of wine. "I am so excited, Papa.

I'm a bit nervous too especially as Madeline used her contacts to get me the job. I just don't want to let you guys down."

I reached across the table to take her hand. "Darling, you honestly will never let us down. We are so proud of you getting the job. All I did was get your foot in the door. The rest was down to you."

I adore my stepdaughter's humility. It's so refreshing especially compared with my normal work environment which pounces on any sign of weakness.

"Well thank you again, Madeline. I will work so hard to repay your faith in me. I had a call last Friday with Gerry who will be my mentor for the first few months. It sounds like I will be thrown right in at the deep end." Amelia's face lit up with the excitement. "I will be shadowing him for the first couple of interviews and then it will be up to me to write the article for his approval. It feels a bit like being back at university and I guess I won't get two weeks to write it," Amelia laughed.

"Best way to settle is to get stuck in," said Charles. "I really don't like long induction programmes, do I, Madeline? Get them working as soon as you can and learn on the job."

"I agree." I am nodding as I consider the best practice we employ at Saville's. "You will fit in so well and if you can turn out a couple of good, quick articles then you will build your reputation. I'm sure magazine work is fairly ruthless, but just be you, Amelia. They will love you."

"I forgot to tell you," Amelia was reaching for her phone. "I got a lovely email from your friend who provided me with that introduction. It was really sweet of him to do that. Look."

I could feel my handshake as I took the outstretched phone. I took a big swig of wine to calm my nerves. How dare Dave overstep the mark and contact my family. I really can't believe he would do that. I read his email.

Dear Amelia, just a short note to wish you the very best of luck in your new job. I am sure Dennis will keep me updated on your progress and if you need any further support at all do let me know. Kindest regards Dave Roberts

Nothing too controversial about his message but I'm still angry. I had acted as liaison between Dave and Amelia as I wasn't keen to expose my family to my lover. There are rules to follow and Dave certainly should know better.

I can see that Amelia and Charles are waiting for some form of response. "Oh, that is very kind of him to message you. I'm not sure he will be of any further help to you, but it's nice of him to offer." I was desperate to close down that avenue. The last thing I wanted was for any further communication. "Will you excuse me?" I continued as I stood up. "I am just going to use the bathroom."

Winding my way through the busy restaurant I find the restrooms. Pulling my phone from my jacket pocket I rush off a text to Dave. 'Please don't message Amelia again. I do not want my family involved PLEASE.'

His reply is swift. 'Sorry Maddy, didn't mean to upset you. Just wanted to say good luck. Message understood. Missing you Love D xx.'

Still bristling with anger, I respond with a perfunctory kiss and turn my phone off.

This latest situation has just helped to confirm to me that it is time to end it.

Dave is starting to put my relationship with Charles at risk. I will never allow anyone to come between me and my husband.

This relationship is over.

I just need to strike the death knell on my return to the UK.

CHAPTER FIFTEEN

"Stacey, that's great. Thank you for the update. As usual you have managed expertly without me," I smile across at my PA as we come to the end of our handover session.

It's the first day back at work after the most relaxing time in Portugal. Hot on the heels of the management morning meeting, I have time with Stacey to catch up on my emails and diary commitments. Ever thoughtful, she has organised my diary to ensure I have the morning free now to work through my backlog of work.

"So, did you have a lovely time away, Madeline?" asked Stacey. "I can see the weather was good. You are glowing. Well jeal."

"Oh god, yeah, it was so peaceful and relaxing, thank you. The weather was glorious. Amelia and I spent most of our time on the sunbeds. It gave Charles good bonding time with the little 'uns."

I laughed as I remembered Charles panting after the children as they raced around the pool area. It's not really fair, but I justify it to myself that he doesn't like to sit in the sun. He worked up quite a sweat on daddy duties. The children loved it too. They don't get as much time with Charles so having the opportunity to play together was so valuable.

"Well, you look amazing on it. I'm glad to have you back though. It was far too quiet without our daily gossip. Anyway, let me leave you in peace so you can work through your emails." Stacey stands and starts to back out of my office. "Do you fancy a coffee?"

"You star," I smiled. "Flat white would be perfect. Thank you. Could you field my calls for the next hour or so? Only urgent stuff if that's ok."

My PA, and friend, is very protective of my time and can be assertive to the extreme with anyone trying to encroach on my day. Whilst I had a clear morning ahead there was one task I needed to deal with. I had decided I would ring Dave today and 'eat the frog'. It was a job I really wasn't looking forward to, but I had to get it out of the way. I had spent the weekend contemplating my approach. The email to Amelia was really the last straw.

Our relationship was starting to impact on my family life and that could not happen.

After Stacey had left the room leaving me with a delicious flat white, I closed the door and fished in my handbag for my personal mobile. Charles insisted on business mobiles for his top team so that we could keep work and family life separate. I had never been more pleased of this practice. When you start on a path to deceive your husband it feels incredibly wrong to use the phone, paid for by your employer, to flirt. Especially when your husband owns the business.

The phone was ringing. Tapping my glossy red nails on the desk I wait impatiently for an answer.

"Maddy, this is a lovely surprise." We didn't often call each other at work. For once, I am the one breaking the rules.

"Hi Dave. Sorry to ring you but this just couldn't wait until Saturday. I need to talk. Is now a good time?"

"Ok. I have a meeting in about 15 minutes but I'm good for now. What's up?" Dave sounded distracted as if he were concentrating on something else.

I pushed on despite not getting the right vibes from him. "Look Dave, there is no easy way of saying this. So, I'm just going to put it out there. We need to stop. I can't do it anymore."

"What?" His voice carried an edge.

"Dave, I'm sorry but I am ending our relationship. I can't go on. I'm sorry."

I left it hanging there as the silence became palpable. It was an awkward atmosphere where both parties were thinking of their next sentence.

Unnatural.

Dave broke the silence. He sounded extremely pissed. "Maddy, come on what's wrong. It's not because of that email I sent Amelia? Surely not?"

"Look it's not just that." I paused as I collected my thoughts. "I have loved our time together but we both knew it wasn't going to be forever."

"Maddy, I love you. I know you are married but we could be together. I would do anything for you. You know that."

The frustration in his voice was unmistakable. Another reason why this had to end. He had become too dependent on me. I just don't feel the same way as him. Perhaps I am about to break his heart. I honestly didn't think he was that serious about me. I thought we had reached an agreement about our relationship. It wasn't supposed to be a long-term thing.

It wasn't supposed to be love.

Just sex.

"I'm sorry, Dave. I just can't do it anymore. I love my husband and I don't want to hurt him. If we carry on like this, he will find out and it will destroy him. I can't do that. I am so sorry. I do care about you and I don't want to hurt you either. You do understand, don't you?"

"I honestly don't understand," Dave's voice seemed to have a wobble in its tone. "Look I can't talk now. Promise me you will come on Saturday and we will talk about it. If you still feel the same way after we have spoken, then I will accept that. Please don't do this over the phone. At least speak to me face-to-face. I deserve that at least."

"Ok. I'll meet you Saturday." I really didn't want to meet him but I guess he is right. Dumping someone over the phone is the lowest. "I won't change my mind, Dave. It's been on my mind for a few weeks now. But I agree it's crap of me to do it over the phone. I'll see you Saturday. Usual place and time?"

My stomach is churning as I replaced the receiver. I hadn't planned that outcome at all. Selfishly, I had decided to dump Dave as soon as I could after the holiday. In my head I had moved on. Done. Now back to my safe life with Charles. I hadn't really thought about Dave or how he would deal with the news; that's not my problem.

Is it?

He knew what he was doing when we started this affair. He must have known I was never going to leave Charles. We had no future. It was just a bit of fun.

Wasn't it?

Ok, having to meet up delays the decision a few days. It won't change the decision. But I have signposted my feelings to Dave. At least he knows what's happening now.

It will soften the blow, I guess.

How wrong could I be?

CHAPTER SIXTEEN

The door was resting on the security latch, allowing me to let myself in.

I knew things were going to be tough as soon as I stepped into the hotel room. Not that I was looking forward to our meeting, not in the least. I had been worrying about it since the phone call. Playing our conversation over in my head, I had been practising my challenges for the upcoming argument. Because it is going to be an argument. I can feel the tension already.

Dave was sat on the desk chair rather than relaxed on the bed. He had his arms crossed across his chest in an obviously closed body vibe. He didn't smile at me; just stared right through me. As if I was invisible. I made a fuss of closing the door properly and taking off my jacket, hanging it on the back of the door. My mind was swirling around with pre-planned thoughts. Despite going over the conversation numerous times, I didn't know how to start it. I turned slowly and smiled self-consciously at my lover. Before I could start, he took over.

"Maddy, I have to say I am disappointed in you. I had expected better of you. I didn't think you would wimp out at the first sign of trouble. I honestly thought we had a good year of fun ahead of us."

Dave rocked back in the seat and continued to glare at me. I felt like I was standing in the headmaster's office waiting for a bollocking. How had he taken control of the situation and turned it round on me? Honesty was the best policy, so here goes.

"Look, I'm sorry Dave. I know you are disappointed but I have wrestled with my conscience and I really cannot go on. I am so very sorry." I tried to reach towards him to touch fingers but his hand moved away as if I were contaminated.

"I don't want your apologies, Madeline Saville. As I say, I am disappointed that you have decided to finish my fun before I am ready."

"I thought you said you loved me, Dave. If you loved me you would understand."

I sounded pathetic pleading for his understanding. The situation was turning nasty quickly. Again, this is not how I had planned it. Or practised it. Where had this venom come from? The other day on the phone he was spouting his love for me. Now he sounds far more clinical and definitely angrier.

This is all about who is in control now.

"Love! Don't be so fucking stupid woman." Dave's face had turned puce with rage. "I don't love you. I was just playing you."

I sat down heavily on the bed as I tried to absorb the change in the man. He genuinely seemed to hate me. Where had my gentle lover gone to and who was this man he had been replaced with? Perhaps it's his way of saving face. Nobody likes being dumped, so I guess I shouldn't be too surprised if he wants to make it personal. Now is the time to exit stage left, I surmise.

"Ok Dave. Let's just leave it there then. I will pay for the room on my way out. I'm sorry. OK?" I picked up my handbag making ready to go.

"Not so fast. I have something to show you before you go." Dave grabbed hold of my arm and pulled me over to the desk.

"Stop it." I cried as I tried to pull my arm away. "You're hurting me. Get off me."

Dave got up from the chair and pushed me down into it. His hands held me down by the shoulders and I could feel his fingers pinching into my skin. His phone was placed on the desk with a video ready to play. He hit the play button and pushed the phone into my eye line.

The video focused in on me. I am naked. Sat on top of Dave with his cock in me. Slowly I moved up and down his shaft with a look of sheer longing on my face. As I watched I could hear our lovemaking groans as we both reached our orgasms. It was beautiful and sinister at the same time.

"Fifty grand. That's what I want." Dave pressed pause as he sneered at me. "Did you really think you could get away with it, Madeline? Fifty grand by the end of next week or I send this little performance to Charles. I've no doubt he will recognise his lovely wife." He paused. "And there is more. He will get to see all the varied positions we enjoyed on our Saturday morning yoga sessions. It's quite a performance. You should be proud of yourself." Dave laughed as he watched my face crumbling.

"Why?" I whispered. "Why would you do this to me?"

"I saw you coming, love. I knew who you were when I got on that train. Oh God, you played right into my hands. So bloody easy. You must have been so starved of sex. You fell right into my lap."

"What?" I screamed. "Are you seriously saying you set me up? That you came onto me for money?"

"Of course, Madeline. Did you think I fancied you? Did you really think I was in love with you? Oh dear me." He laughed. A malicious laugh full of menace. "Yes, it was nice. You are good in the sack. It made the job easier. If you had been a right munter then I probably would have gone for more money. Take it as a compliment that it's only fifty grand."

I am stunned.

I sat paralysed with shock and stared at this man whom I had made love with for weeks. OK, it wasn't love but I thought we had cared for each other. How could I have got this so wrong?

I had been played.

And now he was threatening me with disclosure.

I feel sick.

"What makes you think I have that sort of money? My husband may be the rich one, but I can't just get fifty thousand pounds out of our joint account. Seriously?" I spoke with more confidence than I felt. I was struggling to contain the bile which was rising up my throat. I could hear my heart beating frantically as panic set in.

"Don't even try that one on me, Mrs Saville. You have the money in an account in your name. An inheritance if I remember rightly."

"How the hell do you know that?"

"Oh don't ask a con artist to reveal his sources, darling. Just know that I have a great deal of information on you which I will use if I don't get my money by next week. Now. Off you pop." He waved me away towards the door with contempt. "I will be in touch with bank details. And it goes without saying that if you go to the police, the sex tape goes to Charles." Dave opened the hotel room door and stood to the side, gesturing for me to leave.

Grabbing my bag and jacket, I fled from the room and charged down the corridor to the lift. My heart was racing as the lift doors opened.

I feel I will vomit any minute.

I just can't believe what has just happened. What an idiot I am. I fell for him, hook, line and bloody sinker. What the fuck am I going to do? I could feel my blood pumping at speed around my body and a heat was rising in my cheeks as I contemplated the shame.

As the lift opened into the lobby, I scrolled my phone for Stacey's number. She answered almost immediately.

"Stacey, I need to see you. Can we meet?" I gasped out my words continuing to swallow down the bile in my throat.

"Hey Madeline. Are you OK? You don't sound it." My friend's voice was full of concern.

"No. I am in a mess. I need to talk to you. As a friend. Can we meet?"

"Of course we can. How about The Grapes?" Our favourite wine bar was mid-way between our homes so the perfect location for when we met outside work.

"Thanks Stace. I will be there in 10. Thank you."

As I hurtled out of the hotel, my mind was racing. What the hell am I going to do? I could never have contemplated what happened today. It's the stuff of nightmares. This sort of thing doesn't happen in real life.

Surely not?

My body starts to tremble as the reality of the situation sinks in. Sobs catch in my throat as I feel the waves of panic attacking my brain. I want to dissolve right there on the pavement but that is not possible.

I desperately need a shoulder to cry on. I need advice and alcohol.

CHAPTER SEVENTEEN

I spotted Stacey as soon as I walked into The Grapes.

She had managed to grab a booth which would give us an element of privacy. I know I have to tell all to my dearest friend and hope that she understands. I expect her loyalty at work, but I can't just expect her support as a friend. It doesn't work like that. True friendship comes from years of getting to know each other, socialising, and sharing secrets. Dave had been the one secret I had failed to share with my best mate. Would she ever forgive me for that?

I threw my bag onto the far side of the booth and scrambled in. Stacey had already grabbed a bottle of wine and two glasses sat filled with the sweet nectar. She reached across the divide and took my hand in hers.

"Madeline, you look like you have seen a ghost. What the hell has happened? Is it Charles? Or the kids?"

I took a long slug of drink before attempting to speak. "Oh Stace, I have been such a fool. I cannot believe what an idiot I have been."

"Tell me what has happened, Madeline. You are starting to worry me now. This is just so not you." My friend continued to hold my hand encouraging me onwards.

"I'm sorry. I am going to put you in a crap position but I need to tell someone. You can't tell Charles what I am going to tell you. Please Stace. I know it's not fair but." I pause as I try to gauge her initial feelings.

"I promise," she whispered.

"You don't know what you are promising. You may hate me once I tell you what I have done."

"Look just spit it out, Madeline. You are my best friend and if you can't talk to me then you can't tell anyone. A problem shared?" Stacey had a calming way about her that could settle the most anxious of souls. Just what I needed as my head is a swirling maelstrom of thoughts.

"Ok, here goes. Please don't hate me. I have been so stupid. I met a guy at that conference back in April. It all got out of hand. We became lovers. I have been such a shit," I paused to take another huge slug of wine, bolstering my nerves. "It's been going on for three months. Charles knows nothing about it and I can't let him find out. It will destroy us."

"Oh Madeline," replied Stacey. "How have you managed to keep this secret from us all?" The look of disbelief on her face was clear. "Shit, Madeline. Why? I thought you and Charles were solid."

"I honestly can't explain it. I was happy with Charles. It just happened." I shake my head slowly as I try to find the words to explain my foolishness. "It was unreal. Just a fantasy which got out of hand. Before I knew what was really happening I was in too deep. I'm just a bloody fool."

Stacey looks stunned. I'm sure she is judging me. I don't blame her. It's just not the sort of behaviour either of us would expect of the other. She takes a sip of wine before she says anything else.

"Shit, Madeline. I am shocked. I had no idea. No suspicions so I guess Charles hasn't found out yet."

"No. Charles knows nothing and I am determined to keep it that way. I cannot hurt him. He is my world. It will end us if he finds out."

"I hope you don't mind me saying this, as a friend. Surely you should have thought about that before you started this fling?" Stacey gives it to me, both barrels. I deserve it.

"Oh God. I know. I really wish I could go back in time and do it all again differently. But life isn't that simple. You fuck up and you pay the consequences."

My wine glass is already empty, so I refill and take another large gulp. I'm not really tasting the wine. It's like a soothing drug taking the edge off my shame. Stacey is my best friend but that doesn't make it any easier telling her what an idiot I have been.

"I'm so ashamed of myself. Trouble is, when you start to deceive, you weave this web of lies which all becomes so believable. I used my weekly yoga classes as cover for us to meet up. It's a dirty and sordid secret. I just don't want to hurt Charles. I have been such a fool and now I'm right up shit creek without a paddle."

"What's happened?" Stacey had taken her hand back and was sipping on her wine. I couldn't work out from her face what she was thinking, but decided to push on with my embarrassing story.

"I decided when we were away on holiday that I was going to end it. Dave seemed to be getting too emotionally involved and I didn't feel the same way. I know you will think me dreadful but I wasn't after something serious. I was just enjoying the sex." I dropped my head in my hands as I imagined how disgusted Stacey must be. "You hate me, don't you?"

"I am finding it hard to understand, Madeline. You and Charles are a great team. How could you have risked it all for sex? I know you are still a young woman but really. Why? What about the kids? You could lose them if Charles found out."

I groaned thinking about Sophie and James. My shame is complete. "I am such a fool. I don't know what I would do if Charles took the children away from me. My life would be over."

"Look Madeline. I'm your best friend. I may not approve of what you have done. But that's really none of my business. I can't judge you for something I have never done or been tempted with. No one else knows what goes on in another person's life." Stacey reached across the table again to hold my hand. "I can say this to you as a friend. Charles must not find out. It is your secret to keep. Even if you feel dreadful holding that secret. You will have to live with it."

"That's the problem. It may not be my secret to keep anymore. I really don't know what to do." Pausing to get my thoughts together, I knew I had to share the worst part with my friend. "I saw Dave today to break it off. He insisted on me doing it face-to-face. I tried to dump him over the phone last week, like a coward. Now I know why he wanted to see me. He has a fucking video of us in the act. And he wants money for it or he will send to Charles."

Stacey's face turned a shade of puce. "Shit. What the hell. That's blackmail.

You must go to the police Madeline."

I shake my head in resignation. "He said if I involve the police he will send it to Charles anyway. I cannot let Charles see that tape. It's disgusting. He will leave me if he sees it. I know I probably deserve that but I cannot do that to the children."

"Unbelievable. Do you think he is serious? Surely he wouldn't do that." Stacey was struggling to understand how anyone could be so cruel.

"To be honest it's like I never knew the bloke. He turned on me like some sort of animal in a snare as soon as I tried to end it. He was so bloody nasty. The things he said. I think he set me up from the start. It was never an accident us meeting up. He planned it all." The harsh reality of how I had been ambushed and used by this guy both hurt my pride and shamed my conscience.

"How much money?" she asked.

"Fifty thousand pounds. My deceit is worth fifty grand. That's how I know I've been set up. He sought me out and set me up and I fell for it. What a bloody idiot I am."

"O-M-G that is dreadful, Madeline. What are you going to do?" Anger against Dave had replaced the disappointment Stacey had previously felt for my behaviour. I could sense her coming round to my side. I seriously don't deserve her loyalty.

"I'm going to have to pay up. Somehow he knew that I had that inheritance from my parents. How the hell did he find that out? He knew I have some money I can pay out without Charles knowing about it." My painted nails tap irritably on the table. "It just makes me feel sick that he found out things about me and then seduced me and I was stupid enough to fall for it."

"Look Madeline, if you pay him this money, what's to stop him coming back for more? You need to protect yourself if you are going to do that. Legally."

"Easier said than done, Stace. How can I use Charles's legal team without putting them in a prejudicial position? Can you imagine me sitting down with Gerald and talking him through the sordid details? I couldn't ask him to keep it from Charles. They are the oldest of friends."

"I know what you mean. That wouldn't work." Stacey paused thoughtfully. "Look I have a mate who's a specialist family lawyer. Do you want me to talk to him, off the record? The very least you need is some sort of legal agreement that stops this snake from coming back for more money." She pulled her mobile from her bag as she continued. "Something like a secrecy agreement or non-disclosure or even some sort of restraining order. You cannot just give this guy fifty grand and hope that he sticks to his side of the story."

"Stace, would you? You are right. I need to protect myself from this guy or he can keep coming back and threatening my future. To think I made love to him and he could do this. Bastard."

I shake my head in disbelief. I still can't get my head around what's happening. Who in the hell does stuff like that?

"Leave it with me. I will ring my mate, Adam, this afternoon and get his take on it. If he can help, we can perhaps meet up with him during the week. When do you have to go back to the snake?"

"He wants the money by next weekend or Charles gets to see my explicit performance."

"OK. I will message you later once I've spoken to Adam. Now you'd better get back home before Charles wonders where you are."

Stacey was already on her feet. I could sense she had the bit between her teeth and was in protection mode for her friend.

"Thanks darling. I honestly don't know what I would have done without you. I did message Charles to say I was meeting you for lunch. He was taking the children to Pizza Hut for a treat so at least I have some time to get my shit together before I have to face them all."

We embrace as we gather our bags and coats together. I am so glad I turned to my closest friend for support. I knew I could count on her to stand by me. She may be disgusted in my betrayal of my husband, but she knows me as a good person and hopefully understands how stupid I have been. I'm not malicious. This mess is caused by stupidity alone. And my secret attraction to that bastard.

I never meant to hurt my husband. I never meant to keep secrets from my best friend. I got caught up in the moment, enjoying the excitement of something new. Something risky. And now I am going to pay the price for my poor judgement. This man hooked me in and now has me dangling on the end of a rope.

Stacey rubs my arms, encouraging my inner courage. I know she has my back and will support me through the weeks ahead. As we turn to go, she pulls me back with a cheeky grin on her face.

"On another note entirely. Was he any good?"

It seems ridiculous that we could share black humour at such a time. It's sick, but I can't help laughing. Gallows humour, I reckon.

"Bloody amazing. Never had sex like it. Not sure it was worth the money though."

CHAPTER EIGHTEEN

Adam Scott's office is something else.

One side is floor-to-ceiling glass which sets off the view of the Thames, meandering its way through the capital. The clock tower of Big Ben is visible in the distance. His office is on the tenth floor so the view over the tops of other office buildings gives an uninterrupted view of the river leading down to the Houses of Parliament. The room is dominated by a vintage mahogany desk with patterned green panels on its surface. Despite the office being modern in design, the beautiful desk complements the surroundings and gives its occupant an air of seriousness and competence. One wall is covered with a mahogany bookcase, stuffed with legal documents and tomes.

Adam is probably in his mid to late 30s, similar in age to Stacey and me. He is tall, around 6 foot tall, with close-cropped black hair. A pinstriped suit sits well with the legal image. He wears his reading glasses on the tip of his nose, with a chain dangling around his neck, as his concentration is focused on the papers in front of him. Adam is sat in the biggest leather chair imaginable which is ergonomically designed for comfort. Stacey has taken the sofa seat towards the back of the room, leaving me sitting opposite my new solicitor in a much less comfy seat. I don't really notice the lack of comfort as my mind is alert and expectant with the discussion to come.

Stacey had been good to her word and spoken to Adam at the weekend. He had agreed to work as a legal go-between with Dave. His initial counsel, via my friend, was that I shouldn't cave into bribery. With the basic details of the case I had provided him with, he understood my position that I was just not prepared to risk the tape of my misdemeanours falling into my husband's hands. Our meeting was to finalise the details before he reached out to Dave and his legal counsel.

I had spoken to Dave the day before.

I don't know how I had got through the conversation. Rage was eating me up inside as I listened to his smarmy voice. How quickly a relationship can turn from one of fun and mutual respect to disgust and hate. In a heartbeat.

I had shared intimacy with this man and now the very thought of him turned my stomach.

The conversation was an example of bluff and counterbluff. Dave was reluctant to involve any third party in our sordid business. He wriggled against my demands for a formal document renouncing any right to further funds and guaranteeing no further copies of the dirty tape were available. He was to hand over the original and all copies to me. He cited threats of disclosure to Charles unless I agreed to drop my demands.

Adam had prepared me for this eventuality and, with his support, I had remained firm, knowing that what Dave was after was my cash. If he walked away from the deal what would he have? The satisfaction of ruining my marriage. Not going to satisfy him for long, I guess. But my cash will. Hopefully.

"Right, Mrs Saville." Adam looks up from his papers and fixes his gaze on me. "I spoke to Mr Roberts's solicitor this morning. He is meeting with his client as we speak and will arrange for the non-disclosure document to be signed and witnessed. Once I have an electronic version of the agreement then we will release the funds via our client account. That way Mr Roberts has no details of your bank account. I am confident that once we have completed the transaction you will be free of this nasty individual."

"Thank you, Adam. Please call me Madeline." I smiled. "I really appreciate your assistance. I feel much more in control of the situation now. I honestly can't thank you enough."

"Thank Stacey; not me. It's not a normal case by any means, Madeline. I've been in this business for over 15 years and never seen a case like it. It wouldn't normally be something I would touch but Stacey can be very persuasive." Adam nodded across to his friend. "However, I have to say I am pretty disgusted with Mr Roberts. I am never surprised by the lengths people will go to when they want to hurt another human being. This just seems really extreme. I just wonder how the guy sleeps at night."

The phone broke into our conversation. Adam answered and once he established the caller, pressed the handset to speaker mode, allowing me to listen into the call.

"Mr Scott, it's Humphrey Jones from Jones and Wright Solicitors. I have my client David Roberts here. We have reviewed the document you have shared. My client is not comfortable with the format of the document but, having discussed the implications with my client, he is comfortable with signing it. We have two copies of the signed document which I am just about to email over to you, and I will have the original couriered to you this afternoon. Does that meet with your requirements to complete the transaction?"

"Let me just confirm with my client, Mr Jones. One moment." Adam pressed the secrecy button as he looked enquiringly across the desk divide. "As your legal counsel, I am comfortable that we don't have the original in our hands prior to releasing the funds. There is an agreement between solicitors to cover this type of eventuality and I know Jones and Wright. They are a reputable firm. Are you happy with that Madeline?"

"I trust your judgement, Adam. Let's just get this dreadful business over with."

"Mr Jones, my client and I are comfortable with that approach. I will instruct my team to transfer the money across to your clients' account. If you can confirm receipt to me. Once I have the original document in my hands, I will call you so you may release the funds to your client. Agreed?"

"Agreed. I think that concludes our business today then. Thank you, Mr Scott. Goodbye."

Adam put the phone back on the receiver as my head dropped into my hands.

Stacey was across the room and crouched before me rubbing my shoulders. "It's over, Madeline. It's all over now."

"Thank god," I whispered. "Thank you, Adam. Thank you, Stacey. I really appreciate all the help you have both given me to get out of this mess."

The nightmare was over.

A wave of emotion swept over me. It took some time before I could compose myself enough to look up at Stacey and Adam. The shame of sharing my foolishness with my best friend and her old school friend was toe-curlingly embarrassing. I had swallowed my pride in asking for help and having to share the sordid details of my behaviour.

Two faces of concern, not judgement, looked back at me.

It was over.

An expensive and embarrassing end, but God, had I learnt my lesson. I honestly don't understand how I could have put all that I held dear to me at risk, over a man. My fingers have been burnt. Expensively. But now I can put the biggest mistake of my life behind me and move on.

I had some serious making up to do with my family despite them knowing nothing about this nightmare. They will never find out how stupid I have been. The financial penalty will at least ensure that I have protected them from the fall out. I was determined to spend the rest of my life making it up to Charles and my children.

I will be the model wife and mother from now on.

No matter what it takes.

CHAPTER NINETEEN

Hampton Court Gardens are a beautiful place to stroll on a Saturday afternoon.

Looking out from the side of the palace, the gardens are laid out in formation with small conifers standing in salute. An abundance of colours filled the beds in between the expertly groomed grass carpets. Intricate patterns had been cut into the lawns adding definition. To the left, a couple of gentle banks of grass rise from the main lawn, protected by taller conifers. To the right a heavily laden rosebush marked the end of this section of the garden.

We were walking slowly towards the impressive fountain which was spouting a welcoming spray in the July heat. We had spent a wonderful morning in The Maze. Sophie and James had been full of giggles as they chased Charles through the hedge-lined paths. I had struggled to keep up, being in charge of the strollers, but could follow their voices as they screeched each time Charles jumped out to scare them. By the time we had made it to the middle of The Maze both children were hiccupping with excitement. It was so good to watch Charles playing with Sophie and James. At work he is extremely grown up and serious and his colleagues would not recognise the man growling like a bear at his younger children.

Once we had navigated our way out of The Maze, we explored The Magic Garden. Charles was again brilliant as he brought the mythical magic of the place to life. He adopted different voices as he recounted tales of strange beasts, warriors of old and mythical beings. Whilst in the Mythical Beast Lair, Sophie was determined to find every carving of the strange creatures which I delighted in helping her with. Nearby was the Crown which was built to match the design of Henry VIII's adornment. The children squealed with wonder and a small element of fear as Charles became the showman, pretending to be that notorious monarch.

I could not love this man more.

Somewhere along the way I had lost touch with the man I fell in love with. He is the perfect father. My friend. My confidant. My lover.

A COSTLY AFFAIR

How could I have ever put that relationship at risk?

We had lunched at The Tiltyard. Charles and I had indulged in large salad bowls whilst the children had enjoyed the specially prepared lunch boxes with small sandwiches and fruit pots. Indulgently we had shared a bottle of cold cider. The sweet apple taste remained on my tongue as we walked. Exhausted from excitement, the children were asleep in their strollers, gripping onto their new Beefeater teddies. Us adults knew we would have some time alone to enjoy the classic gardens without entertaining Sophie and James at the same time.

Charles reached across, gently scooping my hair behind my ear. "Darling, are you OK? You have seemed a bit remote for the last few weeks. Have I done anything to upset you?"

The look on my husband's face told of his concern and trepidation at asking the question. I flushed with the memory of recent events and the shame of deceiving this wonderful man.

"Charles, I'm fine darling. More than fine if I am honest. I have had the most wonderful day today. We really should do this more often," I responded.

"It has been wonderful. The children have really enjoyed the trip and it's done me the world of good after a tough week in the office. But seriously, Madeline, are you OK? Is something troubling you?"

"I'm sorry you think I've been a bit remote recently, Charles." I paused. I'm not sure how to open up to my husband without distressing him. "I have had a lot on my mind recently. Nothing to trouble you, darling. Just women's things. My biological clock has been ticking."

"Now you do have me intrigued. Tell me more."

"I am going to be 37 in a few weeks' time. I just can't imagine how quickly the years are flying by and before you know it, I will be in my 40s. If we want another child, the years are not working in my favour. I guess my body has been telling me to make a choice."

My troubled conscience was trying to find a way for me to make things up to my husband. Since things had ended with Dave, I had been searching my soul to find a way to atone. We had wanted a big family but since James had arrived, the thought of going through childbirth again had been low on my list of things to do. I had a tough labour with James and that had followed a dreadful pregnancy with sickness and blood pressure issues.

"Do you want another baby, Madeline?"

"I'm not sure."

I realised I was speaking the truth. If my husband wanted another child, could I do this for him? Perhaps it would make up for the unknown hurt I had done him. Perhaps it would be my penance. Allowing my husband the gift of another child even if that wasn't my first priority. I owe him emotionally.

"Darling, I know we talked about having four children but I am more than happy with Sophie and James. Unless you are desperate for more, I am happy. We have a perfect family unit. Whatever you want to do Madeline, you know you have my full support."

"Are you sure, Charles? I know it's something we talked about but I just don't think I'm ready to step back from work again."

I realised I had been holding my breath waiting for his answer. I surprised myself with the relief I felt at his words. I think I would have done it for Charles, but maybe not for myself.

"I'm certain. Madeline, you have made me the happiest man ever. As long as I have you in my life, it is complete. I love you so much darling. I want you to be happy and I will do anything to please you."

"Oh Charles, you make me so happy. I really don't deserve you."

We held hands as we continued to stroll.

With this man at my side, we would put the past behind us.

Over the last few days our relationship had seemed to move to another level.

I don't know whether it's my subconscious shame of my deceit or whether its Charles worrying that something was wrong. Our love making had become more frequent and more interesting. Slowly we had experimented with our bodies, prolonging our enjoyment. It was an unspoken change. Charles is not one to discuss sex. Gradually, I have led him down a path of passion which he seems happy to follow. His previous inhibitions have fallen away as he is eager to please.

It seems crazy that it has taken my affair to see the value of what I have in front of me. Charles is an adoring husband, a kind and gentle father to my children and now an experimental lover. Deep down, I know our relationship is safe.

It has survived the threat which Charles was oblivious to. He will never know how close we came to losing our happy family life.

I will always bear the guilt of my behaviour. But it's a guilt I will carry and a burden I will not share with my soul mate.

PART TWO – THE REVENGE

FIVE MONTHS LATER

CHAPTER TWENTY

It was the Saturday before Christmas.

A typical winter's day; cold and frosty with a hint of snow. The weather forecasters had been building up our expectations of a white Christmas for the last week. The children were bursting with excitement at the thought of snowball fights and perhaps even making a snowman. Jessica had struggled to keep them inside for a change. The joy of a wintry shower was not shared by the adults. We still had a couple of days in the office before we shut down for the festive break, and London Transport really doesn't cope well with the freezing conditions.

Amelia was with us for the weekend. It was her mother's turn to host her for Christmas so we would have an early celebration to allow Sophie and James to enjoy time with their older sister. I could hear the noise of my darlings as they bombarded Amelia with questions. She had literally been in the house five minutes and hadn't even managed to shed her coat. Amelia is amazingly patient with them and even seemed to enjoy their frantic attention. It can't be easy having such young siblings, but Amelia manages that with extreme grace.

The last few months have been incredibly busy at work. My expectations for a relaxing break between Christmas and New Year are at risk, but there is no way I am going to compromise. I will be putting my out of office on and have no intention of breaking the rules. Since the crazy debacle with Dave ended, my commitment to my relationship has been the priority.

Charles and I have reached a new level of happiness. The weekends have become sacrosanct to both of us. We haven't spoken about this shift in our dynamic. It's been instinctive. We have naturally cleaved to each other's side with a greater depth of affection. The 'Charles' of before rarely held my hand in company. He is a very complimentary husband, but over the years this has started to feel false; a habit he has drifted into. Recently his behaviours just seem more natural with a real desire to please me.

We have both changed.

It took nearly losing Charles for me to realise the value of the man I have. I don't want some gigolo who may drive me to heights of passion and ecstasy. I want a man who loves me with all his heart. A man who makes me laugh; who shares my passion for work; who plays with our children, making them giggle until we have an unexpected wet patch on the carpet. Charles is my soul mate. I wish I had realised this sooner. It's so sad that we often don't see what is staring us in the face until it's almost too late.

I risked everything for Dave Roberts.

Why?

With the passage of time, my sense of shame does not decrease. I was an idiot who paid dearly for the pleasure of his body. At night, when Charles has drifted off, I often mull over my mistakes in my mind. Struggling to believe my stupid behaviour. Anger is my best friend during those silent hours. The disbelief of that bastard's behaviour winds me up. How could he target me in that way? He set out to seduce me and swindle me out of my inheritance. What sort of man is motivated by using a woman for his ill-gotten gains? Did he enjoy my body or was it just part of the job? When he cried out in passion was that fake? I really don't know why I am bothered about that. Perhaps it's shame or just vanity? No self-respecting woman wants to think a man is sleeping with her for the money.

I just need to let these emotions go. Whilst my relationship with Charles has reached almost honeymoon heights, inside I am still stressing about what happened. I need to forgive myself and move on. Charles will never know how close we came to losing everything we hold dear. That will be my guilt to hide for the rest of our life together.

That's my penance.

Amelia breaks into my thoughts.

"Hi Madeline, I thought I would find you in the kitchen. Happy early Christmas, my favourite stepmother," her smile reaches right up to her eyes as she pulls me into an embrace.

"Your only stepmother, I hope." I laughed at the phoney shocked expression on her face. "Happy Christmas, darling. I'm so glad you could make it this weekend. The kids have been going wild with excitement." Sophie had refused to go to bed last night, demanding Amelia tuck her in before sleep despite the fact that her big sister hadn't arrived yet.

"I managed to sneak away by bribing them with chocolate. Sorry Madeline. It was only a small piece each, but it worked. I wanted to catch up with you whilst Dad isn't around." As she speaks, she is checking around the corner of the room to try and locate Charles. "Where is Dad anyway?"

"You are in luck. He's popped to the wine merchants to pick up our supplies for the week ahead. He should be back in an hour. Coffee?"

"Love one. I wanted a gossip. And to tell you my news. I've got a new boyfriend." A blush waves across her cheeks as I can tell she is bursting to tell all.

Keen to know more, I busy myself making a fresh pot of Kenyan coffee. Amelia makes herself at home on the kitchen window seat. It's one of my favourite places. A built-in seat, surrounds the bay window, covered with plump cushions.

My stepdaughter is clearly in the early throws of a new relationship. The newness and excitement brings a wealth of emotions and all you want to do is tell your nearest and dearest how happy you are. I can understand why she doesn't want to share her news with her father. He would ask too many questions about background and suitability, whereas I will just listen.

"He's called Peter. Peter McKay. I met him at Tiffany's a few weeks back. He was with a whole load of mates and he had the balls to ask me to dance. I could tell he had been watching me for ages. But not in a perverted way, you know. O-M-G he is gorgeous. Tall, dark and handsome and an incredible kisser." Amelia takes a sip of coffee as she waits for my reaction.

"Wow. Have you been out for a date just the two of you yet?"

I had hated the whole dating scene. University felt like the proverbial meat market and, unlike most of my peer group, I was fussy. Even back at college I had a reputation as the ice queen.

"Couple of times. I'm taking it slowly. With my track record, you know." Amelia did have a habit of falling hard and fast. Many an evening, I had mopped her tears as yet another guy had broken her heart. "He does seem a good one though, Madeline. So who knows?"

"What does he do for work then? Does he live in London?" I was conscious that later tonight Charles would want the full run down so my questioning had an ulterior motive.

"He does. He has a flat in Chelsea. A bachelor pad, he calls it. He's an estate agent, dealing with the wealthy Chelsea brigade. I think he's doing well financially, but can't say I have checked out his bank balance yet." Amelia laughed as we both contemplated her father's usual reaction to boyfriend material.

"I'm so happy for you, darling. I just hope he treats you the way you deserve. It's about time you found a good one. So, when do we get to meet him?" I can't remember the last time we met one of Amelia's sweethearts. Unfortunately, they didn't often hang around long enough for introductions to her family.

Before Amelia could answer we heard the sound of the door from the garage opening. "Soon," she whispered in my ear before launching herself at Charles. "Daddy, Happy Christmas."

Charles struggled to place the wine boxes on the kitchen bar before his daughter grabbed him into a huge hug. Observing the relationship between these two people, who were so special to me, was adorable. She may be a young woman, but she was still the centre of Charles's world. He was protective of her and, in my opinion, struggles to see her as an adult, with adult behaviours and faults.

I guess that's typical of fathers and daughters. This new Peter will face an uphill battle with my husband. It will take time for Charles to accept another man's place in Amelia's heart. I smiled as I thought how sorry I feel for the guy.

Perhaps I will have a quiet word with him when we meet to set expectations. If he wants a place in this family then winning over her father will need to be handled with care.

Walking over to join Charles and Amelia, I grab a bottle of wine waving it before me. "Come on you lot. Time to really toast the festive season. Let's get Christmas Day mark one started. The kids are desperate to open Amelia's gifts."

CHAPTER TWENTY-ONE

Traditions are an important family milestone, especially for children.

Both Charles and I are not overly fussed about turkey, but Amelia is convinced it's not Christmas without it. Even Sophie seems to understand the link between the large bird and Father Christmas or, should I say, the delivery of presents wrapped in glitzy paper.

Like the turkey, we are all well and truly stuffed. Lunch was served mid-afternoon and we were now settled in front of the log burner in the lounge. Charles was settled back in his favourite armchair, whilst Amelia and I were sharing the sofa. Port has been poured; an excellent vintage Charles picked up earlier. That's another thing we have in common as a couple, a passion for good wines. Charles had handpicked the bottles to complement the turkey dinner and traditional pudding. As usual his choice was impeccable.

Sophie and James are the embodiment of patience. As with all traditions, there are those that you hate as a child, but you know they have to be tolerated for the greater good. Whether it was Christmas Day or our early one for Amelia, presents aren't opened until after lunch. Once the stress of cooking was over and the vast feast consumed, the focus would shift to the giving and receiving of presents. Sophie's gaze shifted frantically from Charles to me, waiting to see which parent would crack first. I smiled at Charles and took his slight inclination of the head as agreement.

"Ok Sophie, why don't you look under the tree and find your sister's stocking."

My words galvanised our daughter into action. Another tradition in the Saville household was Christmas stockings. Each child had an embroidered pillowcase which had been lovingly created by Catherine. It shows the maturity of their marriage split that once Sophie and James were born, Catherine insisted on making the exact replica of Amelia's stocking. I treasured them. I valued my husband's ex as a friend. It's an unusual relationship, but it works.

"Let Sophie and James have their presents from me first, Madeline."

Amelia was up and across the room before I could agree. She picked up James, depositing him on Charles's lap and passing her father a large parcel for her baby brother. Sophie sidled up to Amelia, expectantly, with her thumb wedged into her rosebud mouth. She was rewarded with another large parcel and her big sister's lap.

Charles did most of the unwrapping for our son who seemed to be pulling on the same bit of paper over and over with little success. In no time the gift was revealed. James jumped up and down on his father's lap as his excitement built. Amelia had got it spot on. It was a Lego zoo with big chunky animals which anchored to a large base, with differing enclosures designed for the varied animals. The size of all the individual parts made it a safe toy for a toddler, especially one who likes to stick bits in his mouth when playing. The elephant was already making a play for favourite, wedged in between his baby teeth.

Sophie's present was now the focus of attention. The box revealed a brightly coloured dressing table with huge spotlights which pulsated when plugged in. The unit came complete with hairbrush and a realistic hairdryer which simulated a gentle breeze. Inside the centre drawer, Amelia had added some children's jewels including paste necklaces and a huge plastic ornate ring. Sophie threw herself into Amelia's arms squealing with joy.

"I love it, Meli," cried Sophie using the shorter version of her sister's name, which was reserved for her baby brother and sister. "You are the bestest sister in the whole wide world."

"Oh darling, I'm so glad you like it. Now you and Mummy can get ready together. And you can keep all your jewels safe so Mummy doesn't nick them," laughed Amelia.

Both Sophie and James were distracted by their gifts, so the adults were able to exchange presents with an element of peace. Amelia had bought Charles a new leather wallet, which he was delighted with. He liked to use a wallet until it fell apart and his current one is in a sorry state. A Mulberry handbag was my gift and I was surprised by Amelia's generosity. I was shocked at how expensive her gift was.

Amelia spotted my reaction and jumped in. "Madeline, please. I cannot thank you enough for all the help you gave me in getting my dream job. I know you keep down selling it, but I know how much support was on offer. You even fine-tuned my presentation which I'm sure was one of the main reasons I got it."

"I'm just so glad you have settled in so well and it does sound like everything is on the up for you." I winked secretly at her as we acknowledged our conversation earlier.

Finally, Amelia was able to open her main present from Charles and me. Her stocking had been filled with numerous smaller gifts including lipsticks, assorted smellies and underwear. We had found the most gorgeous bracelet of gold, inset with blue sapphires. The stones worked so well with her skin type and they had become her favourite over the years. She seemed delighted with the gift and I beamed with delight as it had been my choice. Christmas is such a special time for me. I enjoy the selection of gifts and seeing the delight on the recipient's face more than receiving presents myself.

Settling back in my seat, I observed my precious family. Charles had relinquished James and was starting to nod, his stomach full and the wine gently rocking him away. Small snores broke from his lips. Amelia and Sophie were playing quietly with the new dressing table whilst James continued to navigate his way around the zoo, introducing himself to each animal.

Christmas is a great time to reflect on the year gone by and be thankful for our blessings. Looking at my family relaxing, a feeling of overwhelming love fills me. I am so lucky to have these people in my world.

I came so close to cocking it all up earlier this year, but that is in the past. My future is centred on Charles and my growing children. My delight that Amelia may have found love is just the icing on the cake for the Saville clan.

Next year will be a better one all round. The bump in the road caused by my disgraceful behaviour did no lasting damage. I can put it all behind me and move on, surrounded by my precious family. A family I risked losing through my wantonness. Thank the Lord I do not have to pay that dreadful price for my behaviour. I know I am extremely lucky that my family know nothing about my betrayal.

And never will.

CHAPTER TWENTY-TWO

Roger Jones called attention by tapping vigorously on his wine glass.

"Guys, I just wanted to say a few words before we dig in." Roger surveyed his audience noting their slight frustration at the delay in indulging, once more, over the festive period.

It was Boxing Day at the Jones's home in Tunbridge Wells. Charles, the children and I had been invited to join Catherine, Roger and Amelia for lunch. Fortunately, it was a cold spread so dinner would not be spoiled by Roger's need to launch into his habitual Christmas address.

"Catherine and I are delighted you could join us for lunch today. Christmas is a time for friends and family and we are so happy to regard you, Charles and Madeline, as our dearest friends. It is splendid to see you and your beautiful family in such good health. So, if I may, a toast. To our friends, the Saville's, good wishes, health, and happiness. Happy Christmas."

"Happy Christmas," we chorused.

I simply adore Roger.

He is such a character and has always made me feel incredibly welcomed into his home. Roger is a stockbroker in a City firm and hugely successful, as evidenced by their impressive house in the suburbs of Tunbridge Wells. A tall slim man, well over 6 foot tall, Roger is a couple of years younger than Charles. He was brought up in the east end of London and his cockney accent has never been an impediment to his successful career. In fact, the cheeky cockney demeanour is used to his advantage.

He definitely dyes his hair as there is no way he wouldn't have a smattering of grey at his age, but whoever does it for him is good. Some men look ridiculous when they don't adopt the silver fox look, but Roger is not one of that number. He's a big character full of genuine warmth, who adores Catherine. Sadly, they haven't had children together. Roger has accepted Amelia into his family and clearly adores her. His generous nature has extended to Charles's second family and the unusual but wonderful relationship we share. It is definitely weird but it works.

Catherine is the antithesis to her second husband. She's a quiet woman who is comfortable blending into the background. To the impartial observer you would probably match Catherine with Charles and Roger with me. Just shows how wrong you can be. Catherine tolerates Roger's loud enthusiasm with a weary smile. In social situations, she enjoys being able to let Roger have his head and she can sit back and relax in his wake. Catherine is 57 so a good 20 years my senior. On the face of it we probably have little in common, except our love for Charles.

Oh yes, she still loves my husband. But as a dear friend.

Unlike her husband, Catherine has allowed her ash blond hair to take on a greying hue. She has it regularly set into short waves. She is most comfortable in an elegant twinset. I don't think I have ever seen her in casual wear. A pearl necklace and matching earrings are standard wear.

I have found a dear friend in my husband's ex. OK, there are things I certainly wouldn't tell her. My recent affair is a case in point. She is far too close to Charles for me to share any concerns in my family life. However, she has been there for me over the years of my relationship with Charles. We share a love for her daughter. Catherine has never shown any animosity to me spending time with her only child. This shows a generosity of character I admire in the woman.

At the table, Catherine has positioned herself next to me at one end. Amelia is sitting between Charles and Roger, leaving my children between us. Catherine is helping Sophie, serving her food whilst I take responsibility for James. Once the children are settled, we have a chance to talk.

"Madeline, Amelia tells me you know about her new chap. What do you think?" Catherine leans into me, conspiratorially.

"I am so happy for her, Catherine. She has only told me the briefest of details but he sounds eminently suitable. Charles has tried to grill me on what I know but I'm afraid I haven't been able to tell him much. She does seem quite smitten though. What has she told you?"

"Well, we had quite a long chat yesterday. He's an estate agent and seems to deal with high value property in the City. I think he's in his mid-30s and, by the sounds of it, is comfortable financially," replied Catherine. "I do worry that Amelia will get caught up with a money grabber, especially if they know her background. I always feel a bit better when I know they are financially self-sufficient. Does that make me wicked, Madeline?"

You would never describe Charles's ex-wife as a snob. She's just a concerned parent. "Of course not, Catherine. I feel exactly the same as you. Amelia is such a caring girl and I worry that she falls too quickly and too often for the wrong guys. Let's hope this Peter is a good 'un. Have you met him yet?"

"Not yet. I have asked her to bring him home for dinner one night. It will be interesting to vet him. You know what Roger is like. It will definitely test whether the relationship has wings," laughed Catherine. "Peter may think he's joining a mad house and run for the hills."

"And then he will have to run the gauntlet with Charles. I almost feel sorry for the guy. I wouldn't be surprised if my husband hasn't checked him out already. Well, at least financially. He does have contacts."

We were interrupted by Amelia pulling a chair up alongside us. "OK, what are you two scheming about?" she said as she gate-crashed our conversation.

"We were talking about you, not to you, darling," smiled her mother. "We were speculating about your new love interest and when we will get to meet this Adonis?" Catherine left the question hanging there as Amelia shrugged her shoulders.

"God, you two. Give it a rest. It's not as if he's my first ever boyfriend. You will get to meet him when I am good and ready," Amelia laughed. "I don't want to scare him off when he finds out I have two mothers he needs to impress."

It is so refreshing that Catherine shows no jealousy when Amelia says things like that. She really is an amazing spirit. At times I do wonder how she and Charles ever broke up. I just can't imagine them arguing.

Charles told me that they married young and just grew apart. It all sounds very civilised and grown up. Surely any marriage break up is full of anger and upset. He assured me they put Amelia at the centre of their decision and decided that they had to behave responsibly in front of their teenage daughter.

As we head back to London later in the afternoon, I reflect further on my unusual family. Charles and Catherine share a special love, one which brought them together in their twenties. Charles had just left university and was starting out in the world of finance. Catherine came from a privileged background. Her family were farmers and landowners who could afford to send their daughter to private finishing school. Girls like Catherine didn't focus on a career but on a good marriage. They met through mutual friends and, once families had approved, their path to marriage was smooth and swift.

Catherine struggled to get pregnant and, from what Charles has told me, that was the start of their marriage problems. She was desperate for a family and, without a child, his wife was lost and lacked purpose. As she approached her thirtieth birthday, she received the best gift ever, finding out she was pregnant. Amelia was a difficult birth and the doctors advised both parents that another child was not advisable. It's very sad but I think they both realised after years of trying to paper over the cracks that they didn't love each other as husband and wife, but as friends. Charles had no intention of finding solace in an affair. I don't think he felt bothered about a lack of sex life. Sex has never been a huge driver in his life.

He was concerned about Catherine though. She was a woman with a huge propensity for love and he felt he was denying her the companionship of a loving husband. He was delighted that she met Roger so soon after they split. You can tell how happy Catherine and Roger are. He knew from the start that Catherine couldn't bear him children, but that was not an obstacle to their love. Amelia accepted him as her stepfather and when I joined the scene, our extended family was complete.

It's weird really that the two families are so close. In the months ahead that closeness will be tested. Would we stay strong together as a family? Or would tribal loyalties drive us apart?

If only we had known what was ahead of us.

Would we have done anything different? Could we have done anything different?

CHAPTER TWENTY-THREE

The video call was drawing to a close as I felt the corners of my mouth curl with an escaping yawn.

It was one of those calls which seemed to have stretched on for hours without achieving very much at all. Because of my role within the company, I couldn't turn off mentally during these audios. My advice could be sought at any time during the agenda and my concentration levels had to be high. However, some of our Business Managers could 'talk for Britain.' They felt it was their opportunity to impress and often their requests for advice felt somewhat fabricated or even already resolved. Were they looking for confirmation that they had handled a situation well and placing it on record so that the bosses could be aware?

Stacey stuck her head around the door having seen my phone extension light disconnect. "I'm just popping out for some lunch, Madeline. Can I get you anything?"

"Oh, you star. I'm going to need to work through today. Got a shed load of notes to write up after that epic. Could you grab me a salad, chicken or prawn? Don't mind which. And a sparkling water please." I wafted a tenner at her.

Organising my notes, I opened a new document and started to capture the pertinent points from the latest meeting. Each week I provided a report to the board covering any issues identified across the business. It was my responsibility to identify any trends before they became a problem. Despite several of the Business Managers' efforts to impress, I had my means of getting underneath the PR and establish early signs of staff issues.

We had a zero policy on bullying within the company, and last year I had been instrumental in dismissing a fairly senior guy who had created a toxic environment. He was one of our best performers and brought extremely good business in, but to the detriment of his people. Charles would not hesitate to put staff welfare over profit. It's what has made Saville's the place to work in the financial sector.

My considered words were dancing across the page when my train of thought was rudely interrupted. The shrill of my mobile cut through the silence. Glancing at the screen I could see it was Amelia calling.

"Hi Amelia, this is a lovely surprise. Everything OK?" I balanced the handset under my cheek as I typed.

"Hi Madeline. Sorry to catch you at work but I wanted to see if you are free next Wednesday. We were hoping you and Dad would join us for dinner."

"Oh, that would be lovely. I honestly don't think we are doing anything but just need to check Charles's diary. Let me do it now." I pulled up my husband's calendar to double check his movements for that day. He was in the office Wednesday. "It looks good, darling. I will speak to him tonight and text you. I presume we are getting to meet the lovely Peter?" I smiled with anticipation.

"You guessed right. Peter suggested it actually. Think he is keen to meet Dad and get that out of the way. We were going to book a table in Covent Garden if that works for you guys?"

It had been a while since Charles and I had enjoyed a night out and the prospect of meeting the new love of my stepdaughter's life was an added bonus. Covent Garden is another favourite destination which hopefully meant Peter was our type of person.

"Thank you, Amelia, that would be splendid. I will confirm tonight. Really looking forward to meeting Peter."

We spent the next five minutes chatting as I caught up with the latest developments at The Sunday Times Magazine. Amelia seemed to be making a great first impression and was being given increased responsibility. I was so pleased that she had found her niche. Given the chance of a career at a prestigious magazine was proving life changing. She appeared more confident and certainly had a spring in her step. And now a new boyfriend who made her smile. Life was on the up for my beloved stepdaughter and I couldn't have been happier for her.

As we drew our conversation to a close, Amelia had a final request. "Madeline, I know you are super cool with Peter but can I ask a favour.

Can you work on Dad? I don't want him giving Peter the third degree at our first meeting. I do understand Dad only wants to protect me, but you know what he's like. It can be a bit overwhelming."

"Don't worry darling. Your dad will be on his best behaviour. Leave that to me." I smiled as I anticipated the conversation. Charles doesn't think he is intimidating at all, but he can come across as the judgemental father. Any chap would struggle to impress him as future son-in-law potential. "Anyway Amelia, I must go now. I'm working through lunch so really need to crack on. Will text you tonight and hopefully see you next week. Love you sweetheart."

"Love you, Madeline. Can't wait to see you."

CHAPTER TWENTY-FOUR

The evening air was crackling with frost as we arrived outside Clos Maggiore.

We were a bit early and intended to grab a drink at the bar first. Dutch courage for Charles; a moment of relaxation after a busy day for me. The entrance to the restaurant was magical. Christmas trees lined the front, decorated with beautiful white ribbons and baubles. Fairy lights twinkled liberally, inviting guests in. We hadn't been to this establishment before and first impressions were extremely positive. The ceilings were decorated with an abundance of white gypsophila, filling the room with a heady fragrance. Away on the back wall a huge fire burnt, warming the room. A slight fragrance of applewood hit my nose. The combination of smells was welcoming.

It was clear there wasn't a separate bar area as the Maître D' approached us. "Good evening, sir, madam. Welcome to Clos Maggiore. Do you have a reservation?"

"Thank you." Charles said. "We are meeting another couple who have booked ahead. Not sure if the table is in the name of Saville or McKay."

Our host clearly had a good memory of bookings as he didn't need to refer to his records before saying, "Of course. Your guests are not here yet. However, may I show you to your table?"

The Maître D', who I guessed was Italian, made his way, weaving through the tables, to reach a booth on the left-hand side of the vast fireplace. The booth gave an element of privacy which would be ideal for this first meeting with Peter.

"May I organise some drinks for you?" he asked as we settled back on the soft leather seats. His routine was practised. I don't even remember handing over our coats, but within seconds they had vanished with a colleague.

"Scotch would be excellent, thank you," said Charles. "Madeline?"

"I would love a G&T please," I smiled at our handsome host.

He had typical Italian features with an olive complexion and dark wavy hair. He was immaculately dressed and smelt amazing. I am definitely a connoisseur of male fragrances. There is something special about a man who knows the value of smelling good. Charles was a creature of habit and stuck with his Chanel brand. He wore it well though and was one of the first things I had noticed about my future husband.

Once left alone, we glanced around the dining room, taking in the ambiance. Most of the other diners were couples and tables were nicely spaced out to give a far more romantic feeling. Quiet music played in the background, just taking the edge off silence, but not intrusive.

A different, but equally handsome, waiter arrived with our drinks. His approach was professional in the extreme. We didn't really see him arrive and the drinks appeared in front of us without any interruption to our small talk. Interestingly Charles seemed nervous. From his previous discussions with his daughter, he understood how special this new man was to her. Charles wanted to like Peter and his nerves came from a worry that he wouldn't bond with this new partner. It was an unimaginable situation for my husband.

I spotted Amelia as soon as she entered the restaurant. She was glowing with happiness. Her face was alight with a beautiful smile as she handed her coat to the Maître D'. She was wearing a figure-hugging blue dress which fell below her knees and she stood tall in matching stilettos. I waved a welcome, guiding her to where we were sat. As she moved away from the door my heart stopped.

A coldness penetrated me to the bone.

Dave Roberts entered the restaurant behind her.

The shock settled in my stomach as the bile rushed to my mouth.

What the hell is happening?

My hands trembled as I clutched the edge of the table.

He looked straight at me and smiled.

My heart is racing.

Am I going to be exposed?

What the hell is he playing at?

The cold truth hits me like a spade to the gut. Dave Roberts is Peter McKay.

"Hi Dad, Madeline. Please let me introduce you to Peter." Amelia smiled sweetly as she gestured her boyfriend forward. She seemed oblivious to the look of shock and distress on my face.

Fortunately.

"Mr Saville, delighted to meet you." Dave reached a hand out to my husband and shook it with confidence before he turned to me. "Mrs Saville, I have heard so much about you from Amelia. It's almost like I know you already."

He took my hand which was trembling and lightly squeezed it. Nobody noticed me wipe it on my dress as I pulled away. I had to get away. My whole body is trembling with fear. There is no way I can sit here and pretend my world hasn't just gone into seismic shock.

As Amelia and Dave settled into their seats, I made my excuses and made my way to the bathroom. I honestly don't think Charles or Amelia noticed anything wrong, but I could see the smirk on that man's face as I made my way between the tables.

I made it to the bathroom upstairs before the bile in my throat forced my head into the toilet bowl. Luckily, it was just the contents of my G&T which spewed out. I sat on the floor for minutes, shaking as I tried to control my heaving stomach.

I just don't believe what is happening here. In what sick world would you expect your ex-lover to end up as your stepdaughter's new beau. This has got to be a set up. He knew who Amelia was. For god's sake he introduced her to her new employers. Was this always his intention? To have a backup way of hurting me.

This really is some form of nightmare. It just can't be happening. Perhaps I imagined it. I will go back downstairs and find it was all a wicked joke and the guy down there is not Dave Roberts, just someone who looks similar.

Who the hell am I kidding? This truly is a nightmare. I really want to wake up and find it's all over.

How the hell was I going to get through dinner tonight with that monster sitting opposite me?

I can't let on to Charles that I know Peter's real identity. That is just not going to happen. I didn't pay the bastard fifty grand for him to blow my cover like this.

It's some sort of test.

Dave knew what reaction he would get. He played it perfectly for the maximum shock. Letting me see Amelia first then appearing behind. Waiting to see if I gave myself away rather than forcing the issue there and then. Oh no, there is no way I am going to give him the satisfaction of knowing he has wrong-footed me. I will be the proverbial ice queen. There is no way Charles or Amelia will get any idea of the turmoil going on in my head.

It seemed like hours as I sat on the toilet floor trying to calm my beating heart. My fingers were clammy and trembling still. Slowly I fought to control my breathing.

Dave wants me to fall apart.

He wants me to give myself away.

There is no way I am going to embarrass my beloved husband.

Madeline Saville will put on a show to end all shows.

CHAPTER TWENTY-FIVE

"I'm so sorry. Do excuse me," I smile sweetly at Dave as I slid back into my seat.

"Everything OK, Madeline?" asked Charles as he reached for my hand under the table.

"Fine, darling. I'm sorry. I popped to the bathroom and then got an urgent call from the office. It's all sorted now though so no worries." I looked directly at Dave, forcing myself to remain ice cool. "It's so lovely to meet you at last, Peter. I've heard so much about you from Amelia." My smile was forced, but to the casual observer would look entirely genuine.

"I will be honest with you both, I was extremely nervous about meeting you tonight," responded Dave. He took a sip of his beer before continuing. "It's clear that Amelia is so close to you, Charles, and I really wanted you to accept me. And Madeline. Amelia talks non-stop about you so I know she values your opinion so highly."

I cannot believe the cheek of this bastard.

He can sit there and suck up to us when he knows that I know who he really is. My smile becomes even more forced that I imagine my face could crack under the strain of pretence.

Amelia has been watching the opening exchanges trying to determine how it's going. I reached across the table and took her hand, squeezing it reassuringly. The harsh reality of the situation hits me once again. Whatever happens next, my beloved stepdaughter is going to get hurt.

It will be my duty to pick up the pieces of her heart and fix it when this bastard does the dirty on her. It's my fault that her heart is in the balance. My stupidity and this evil man, who is determined to wreak my life because of our pointless relationship. What have I done to deserve this? All I did was wake up to the futility of my affair with Dave and put an end to it.

Why did I ever start that affair?

Why did I fall for some sort of nutter?

It can't be normal to behave like this.

Why would he want to hurt me even more?

He's taken my money; why more?

I am trying to figure out his motivation.

He cannot reveal our relationship to Charles as he had signed away any chance of that when he took my money. So why is he doing this? Did he meet Amelia by chance? Or is she his next victim? Bribery can't be the motive this time. So what?

Or is he doing this to get at me?

Oh, come on, Madeline. Pull yourself together. This is not about you. Surely? Why would he? My mind is in a spin with thoughts flying around.

Somehow, I will get through tonight and then see how we get Amelia out of this toxic relationship.

We fell into a polite silence as each of us perused the menu. My stomach was still performing somersaults under the table as I tried to decide what delicacy I could force down me. The menu looked amazing but the evening is spoilt for me now. I had been so excited to visit this restaurant for the first time and to meet Amelia's new boyfriend.

It all went horribly wrong when that bastard walked through the door.

I still felt sick although a few sips of a full-nosed Bordeaux was helping. After taking time to review the menu, I finally settled on a goat's cheese starter followed by rack of Welsh lamb. Hopefully, the portions would be small enough to help me carry off my charade.

As the waiter left with our orders, I decided it was time to turn the tables on Dave. Let's see how his story stacks up under pressure.

"So, Peter, tell us what you do for a living." I started the conversation off. I sat back and watched as Dave tried to impress Charles with talk of his high-powered job in commercial property. I threw in the odd question to really force him to tie himself up in lies.

He was doing well. I will give him that. Perhaps he does actually work in property rather than HR. Perhaps that was another lie he spun me. If you are going to carry on such a large scale deceit then I guess you need to be a practised liar.

Seems Dave Roberts is a master liar.

To my disgust, Charles appeared to be warming to him. They were deep in a conversation around finance for commercial units. Amelia smiled across at me, obviously picking up the vibes that her father seemed comfortable with her new chap.

This certainly wasn't going to plan. The last thing I want is for Charles to like this guy. It will make my next steps so much more difficult to manoeuvre. He seemed to be one step ahead of me yet again.

"And how long have you known our Amelia then?" I interrupted quite brutally as I tried to turn the conversation away from business. "Tell us where you guys met."

"It was in a nightclub if I remember rightly. Wasn't it, darling?"

Dave seemed sideswiped with the change in topic and certainly didn't seem comfortable. I rejoiced at his discomfort. Let him squirm. Fortunately for him, Amelia took over at this stage to eulogise about their first meeting. She was gushing about their first date when Peter had treated her to a stylish Indian at his favourite restaurant. Well, that was news to me. I could have sworn that he told me he hated spicy food. Oh, those webs are weaving again. Let's hope he gets tied up good and proper on his spinning tales.

The conversation was brought to an abrupt close with the arrival of our starters. My goat's cheese was stuffed with truffles and topped with a wonderful sauce. Despite my earlier sickness, I suddenly felt hungry and enjoyed the mix of flavours. As we ate, Dave started to ask Charles about his business. I relaxed and took the opportunity to catch up with my stepdaughter. I could see that Amelia had lost her initial nervousness and was enjoying the evening. I could only feel sorry for her as this was going to be the calm before the storm of their relationship imploding.

"Madeline, I understand you work for Charles." Dave's remark caught me by surprise. I had started to enjoy my evening, especially the succulent lamb which was draped in a broccoli puree, which was sensational.

"I do. It's a family business so I was delighted to join Charles and support him. We make a great partnership, don't we, darling?"

I made an ostentatious gesture of hugging my husband. It was amusing to see that Charles looks surprised at the spontaneous show of affection. He had the foresight not to question my behaviour, but I knew I would have some explaining to do later. We just don't do inappropriate shows of public affection, especially when in new company.

"You must have felt you had landed on your feet with that job, eh."

Dave managed to convey a meaning to that remark which wouldn't be noticed by Charles and Amelia, but was clear to me. I knew what he was implying and I certainly wasn't going to get drawn into that spat.

"I like to think that Saville's are the winners. They acquired a qualified HR manager and Charles found his soul mate."

My false smile put him in no doubt that I was not falling for his sarcasm. Charles laid his hand over mine on the crisp tablecloth in a possessive gesture.

The conversation continued to flow whilst we tucked into desserts and coffee. If I didn't know Peter as his nemesis, Dave, I think I would have liked the man. He put on a good show, praising Amelia's new job. He had obviously spent months with her and had got to know her way of life and friendship group. As I totted up the dates in my head, it became clear to me that Dave must have met Amelia soon after our relationship came to a nasty end. This just added to my conclusion that poor Amelia was being used in some sick way to get at me.

Somehow, I managed to get through the rest of the evening without making any glaring mistakes. The pressure of my performance was exhausting, but I must admit it was a brilliant performance. Charles and Amelia did not suspect a thing. The harsh reality of Dave's identity remains hidden from those dearest to me.

There is no way this man is getting away with hurting my family. He has to be stopped and I guess it's down to me to do that.

It will be difficult to stop this budding romance. Amelia seems smitten with the creep. It's going to take some careful handling, but I am determined to get this bastard out of my life once and for all.

No matter what it takes.

How profound those five words will mean in the months ahead.

CHAPTER TWENTY-SIX

The toilet flushed as Charles finished his nightly ritual.

My new Jodi Picoult was keeping me company as I waited for my husband to join me in our super king-size. I had already dumped the numerous cushions, which decorated our bed, on the floor and was snuggled against our duck down filled pillows. They were sumptuous, creating a feeling of safety and comfort. I love our bed. It is a place of happiness and tranquillity. Whilst we are not a couple who laze in bed on a Sunday morning, we always seem to be far too busy for that, our bed is our safe space. A sanctuary against the pressures of modern life.

Our night-time ritual is sacrosanct. We tend to be in bed by 10.30pm most nights and spend a good hour chatting through our day and exchanging news. Since my affair with Dave ended, my relationship with Charles has moved up a level. In the past, we had both got used to sex being a duty rather than the pleasure of holding each other, kissing, and making love.

Our lovemaking is now more spontaneous rather than a rigid once a week. Some weeks we just don't feel like it and we both feel in tune with each other. There is no blame if one of us is just not feeling it. Other weeks we seem to be making love every night or just holding each other closely and pleasuring with touch.

Tonight we are later than usual.

We didn't leave London until gone 10pm so our normal routine is out of the window. I am trying hard not to think about the debacle of this evening. I realise I will have to deal with the fallout but I really don't want to think on that yet. I am so tired and another sleepless night due to that bastard Dave Roberts is not a welcoming thought. He has played with my life throughout the last year and I am just so weary of it.

I thought I was free of him.

Well, you know what thinking does!

My stupid mistake is coming back to haunt me. In the most frightening and unbelievable way.

Charles leaves the bathroom and slowly folds his dressing gown, placing it on the antique chair which lives on his side of the bed. He removes his pyjama top and follows the same process. His carefully defined movements are so endearing. He is a man of routine and after the stress of the last year, routine brings me comfort and stability. It's what I need to keep me on track.

Flipping the covers back he joined me under the duvet, groaning quietly as he stretched out. "Oh God, this is late for a school night. I'm going to pay for that last scotch in the morning." Charles removed his glasses placing them on the nightstand.

Without a word he raised his arm and I wriggled over to rest my forehead on his chest. I could hear the rhythmic beat of his heart in time with my own. Even our hearts now beat in unison. Our marriage is precious to me and there is no way that Dave Roberts is going to destroy what we have together. Hell will freeze over before I let that happen.

"It was a good night though, wasn't it?" Charles seeks my confirmation. "I quite like Amelia's new chap. Don't you?"

I paused before I spoke as I tried to figure out the best approach. "Amelia is definitely struck on him."

I decided a non-committal view may work for tonight. There is no way I want to get into an argument tonight. I'm emotionally and physically shattered.

"I hope you don't mind me saying, darling. But you seemed a bit strange this evening. Is everything OK?" Charles was gently stroking my hair as he spoke.

"Strange?" Again, I feel like I'm playing for time.

"Well, you didn't seem yourself. It felt like you were grilling poor Peter. I don't think Peter or Amelia noticed anything but you definitely seemed more on edge than I expected."

"I'm sorry darling. I didn't want to come across too challenging. I guess we both have Amelia's wellbeing at heart." I sat up so that I could see my husband's expressions. "I have to be honest with you, Charles, I am not sure he is the man for her. There was something; I can't put my finger on it; he just didn't seem genuine."

There I have said it. I hadn't planned to.

I dropped the bomb and waited for an explosion.

As usual my husband is a gentleman and rarely argues with me. If he doesn't like something I have said or the way I behave, he has a habit of just shutting a conversation down or moving away from the situation. He really doesn't do confrontation in his personal life, even though he is totally in command of it at a business level.

"It's a shame you think that darling. I like him. He clearly cares for Amelia which is the most important thing for me. Perhaps you will warm to him. I invited them round for lunch Sunday so he can meet the children. Perhaps in a more informal setting it will be easier to get to know him."

Oh God. That man is going to be in my home. There is no way I can sort this situation by Sunday. How in the hell am I going to cope with this? I don't want him anywhere near my children. If I try to stop it happening it will definitely raise a red flag with Charles. I am going to have to find a way round it.

He is not meeting my children.

No way.

"You are right of course Charles. I'm sure it will help to meet informally without the hustle and bustle of a busy restaurant. There was one thing I thought was strange though tonight."

"What was that, darling?"

I could tell that Charles was starting to lose interest as sleep drew nearer. "Peter invited us out for dinner, but you paid the bill. It was very generous of you, but surely you should have let him pay."

"Um. I'm so exhausted Madeline. Can we continue this conversation at another time please?" Charles had already rolled over onto his left side, showing his back to me.

"Of course, Charles. Night night, darling. Sleep tight."

I lay there knowing that sleep was a long way off.

How in the hell was I going to handle this?

I don't think Dave will just going to back off because I ask him to. I'm going to have to play dirty like him. Letting Charles pay the bill is typical of the cheating bastard he is. I bet he is living above his financial station to impress Amelia. The restaurant was beautiful tonight and the food was out of this world. For Dave it probably tasted even better knowing he wriggled out of paying. Are there no depths to which this man would stoop?

He has underestimated me. I am not a woman to take his shit lying down. I will get revenge for the hurt he has caused me and I will not let him hurt my family. What is it they say about a woman scorned? Well, my fury will be his undoing.

As I lay there in the dark, my mind rolled over the problem of Dave Roberts and what I was going to do next to destroy this man before he destroyed my life.

A long night of scheming lay ahead.

CHAPTER TWENTY-SEVEN

It had been an incredibly busy morning.

Back-to-back meetings had tested my organisational skills today. Stacey had been a godsend; keeping me on track and supplying me with endless cups of coffee. I do love days like this though, normally. People think I'm mad, but the cut and thrust of switching my mind from topic to topic excites me. The stimulus and adrenaline high will keep me focused until the climb down at the end of business. That's when the tiredness will kick in but, until then, I will ride that motivational high.

Stacey popped her head around the door as I placed the handset back on the receiver. "Madeline, sorry to interrupt you. I have a call on line one. Peter McKay. Are you OK to take it or shall I take a message? He says it's urgent."

My head hit the desk as I bury my forehead in my hands. "Oh shit."

Groaning I looked at Stacey for support, needing to see a friendly face. Because of my busy schedule today the chance to update my confidant about the extraordinary events of last night had passed us by. I can see that she looks concerned at my unusual reaction. It's clear this is no normal business call.

"Stace, put him through and I will explain later. It's Amelia's new boyfriend."

I'm not going to try and tell her the horrific details just yet. That will require a glass of wine perhaps after work tonight.

"Ok Madeline. I'll put him through and if you need me to interrupt at all then just give me a wave."

My PA was brilliant at saving me from the most verbose of our team. She would have my back if this conversation got sticky. I seriously can't imagine it's going to be enjoyable for either party.

"Madeline Saville speaking." I certainly have no intention of making this easy for him.

"Maddy, Peter here. How are you doing?" Smarm drips from his mouth, turning my stomach.

"Peter or should I say Dave?" Sarcasm is obvious in my tone. "What do you want?"

"Oh, don't be like that Maddy. It was lovely to see you last night. I have missed you." Two can play that game of sarcasm. "I do like your husband. He seems a nice guy. Such a shame he doesn't know what a slut you are."

"Look Dave, I honestly don't know what your agenda is, but do me a favour. Get out of my life and leave me and my family alone. Don't forget I paid you off and you signed an agreement, so unless you want to hear from my solicitor I suggest you back off now." My hands were trembling as I tried to stay calm and firm in my resolve.

"Maddy oh Maddy. You are so naïve. I'm only just getting started. Young Amelia is one sexy woman and it's a nice diversion for me. She's not as good in bed as you were darling, but she will do. And Daddy is extraordinarily rich, isn't he?"

"Dave back off. End it with Amelia before you break her heart. She is innocent in all this and doesn't deserve your cruelty."

Rationalising with this man was never going to work. I'm treading a fine line between anger and persuasion. My head was fuming with the sheer cheek of him. I feel like giving it to him with both barrels, but at the same time I need to keep in charge of the conversation.

"Darling, I'm doing nothing wrong. Amelia is a bright, young woman. She can make up her own mind who she sees. I'm sure your solicitor will confirm that. So play nice."

What an evil bastard.

He was playing with me and enjoying every minute of it. I'm convinced that he set out to ensnare my stepdaughter. There is no way this is a coincidence. I cannot control what he does with Amelia. And he knows it. I have failed to protect her from his vile behaviour. He will break her heart and I will just have to sit there and watch. But I can influence who sees my children. There is no way they will be exposed to the devil.

"Play your games with Amelia if that's what you want, Dave. She will find out what type of man you are in good time. I can't stop you hurting her, but you will keep away from Charles and my children."

"But your charming husband invited me to lunch on Sunday and I really can't turn him down. You will just have to suck it up Maddy and play along. You really wouldn't want to give your dirty little secret away. What would Charles think, knowing I have had both his wife and his daughter? I do hope he has a strong stomach for the scandal that will unleash." Dave chuckled as he enjoyed my discomfort.

"You bastard," I whispered. "I hope you rot in hell for what you are doing. I honestly don't know how you sleep at night you evil little man."

Dave laughed loudly in my ear. "Oh, I sleep so well, Maddy. It's easy to sleep with Amelia's nubile breasts thrust in my face. She really does have a beautiful body. It's certainly no hardship fucking her. I've had worse jobs."

It was at that low point that I slammed down the handset. I couldn't give him the satisfaction of any more of his twisted drivel. He is truly an evil man. In my world, friends and family have standards of behaviour. I broke those rules when I met Dave Roberts. But surely I don't deserve this level of punishment.

The crime is not worthy of such anger and revenge.

"Stace," I connected with her extension. "Cancel my 2pm meeting would you and once you have done that, grab your bag. We are going for a glass of wine."

CHAPTER TWENTY-EIGHT

The lunchtime rush was drawing to a close.

Swiping my card, I juggled purse and two wine glasses as I made my way across the emptying bar area to a table set in a bay window. Stacey was reviewing her phone as I joined her and she quickly popped it back in her bag.

"Come on then Madeline, spill the beans. What happened last night?"

Taking a glug of wine, I organised my thoughts. "You seriously could not make it up Stace. Peter McKay, Amelia's boyfriend, is actually Dave Roberts."

"What the hell. How?" The look on Stacey's face would be highly amusing if it wasn't for the seriousness of the situation. The expression gobsmacked came to mind.

"He just walked into the restaurant behind Amelia like he had no cares in the world. I honestly don't know how I didn't give away the whole sorry tale right then. I had to rush off to the loo. Threw my guts up." My stomach grumbled at the memory. "Then I had to go back and face him and pretend he was who he said he was." In frustration I tugged at my hair in an attempt to tidy a loose tendril which was poking out above my ear.

"Shit Madeline. What sort of sick joke is he playing?"

"My thoughts exactly. Amelia first told me about Peter about a month before Christmas so it can't be that long after I paid him off. He must have gone out to target Amelia to get back at me."

"But why would he do that? You paid him a lot of money to get him off your back." Stacey was shaking her head with disbelief.

I totally get her confusion. The whole situation is a nightmare. It's beyond belief. To most sane people, of course. But this creep is not normal. As I am finding out.

"He is one sick bastard. And a clever bastard at that. Those documents Adam got him to sign restrict him from threatening to expose me to Charles. They don't stop him from wheedling his way into my family via my stepdaughter."

"I'm shocked, Madeline. I just don't understand why he would do this. Surely he has hurt you enough without doing this?"

The same question had been rolling around my thoughts for the last twenty-four hours. He did enough damage to me before. Making me admit my shame to my friend, taking me for a gullible fool and punishing me in the wallet too. And now this.

"I have tried to work it out in my head, but I don't think I can. I don't think we are dealing with a normal person. There is something wrong with him. He doesn't think or act like a normal person. I thought he was just a con man, but I think there is something more to it than that." I took another slug of wine as I framed my words carefully. "I'm scared Stace."

The conclusion I had reached in the early hours of this morning was that perhaps he is some sort of psychopath. This isn't normal behaviour. This speaks of some form of mental health issue and a dangerous one too.

"Oh God, Madeline. I really don't like the sound of this. What the hell are you going to do?"

"That's the problem. I don't have a bloody clue." I took another large slug of wine as I tried to think about the enormity of what I was facing. "He's got me. I can't say anything to Amelia. She seems pretty smitten. Poor cow."

"Amelia is so close to you. Do you not think you could talk to her in confidence?" Stacey threw out the suggestion more in hope of a solution than the reality of how difficult that conversation would be.

"I can't do that. No. It will devastate her and I will be asking her to keep secrets from her dad. I may be close to her but can you imagine telling her I have done the dirty on her dad and the guy is now her boyfriend? She will literally lose it."

We sat in silence for some time.

None of what's happening makes sense. It's a nightmare that just keeps giving and giving. I'm not dealing with a normal man. There is something seriously wrong with him if he is getting his kicks out of this. And deep down I'm scared. This is bigger than money now. He wants to hurt me. Perhaps he wants to destroy my happy family life or just destroy me. The problem is that, without understanding what drives someone to do such evil, it's so hard to comprehend their thinking. He must really hate me to behave in this extraordinary fashion.

I honestly don't know why he is so determined to do this to me. OK, I made a mistake when I slept with him. Well, I made a load of mistakes. Every week. But we were both consenting adults. I didn't force him to do anything he didn't want and he hardly seemed heartbroken when I ended it. So why?

"Madeline, why don't you ring Adam this afternoon? Perhaps he can suggest a plan." Stacey was already pulling out her mobile to check my diary for the rest of the day. "You have a free slot at 4pm. Why don't I text Adam and see if he can spare you 5 minutes?"

"OK thanks. It's worth a try, I guess. Not sure whether he can magic something out of this mess. Dave seemed to think that he is untouchable, legally, as the document he signed only covered me and Charles. Never in my wildest dreams did I think he would go after Amelia."

"This whole situation is just crazy" Stacey said as she multitasked, texting Adam. "What about going to the police? This must be harassment or something?"

"If I go to the police then the whole damn mess will blow up in my face. I just can't do it to Charles." I groaned resting my forehead against a clenched fist. "I have to make a choice between hurting Amelia or destroying my marriage. I'm sorry but it's a no-brainer in my book."

I felt an absolute bitch saying those words.

Amelia had waited such a long time to find a decent guy and now she is mixed up in the worst kind of mess imaginable. But she's a big girl now and

I can't protect her without doing extreme damage to my own life. I'm going to have to let it run its course with Dave. Perhaps he will get bored and move on. Perhaps she will see the nastiness of his soul and dump him.

Either way she will have to deal with it.

On her own.

I need to protect Charles and my children from the consequences of my stupidity. And it starts this weekend. There is no way Sophie and James will be at home on Sunday. If Charles doesn't like it then I will cope with that fall out. It's for the greater good. Once Sunday is out the way, I will do all I can to avoid any future contact with that slimeball and keep my fingers crossed that Amelia sees him for the rat he is.

CHAPTER TWENTY-NINE

The doorbell sounded my death knell.

The moment I have been dreading for days had arrived. Staying put in the kitchen, I leave it to Charles to greet our guests. I can hear the noise of welcoming chatter as Amelia and Dave remove coats and shoes. It will be some moments before my absence is noted and I will use that time effectively to paint a smile on my face, which will be as false as my welcome.

True to my word the children are out. I had a quiet word with Jessica and she agreed to take Sophie and James with her to Bella's flat. I made up some story about not wanting the children to get too attached to Amelia's new boyfriend, just in case he went the way of most of her previous beaus. We had kept it low profile with the children so they didn't think they were missing out on anything, and there were actually over-excited about the chance to visit Bella's home.

Charles was pissed with me over my decision but as usual he can't stay angry with me for long. I think he wanted to show off the children. They are both adorable and win over the hearts of most of our friends. He doesn't understand why I have such a reluctance to expose them to Amelia's Peter. If the guy was just Amelia's Peter, then of course I would go along with it. But I know his true identity and that is a completely different kettle of fish.

Stacey had got me some time with Adam, but unfortunately there doesn't appear to be an obvious course of action. Talking to him I was overcome with despondency. We had worked up the previous documentation believing Dave was a con man who was after money. We are not dealing with a con man now. This is a whole new level of manipulation. Without getting the police involved, the chances of stopping Dave by using a legal route seems slim. Any attempt to try court injunctions would lead to uncomfortable disclosure which I am not prepared to agree to. To go down that route I may as well come clean with Charles and risk ending my marriage.

The harsh reality of the present situation remains that I have only one option. Live with the lie and somehow go along with Dave. I must pretend I don't know him and wait for Amelia to end it. I just can't see him keeping up the pretence for much longer. He will get bored and move onto the next victim.

I hope.

I've left it long enough and can no longer hide in the kitchen. I can hear Charles showing our guests through to the formal lounge so, untying my apron, I make my way to join them. Passing the hall mirror I catch a glimpse of my profile. Not a hair out of place. A quick touch up of my lippy and I'm ready to face my foe.

Entering the lounge, the smile is fixed on my face. I will act the perfect hostess for the next few hours. "Peter, Amelia, welcome. So lovely to see you both."

The dishonesty in my voice was laughable.

As long as Charles and Amelia don't notice then I will get away with this. I exchange a warm embrace with my stepdaughter and offer an ice cold cheek to that bastard, Dave. Now that's one thing I will need to concentrate on. The last thing I need is a slip of the tongue and getting the names mixed up. The whole house of cards will fall down on my head if I'm careless.

Charles took the lead in the conversation as he served pre dinner drinks. He was discussing business with Peter as Amelia remains fixated on her boyfriend's every move. It's quite pathetic to watch and I cringed internally with embarrassment. The poor cow has no idea. She is clearly smitten which makes the stakes even higher.

Rather than watch her making a bigger fool of herself than necessary, I grab her attention. "Amelia darling, why don't you join me in the kitchen and we can leave the boys to their chat."

Amelia initially seemed reluctant to leave Peter with her father. I left her no choice by making my way out of the room and almost forcing her to follow. The dinner needed little attention as a casserole is bubbling away in the slow cooker. Just the vegetables which need steaming and a quick turn of the potatoes. It does, however, give me the opportunity to talk to Amelia in private for the first time since I found out about Dave's deception.

"So, how's it all going with Peter?" I asked.

Amelia was sipping her white wine as she slid her bottom onto a breakfast bar stool. "It's amazing Madeline. I think he's the one." The silly girl blushed as she talks. "I know we've only be going out a month but I think I'm in love."

Inside I groaned whilst the smile on my face doesn't waver. "Oh darling. I don't want to piddle on your bonfire but please be careful. You are such a caring girl and you are so quick to share your emotions. Just be kind to yourself and take it slow. Please."

I reached across to take her hands in mine. My worst fears are bubbling under the surface. Amelia is not a great judge of character and she has been hurt so many times before. She doesn't have the strength, or is it cynicism, to peel the layers from an individual's character to get to know the inner core. She takes people at face value, believing that they are showing their true colours. It's an endearing quality which I love. But it's one of those qualities dangerous for the heart. She sees the good in others and naively believes that everyone has the same values and behaviours as she holds.

"I know, I know. Amelia's heart is running away with itself again," she laughed, watching the expression of frustration on my face. "I know I don't have a great track record with relationships but I think that's because I have been wasting my time on guys my own age. Peter is a grown up. It makes such a difference."

"I totally get that. Older men can be so much more attentive and appreciative. I can speak from experience with your dad. My advice is to take it one step at a time. You are in no rush so just enjoy things and see how things develop."

"You are so sensible, Madeline. I do appreciate it. Mum just wants me married off I think, so every time I meet someone new, she's out buying a new hat."

We both laughed at this remark although Amelia's laugh is genuine whereas mine is forced. Perhaps I should have a word with Catherine and try to get her to cool down the pressure on the marriage stakes.

Before long, the dinner was ready and it was time for us to join Charles and Peter. Once the food had been served the conversation moved between us, with Charles conducting the dialogue like an orchestra. It's another one of his qualities; the ability to bring individuals into the discussion and making their contribution feel valued.

I feel like I'm on the periphery of the conversation for most of our main course as I observe the interactions between my husband and ex-lover. Seeing them together is a stark reminder of my deceit. I am staggered that I was willing to risk everything for a few nights in the sack with Dave. Just looking at him makes me sick to my stomach. Whatever did I see in him? He just cannot compete with Charles. Charles is a gentleman in the true sense of the word. He is gentle and kind and has the natural ability to make me feel precious.

My silence was becoming obvious and I decided it was time to stir the pot. It's wrong but I want to see how the guy copes under pressure. He has spent the last few months making my life hell so let's see how he handles the tables being reversed.

"Peter, I can't get over how familiar you seem. You must have a doppelgänger out there. When we met at dinner last week, I could have sworn we had met before." My smile was sickly in the extreme.

It's pleasing to see that Dave looks decidedly uncomfortable at this change in direction. It takes him a few moments to compose himself. He wasn't expecting that. Let's see whether he decides to crank the pressure back onto me. A bit of psychological ping pong perhaps.

"I honestly can't imagine another one of me out there." He laughs. "I don't think we have met before. I certainly would remember such a beautiful woman. Sorry, Amelia." Dave smiles across at his girlfriend.

"Oh, don't apologise," responds Amelia. "I should have warned you how stunning my stepmother is. She's certainly no wicked witch with a poisoned apple."

We all laughed.

Flattery is not getting him off the hook now. Dave still looks decidedly uncomfortable. His face has a sheen of sweat developing across his top lip. A flush is creeping up his cheeks.

I am actually enjoying this now. Is that wrong?

No definitely not. He has the brazen cheek to come into my home, my inner sanctum. He deserves to feel awkward.

"It's just I could have sworn I saw you at one of our HR conferences in Manchester earlier this year. But it can't be as we didn't have any property experts at the event. Must have been your doppelgänger."

I smiled sweetly across the table, making eye contact with a swagger. Fifteen Love. Over to you, snake. Get yourself out of that one.

Dave coughed and ran his finger under his collar in an attempt to loosen it. The tension between him and me goes up a notch. Charles and Amelia luckily have no idea about the underlying atmosphere.

"Interesting. Definitely not me. Can't imagine anything worse that a group of HR experts contemplating their navels." Dave coughed again and took a sip of water. "They do say that everyone has an exact double somewhere in the world. I guess mine is in Manchester."

Fifteen all. I'm actually quite enjoying myself now.

"Well, if you are going to have a double of yourself, then Manchester is a lovely city for it. I hear the nightlife there is exciting, if a bit wild," I add. "Although that particular conference was not blessed with any action. I have definitely had better." The pause is loaded. "As expected, a whole load of HR professionals spouting their theories. Nothing special at all."

This game of innuendo tennis is getting interesting. Dave smiled sickly at me. He knows my game and despite his plan to make me squirm with his presence in my home, it's starting to look like the shoe is on the other foot. It's clear he doesn't want his game exposed too soon. I want him to know that he has an equal adversary in me. I am not going down without a fight.

Bored with the fight now, it was time to move on. I've had my fun and put a shot across his bows. At least he knows I'm not going to take this torment without a fight. But I need to be careful. The last thing I want was for Charles to pick up an unnecessary vibes.

Be a good girl now and shut it. Change the conversation completely, I think.

"Is everyone ready for sweet? Apple crumble and crème anglaise coming up."

As I left the room, I could swear Dave winked at me. He is onto my game. And knowing Dave as I do, he is probably getting off on it.

The bastard.

CHAPTER THIRTY

My blades cut through the fresh snow sending a powder of ice skywards as I perfected the turn.

It was a perfect day for skiing. Sunlight was beaming down on us taking the icy chill away. It was early enough in the day for the sun to complement the slopes, adding brightness and warmth. Later this afternoon it will wreak damage on the piste making it slushy and more challenging, especially on the lower and busier slopes. Motes of light glimmered through branches of pine needles which populated the run as we made our way to the bottom of Hochgurglbahn.

Charles and I had spent the morning traversing the red and blue slopes around Hochgurgl. This part of the resort was slightly quieter than the main area of Obergurgl where our chalet was located. A short bus ride away to Hochgurgl, although we had decided to grab the cable car this morning to speed our way across resorts and avoid some of the crowds. We had arranged to meet Jessica and Bella at the Top Mountain Star for lunch. We were looking forward to a bit of quality adult time. The children were in ski school until early afternoon.

My skiing certainly wasn't as competent as Charles's, who had fine-tuned his skill over years of annual ski holidays. He and Catherine used to travel around the world seeking out the best resorts. Amelia had learnt to ski almost as soon as she could walk, so Charles was keen to replicate that skill with our children. I had picked up some intense lessons on our first holiday together and I impressed myself that I could just about keep up with Charles. I didn't possess his confidence but had managed to gain a level of competence which allowed me to try most slopes. I draw the line at steep black runs. Those were the exclusive domain of my husband. I could stand at the top of a black slope and all my training and confidence would be sucked out of my heart. I had found my level and was happy with that.

In synchronisation we swirled to a stop at the base of the cable car. A group of boarders hung around the entrance gates, blocking the way in a fashion only teenagers can. They didn't seem to understand the urgency of skiers. The difference between the two disciplines. Skiers accepted the cable car or chair lift as a necessary evil to get back to the top of the mountain. An opportunity to rest weary legs and discuss the next route down. The boarders had a whole different social scene which seemed to involve meeting up in larger groups and enjoying their sport as a group.

I guess that's why Charles is a skier. He is so much more comfortable in his own company or with a small group. He could never be described as the life and soul of a party. That was the principal reason why we hired a chalet rather than book into a hotel. Despite the expense, he would insist on our own chalet with maid to make our stay perfect. This year we had invited Jessica and Bella along. I really appreciate all the little extras Jessica never complains about doing for me. This was our little way of thanking her. Both girls had the rudiments of skiing in their back pocket. The added bonus was that they could spend time together whilst the children were in ski school.

I was determined that Jessica did not see this holiday as a working gig. Once ski school finished each day, I would meet Sophie and James back in resort and spend the afternoon back at the chalet. Most afternoons they were shattered from their exploits and James, especially, would end up napping. That gave me the chance to snuggle up in front of the open fire with a decent novel and possibly a warming draft of mulled wine. Sophie would curl up beside me, determined to interrupt my peace with her observations on the morning lesson.

Charles, Jessica, and Bella would be out on the slopes until the last lift of the day. The girls shared my husband's passion for the great outdoors and saw any time back at the chalet during daylight hours as a waste.

Pushing our way through the teenagers, we made our way onto the cable car. Charles grabbed both sets of skis and loaded them into the exterior storage space. We pushed our way into the cabin, picking seats nearest the exit for a quick release. I pulled off my gloves, rubbing my fingers together as the blood rushed to my fingertips. The pain was exquisite. The sun may be beaming but the temperature was in the minus figures so, when you stopped for a period of time, the harshness of the cold could chill you to the bone.

Pulling out my phone to check my messages, I could see one from Jessica to say they were already at the top and had grabbed a table. I wafted the phone towards Charles motioning him to read the message. The noise in the cabin was deafening. Numerous conversations in myriad languages made conversation almost impossible. Sign language seemed the best policy.

The views across the mountainside were outstanding as we progressed to the top. Ant-like shapes meandered their way downwards, evidence of the sheer scale of this resort. At the end of the second stage of the Hochgurglbarn, there was short slope which led to the chairlift which would deposit us at the Top Mountain Star. Clicking our skis back on as we made our way out of the cable car building, we slowly edged down the slight slope. It was clogged with other skiers making their way towards lunch. I heaved a sigh of relief knowing that we would not have to fight for room at the popular restaurant.

The journey up the chairlift was swift. A cold wind had picked up towards the peak and stung my cheeks as it whiplashed across our faces. As we reached the top there was a scramble of bums as we shuffled towards the edge. The art of disembarking a chairlift with grace and poise was a talent which I'm afraid I don't profess to own. With all the craft of a giraffe on roller skates, I wobbled my way clear of the advancing chairs as we cleared the loading area and snowploughed across to the restaurant entrance.

Charles was a dab hand at finding the best place to leave our equipment. Unlike many people in the resort, we owned our skis and poles so would do all in our power to ensure they were stored apart from the general crowd of rental equipment.

The Top Mountain Star was a circular building with a huge bar area in the centre which was heaving with those looking for a quick drink. Around the perimeter were tables facing out towards the slopes of both Austria and Italy. A few round tables were dotted strategically outside of walkways, to allow those who wanted to dine a level of space and comfort.

Jessica was on her feet waving vigorously to grab our attention. She had managed to find one of the best tables possible which was set back from the bar in the quietest area of the restaurant. It also had waiter service, an added boon as the bar was five deep by this stage.

The act of disrobing began. Helmets, goggles, gloves were stacked on the window ledge. Our ski jackets followed. Settling into my chair, I popped open the rivets and eased the tongue of my boot outwards. The blood rushed to my toes as they were released from confinement.

"Oh God, my feet are killing me." I groaned, committing the faux pas of removing my boots at lunch. I knew I would pay for it later but I just needed some relief. "Sorry girls, promise my feet don't smell."

Jessica giggled as she wafted her own socks in my direction. "Beat you to it, Madeline. Have you had a great morning both?"

"Fabulous skiing," interrupted Charles. He went on to describe the different routes we had covered. With ski map in hand, he and Bella had heads down tracing the various pistes. Bella was a confident skier, much better than Jessica and me. Most evenings she had consulted with Charles about the plans for the following day. The lesser experienced halves of the partnerships would accept and follow those plans.

Discussions were interrupted by the waiter arriving to take our order. We all agreed on the goulash soup with a bottle of Austrian wine to share. There is something about cold, wintery weather to bring out the delights of soup. Goulash is a firm favourite, crammed full of succulent meat and vegetables. Spicy paprika gives an extra kick. I'm not normally a fan of soup, but this particular variety just seems synonymous with our ski holidays.

Our food and wine arrives at breakneck speed. The waiters certainly earn their money as they charge from table to table during the lunchtime rush.

After Charles had poured each of us a glass, Bella jumped into the conversation.

"Charles, Madeline, I just wanted to say thank you so much. I was so touched that you invited me along on your holiday and I really appreciate your generosity. Jessica and I have had the most wonderful time." She raised her glass in salute. "I'm not just saying it, but you guys are seriously the best people ever."

"Oh, stop it!" I blushed at her enthusing.

"No honestly Madeline. I have worked in the nanny game for years now and have experienced some great parents and some dreadful ones. You guys are unique. You work hard in a cut-throat business, but seriously are the loveliest people too. Jessica is so lucky to work for you."

"Defo," added Jessica.

"Also, not many parents would be OK with their nanny being LGBTQ. Most can't cope with any type of relationship," continued Bella. She was on a roll and obviously passionate about the turn of the conversation. It wasn't something that had ever concerned me. Their own business and certainly didn't affect the way Jessica did her job. "I love the fact that you have supported me and Jess when our families haven't been the kindest. You are the best and we love you both."

"Oh, Bella. That's so kind of you to say. Being a working mum is never easy. I think we are programmed to feel guilty from the day we go back to work, leaving our children behind. I can only do my job because of Jessica. The children love you both so much. This holiday is our way of saying thank you for all your support and care for Sophie and James."

"Have you lot finished the self-appreciation," laughed Charles. "My goulash is going cold."

As a group, we burst into laughter which had been a general theme of the holiday so far. It was so good to be able to relax and enjoy the company of friends. The chance to forget about the debacle which was Dave Roberts, for a while at least.

We had been exceptionally lucky to find Jessica and bring her into our family. She gave the stability to our home life which made our work experiences fruitful. Before I had conceived Sophie, I had not contemplated the thought of sharing my home with another woman. I used to be very emotionally insecure, so having a pretty young woman sleeping down the corridor from me seemed crazy for my mental wellbeing.

Jessica had never felt like a threat. She was a beautiful person inside and out and we trusted her with our children's lives. She was undoubtedly a surrogate mother to my little darlings.

Selfishly I know she made my life easier. I'm not sure I could have juggled nursery places and a full-time job. Something would have had to give and it wouldn't have been work. I know that makes me sound like a right selfish cow, but it's a fact.

I love my kids, but work is an important part of my life; a part the children had to fit round. People say that the early years fly past too fast and that you really need to enjoy your children while they are young. Before you know it, they are all grown up and ready to make their own life without you. So having Jessica in our lives gave me the chance to not feel so guilty about the gaps.

Imagine if I knew then how much I would come to rely on Jessica in the months and years ahead. Could I have altered direction at any point? Or was I just dragged along to play this dreadful game of cat and mouse with Dave? At least our holiday gave me a chance to avoid Amelia's simpering over that evil man. While out of the country I was save from his nasty machinations.

For now.

CHAPTER THIRTY-ONE

Oxford Street was heaving.

Who decided it was a good idea to hit the West End on a Saturday? Crazy.

Amelia grabbed hold of my hand as she swerved direction and headed off down Regent Street. Panting, I pulled my bags behind me as we weaved through the bodies towards sanctuary. Within seconds, the crowds were behind us and we drew to a stop. God, I must get back in the gym I thought to myself, as I dragged the breath back into my lungs.

"Come on Madeline," cried Amelia ready to go again.

We spotted '& Other Stories', a small boutique and made our way inside. Amelia was in the mood to spend money, especially as it was pay day for her. Her enthusiasm was infectious. I hadn't been girly shopping for ages, so was great to follow her around her favourite stores. I was making good headway on my credit card bashing. Already had a new pair of jeans and some stylish, black, heeled boots in my bags. The children would benefit from a trip to Hamleys shortly, once Amelia had her fill of clothes.

It was clear that my stepdaughter was in the mood to try on some more outfits. I was soon absorbed in flicking through the rails to find some suitable items to play with. Interestingly the shop held myriad beautiful and stylish outfits. I can't believe that I hadn't explored this one before. It didn't take me long to find a number of outfits to join Amelia in the dressing room.

Amelia has no embarrassment about her body. She insisted on sharing a cubicle so we can compare and contrast our looks. Within moments she was standing there in her bra and thong surveying which item to try first. Shrugging my shoulders, I decided it was best to join in the 'all girls together' look.

We spent a fabulous half hour wriggling in and out of outfits.

Amelia has excellent taste. She could look stylish in a bin liner. I guess there is something about being born into wealth. Going to the right schools, where deportment is on the curriculum, as well as the traditional subjects, must help. She has a certain type of class about her. I felt a tad awkward at first as my first couple of choices are just so wrong. They barely flatter my figure and I wonder how I ever thought they would be suitable.

Before my frustration leads me to give up, I noticed a royal blue slimline dress I had picked up as an extra but had discounted. Pulling the beautiful material over my head, I smoothed the folds down over my body.

"O-M-G Madeline. You look hot." Amelia stepped back in admiration as I looked at my profile in the full length mirror.

"Blimey. It does suit me," I replied with an element of shock in my voice. It really wasn't my normal type of outfit but it certainly does something for me. "You are naughty Amelia. Now I am going to have to buy it."

"Oh, as if you need much persuasion!" Amelia was wriggling out of her latest outfit. "I'm done, I think. You?"

"I think so. Just this dress I think for me. How many are you getting? All of them at a guess."

Amelia sorted through her hangers discarding a couple, but there were definitely more in the buy pile than not. As we changed back into our own clothes, Amelia suggested lunch. Shopping had been a tough gig today so I was hungry and needed a rest. At the cashier desk I was not surprised to find Amelia was putting the best part of £500 on her credit card. It is not my place to express caution at her spending so I bite my tongue. My paltry £150 on one dress doesn't seem so bad then.

Moments later we pushed open the doors of the Slug and Lettuce on Hanover Street. Whilst the place seemed busy, it wasn't hard to find a quiet table. Amelia opened up the menu and gave it her full attention.

"Let me get this," I said. "I think you have to go order at the bar." I glanced around the restaurant checking whether I was right. A lack of waiters confirmed my assumption.

With Amelia's order in my mind, I squeezed through the surrounding tables to reach the bar. A tall, skinny girl with lank hair turned as I approached.

She was chewing gum and had an expression on her face which was far from welcoming. In fact, she looked terminally bored.

"Table number," she growled.

"Oh gosh. I don't know the number. It's that one over there." I pointed towards Amelia. The ignorant madam had the nerve to huff as she entered the table number into her computer. I seriously don't know how she got the job.

"What ya want?"

Wow, this gets better and better. If it wasn't for the fact that we are both hungry and tired I would walk out right now. I spot her name badge, making a mental note. "Kylie, I would like a Chicken Caesar salad, a Goat's Cheese and Fig salad and two glasses of Chardonnay please." The sarcasm in my voice is lost on this dimwit.

"£36.90 then." Kylie, full of charm, wafts the card machine at me. Not so much of a thank you. Once the transaction is approved, she tears off the receipt and hands it to me. "Cutlery is over there." She gestures towards the end of the bar without making any eye contact yet again.

"Oh, thank you so much Kylie. You have a good day, won't you?" I turn from her and grimace at Amelia who is watching me with a grin on her face.

"What a delightful young lady," I laugh as I joined Amelia back at our table. "God knows how these businesses survive when they employ staff like her. What an ignorant bitch."

If there is one thing that really can get my goat it's poor customer service. I don't care if it's a five-star restaurant or a chain, the customer should always feel special. Good service costs nothing.

"Anyway, relax now Madeline. Don't let the silly cow spoil our day. Tell me all about your holiday. How did the kids enjoy skiing?"

I was glad to change focus. "Oh Amelia, you should have seen them. They loved it."

This holiday had been the first time we had put Sophie and James in ski school. Previous holidays they had only enjoyed the delights of the crèche. "They had the best ski school ever. They had lessons for a couple of hours every morning, then the same group of children went into crèche for the rest of the day. It was amazing. They settled in so well with the other children."

"Did you get to see them skiing at all?" Amelia was passionate about the sport.

"Yes, it was so sweet. They had these little bibs on with a yellow balloon on their backs so the coach could recognise their group. I know it was just the nursery slopes, but I felt so proud seeing them make their way down the slope. And so funny watching them fall over."

I smiled remembering the numerous tumbles. Luckily both children were so near the ground already they didn't have far to fall.

"How adorable. Before you know it, they will be racing you down a black run. What about Jess and Bells? Did they have fun?"

"I think so. We didn't cramp their style. Most of the time they were out together. We met for lunch on the odd day. The evenings were great though. We had a beautiful chalet and an amazing chalet girl called Rachel. She cooked the best meals."

It had been lovely to kick back in the evenings and let someone else pamper the family. Each night we had a three-course meal which was at restaurant-level standard. Rachel was a talented cook and baker. Every afternoon there was a different cake prepared for our return from skiing. Thank goodness I had been getting plenty of exercise or I could have looked like a blimp by the time I got home.

"Wow sounds like you picked a good chalet then. How about you and Dad? Skiing good." Amelia balanced a piece of chicken on her fork in anticipation.

"Your dad loved the resort. You know what he's like. He was out as soon as breakfast was done. He would stick around the local slopes until I had dropped Sophie and James off. Then we were off all over the resort. It was hard enough getting him to stop for some lunch. I would leave your dad after lunch to pick the children up so he wouldn't be back until last lifts."

"Don't you mind getting all the childcare responsibilities Madeline? Surely Dad should do his bit with them?"

Amelia had been used to seeing her mother, who didn't work, taking all the care responsibility and was concerned that the beloved dad was taking his second wife for granted.

"Oh, I honestly don't mind. I really can't manage a whole day skiing and I know how much your dad loves it. To be fair I really enjoyed the afternoons, snuggled up with Sophie in front of a raging fire." James loved an afternoon nap. "She is becoming quite a conversationalist for a four year old. Chatterbox more like."

"Oh, bless her. She is a love," said Amelia who had a soft spot for her little sister.

"Changing the subject, how is your love life?" There. The elephant in the room is out of the proverbial bag.

"Good thanks. I really like him, Madeline. I know you said I should take it slow but I don't think I can. I think he is genuine. He really cares for me and we have such a great time together."

My heart drops hearing her eulogise about that rat. Conscious of being two-faced I continue, "I'm happy for you darling. You deserve to be happy. I just hope it all works out well for you."

"Well, the sex is pretty damn mind-blowing," laughed Amelia. "Another reason for having an older boyfriend. They are just so much more considerate of the woman's needs."

"Too much information darling." I closed that conversation down with a bit of humour.

The last thing I want to do is exchange notes on Dave Roberts's love-making skills. I know to my own shame what a great lover he is. The difference is that I know the real man behind that mask. It's all a show for him. I'm sure he doesn't feel anything for my gullible stepdaughter. No different to the way he used me and then hurt me. He will do the same to Amelia in time. I just wish I knew how to protect her before this goes too far.

I quickly move the conversation on to work. I'm not ready to hear about my stepdaughter's happiness.

It is all false. He is playing her and unfortunately Amelia will be the last to know it.

One day soon she will find that out.

For now, ignorance is bliss.

I do feel a cow letting her fall for the bastard but what can I do? I'm being selfish but my marriage is more important to me than Amelia's stupid love affair. She will have to shift for herself.

CHAPTER THIRTY-TWO

A fine drizzle clings to my hair as I leave the office. It's that type of rain that doesn't warrant a brolly but will cause havoc with the frizz.

I'm meeting Catherine for a spot of lunch. She's enjoying a shopping trip in the West End and has agreed to meet for a break in her spending spree. I have juggled my diary and booked a restaurant near St Paul's Cathedral, a suitable halfway point for us both.

Work has been incredibly busy over the last few weeks and I really haven't found the time to check in with Catherine. We've exchanged a few text messages about Amelia and her new boyfriend. As my stepdaughter had enlightened me, her mother seems very keen on Peter and is definitely playing the advocate. Somehow it feels like a disguised reprimand that I'm not fully endorsing the new relationship. Or am I being hypersensitive?

This conversation will take some careful handling. I certainly don't want to flag any motherly suspicions but I want to try and place a slight element of doubt in her mind. Just enough to make her think about applying the brakes on her overenthusiastic encouragement of this relationship.

I arrive at the table ahead of Catherine and order a bottle of Rioja, her favourite, and a bottle of sparkling water. Drinking at lunchtime is another bad habit I've picked up since meeting Dave Roberts. Whilst waiting, I take the time to peruse the menu. Catherine has an amazing ability to know exactly what she wants to eat as soon as she seats herself. I have learnt that from the numerous times we have met for lunch.

The casual observer would never know that we were both married to the same man, albeit at different times. We are firm friends. Over the years we have met up independently of our partners because we enjoy each other's company. The age difference between us doesn't matter. We have an almost unwritten rule that we don't talk about personal stuff especially around Charles. It's not really that we are uncomfortable about it. It is more that we don't want to put the other person in a difficult position taking sides. If Charles and I have argued, it just wouldn't be appropriate to share that with his ex-wife, despite us being good mates. It's just not cricket as Charles would say.

Catherine enters the restaurant in a whirlwind of bags. God knows how much money she has spent; the evidence is irrefutable. Each bag bears the name of an expensive boutique. Roger's credit card will probably need a defibrillator when she gets home. Although Roger can refuse his darling wife nothing.

"Madeline, darling." Catherine envelopes me in the most enormous hug, drowning me in her perfume. Once she has squeezed me within an inch of my life, she drops to her chair with a sigh. "I'm exhausted. Shopping is such hard work. These men don't know how lucky they are. Not only do we shop for ourselves but we do theirs too. I got some lovely new shirts for Roger. I'm sure he will love them." Catherine giggled as she helped herself to a generous glass of wine.

"Catherine, it's so lovely to see you. I do hope I'm not pulling you away from the boutiques though."

"Don't be silly," she laughed in response. "I think I'm done in, so this is a lovely excuse to stop and rest my poor little toes before I head back on the train. Have you ordered?"

"Not yet. Was waiting for you but I have chosen."

As if by magic, a waiter appears to take our orders and we make small talk as we wait for food. Catherine is full of gossip from the golf club. Roger is a keen golfer and, whilst Catherine has never played, she loves the social life at his club. She's normally at the centre of arrangements for any events; loving the hubbub of social organisation.

"How was your skiing holiday, Madeline?" Catherine changes the conversation as our food arrives.

She is delicately cutting her food into smaller pieces so she can use her fork to spear the tiny morsels one by one. I have noticed that behaviour in her before. I'm sure she thinks it helps her eat less. Catherine worries about her weight. She has a healthy appetite normally and does like too much wine, which doesn't help to reduce her calorie intake. Personally, I think she looks gorgeous as she is. Why worry when your husband is totally smitten with you and especially as, in all other matters, Catherine doesn't seem to give a damn what others think of her.

"Excellent. Although it seems a distant memory now." The busy weeks back at work have taken their toll.

"I saw some of the pictures on Facebook. Looks like you had some good weather. How did the little ones enjoy it?" Catherine had to give up skiing a few years back when she had a complex operation on her kneecap. After the pain of the recovery, she couldn't let herself risk the chance of having to go through that again.

"They did love it. Charles is delighted as you can imagine. If they had hated it, I honestly don't know how he would cope," I laughed.

"Oh God no. Charles had Amelia on skies as soon as she could walk. I am sure he thinks that if his children share his passion, he will always have someone to go on holiday with. Well, it's good to see you in one piece anyway."

"I think I only had one tumble this time." Grinning, I took a sip of wine. "How are things with Roger? Is he busy at work?"

"No change there. He has been up to his ears in new business. Which is always good news, especially with my spending!" Catherine belly laughed so loudly that the couple on the next table glared across. Catherine raised her glass to them in a sarcastic salute.

"I went shopping with Amelia last weekend. I think she has your spending gene. I just couldn't keep up."

"I'm not a great example unfortunately. How was my darling daughter? I haven't seen her for weeks. She always seems to be out with Peter and never seems to have time for her old mum at the moment."

"Oh, sorry Catherine. I didn't mean to rub your nose in it. I think she wanted company to spend her latest pay cheque."

"Honestly don't mind me. I could see more of her if I was bothered to come up to London at the weekend. Never the best time for me as there's always something on recently. In the past Amelia would come for Sunday lunch at least once a month, but no longer. I haven't seen her properly since Christmas."

It was the first week in March so finding out that Amelia hadn't been home for over two months was a shock. She hadn't been to ours for a month; that disastrous occasion when I had to welcome Dave into my house under the guise of Peter McKay.

"Well, she's a young lady in the first flush of love. I suppose she has better things to do than see her parents. Charles hasn't seen her since she brought Peter round for lunch in January. What do you think of the guy, Catherine?"

Catherine seemed to take her time before she answered. That is so unlike her as the conversation is always conducted at 100mph; it's hard to keep up normally.

"When we first met I was charmed. He seemed such a gentleman and really seemed to care about my darling girl. Now I'm not so sure."

Well, I wasn't expecting that. Amelia had gone on at me about how much her mother adores Peter. The vibes I am getting from Catherine are way off the mark.

"Has something happened, Catherine?"

"Nothing I can put my finger on. I haven't seen them together so hard to judge, but I don't like the sound of some of the things Amelia's been telling me."

"Really. Like what?" This conversation is starting to trouble me now.

"I get the impression that Amelia is doing as she is told. You know my daughter. She's always been very independent and sure of herself. Every conversation we have starts with, Peter says this, Peter suggested that, we are going to do this because Peter wants to. Have you noticed that at all, Madeline?"

"I will be perfectly honest with you, Catherine, she seems to be cautious in telling me stuff other than everything is great and the sex is amazing. I made the mistake of suggesting she slows down and doesn't fall head over heels in love. I think that has made Amelia a bit cautious in opening up."

Catherine nodded. "I'm just not sure I like the changes he is encouraging in her. I may be over-worried and it's hard to prove any evidence of coercion. Something just doesn't feel right. Mother's intuition perhaps."

"I can certainly see why you are concerned. It's good to see her so happy, but there is something about Peter that just doesn't feel right. I didn't warm to him when we first met, but would have hated Amelia to find that out."

There, I have put it out there. Let's see how Catherine absorbs that and whether she picks it up and runs with it. It sounds like I'm being manipulative but, trust me, my motives are genuine. Protection of Amelia is top of my agenda despite the damage the reveal could do to my relationship with Charles.

"Oh Madeline, we are so on the same page. I seriously cannot put my finger on it but I'm not sure I like Peter McKay. Shit, that sounds bad, doesn't it?"

"No, it's honest, Catherine. You can't be forced to like Peter just because Amelia does. Have you talked to Charles or Roger about how you feel?"

"I have spoken to Roger. He agreed with me that he has his doubts. But I never know with Roger. He may just be saying it because I have. Bless him."

I do see that. Roger is very compliant when it comes to his wife. For a successful businessman, he is putty in her hands.

"Did you want me to speak to Charles? I could encourage him to have a word with Amelia. Although if you would rather speak to Charles, then do feel free."

"That would be splendid if you could Madeline. I'm happy if you share my concerns and perhaps he could feel out the situation. Amelia has always been so close to her dad, so if anyone can figure out what's really going on, it's Charles."

When I planned this meeting today, I really thought I would have my work cut out with Catherine. Amelia either spun me a line about how her mum felt or honestly hasn't picked up on the vibes. I do feel better knowing that Catherine has her doubts. I would hate to fall out with my friend over her daughter and the rocky road which lies ahead.

Now to tackle my husband. 'Operation Save Amelia from that Bastard' is now in full swing. I have her mother's blessing. Now to get her father on board. Amelia needs to see that this relationship is not for her and I cannot be the one to enlighten her.

CHAPTER THIRTY-THREE

Family Sunday mornings are slow paced.

Creatures of habit, we love to spend Sunday morning with the papers. The paper of choice is The Sunday Times, along with the added benefit of perusing Amelia's latest work. The children enjoy PJ time. The one day of the week where they can stay in their bedwear until lunchtime.

Our kitchen sweeps into a snug area littered with comfy sofas and chairs, with a huge box of toys. Whilst Charles and I sup coffee and work our way through the papers, the children are happily playing on the floor. A huge pile of Lego is the focus of their attention for now and hopefully will keep them gripped for some time yet.

I love time with the papers, probably as much as time with the children. God, that is too honest and makes me sound like a terrible mother. I'm not going for any awards as Parent of the Year or anything like that. But being bluntly honest, I need 'me time' as much as I need time with my kids. Funny how you don't realise how important some things are until you've lost them.

But that's for later.

"Darling, would you like more coffee?" Charles looks up from the business section as he speaks.

"Oh yes please darling. Those new Kenyan beans are wonderful."

I'm currently reading Amelia's article on a famous US actor. It is an excellent piece of work. I'm really impressed how well she has settled into her new role. It didn't take long for her to be trusted with some high profile interviews. Last week she was in New York for a few days to shape out the latest interview. She had rung me from the top of the Empire State Building, full of excitement and enthusiasm. It was her first visit to the Big Apple and she had taken some time out to do the major tourist attractions before catching the red-eye back to post her piece.

Finishing the article, I place the magazine back on the coffee table as

Charles hands me a fresh cup of coffee. "That was a great piece by Amelia. You must read it Charles."

Charles picks up the magazine and starts to flick. I know he scan reads the parts of a newspaper which don't necessarily appeal to him. Hollywood gossip is really not his thing. He will read the piece purely because his daughter has written it. Clearly he will be examining her writing skill and use of words rather than any particular interest in the subject matter. Before he gets too engrossed, I turn the conversation to Catherine's request.

"Charles, I met up with Catherine the other day for lunch," I start.

"Did you?" He's only half-listening. I can tell. Charles has an annoying habit; tuning out but pretending he is listening. The number of times I catch him out is quite embarrassing.

"I think she's a bit concerned about Amelia and her new relationship."

"Oh yes." His interest is being piqued.

"From what she told me, Catherine has some concerns about Peter's emotional hold over Amelia. She thinks Peter is influencing some of her decisions at the moment. That's a bit worrying, isn't it?"

I can tell that Charles is now fully engaged with the conversation. He slowly puts the magazine back on the coffee table and leans forward, making eye contact as he listens.

"Catherine did ask me to speak to you. She was wondering if you could have a quiet word with Amelia. You know how much she values your opinion. She may open up to you." I paused, watching my husband. The emotions raced across his face from interest, to concern which became the over-riding emotion.

"OK that doesn't sound good. Did she elaborate at all?"

I explained the vibes which Catherine was getting from her conversations with their daughter. Charles is a firm believer in equal stakes in a relationship. He has never tried to influence my thinking or dominate decision making. He has taught Amelia to develop her own mind.

Independence was an important characteristic in Amelia's upbringing.

Whilst Catherine has always sought a partner who takes the lead on most matters, she has strong views and would never let a husband bully her into doing something she didn't want to do. With both her parents sharing a similar view on the pathway they wanted to navigate with their beloved daughter to take her from childhood into adulthood, it strikes me as frightening that Amelia is allowing someone to influence her views in such a way.

But that's the man Dave is. He will find a weakness and pounce on it. Amelia will no doubt be worried that there is something wrong with her. She struggles to keep a relationship going. Dave has seen that and is using it to make her bend to his will.

That's why my stepdaughter is building a picture of domestic bliss when she has spoken to me. Why she has let on that her mother is really keen on her new fella. Why she has been avoiding her father, knowing he will pick up on the nuance of change in her behaviour.

Oh, that man has so much to answer for.

"Right, that settles it." Charles has listened carefully and has made his mind up for action. "I will ring Amelia this afternoon. I need to get her on her own if that's OK with you darling? If I invite her round she will bring that guy with her. This needs a face-to-face father daughter chat I think."

"I agree Charles. Why don't you take her out for dinner one night this week? Just tell her you want to catch up."

Meeting on neutral ground would help to relax them both and hopefully lead to a constructive conversation. The last thing Catherine would want is for the two of them to fall out. If Amelia doesn't feel that she is being played or side-lined then perhaps she would open up more to her father.

"Yes, you are right. I don't want to put her on notice at all so will give her some sort of sob story about missing her. Not really a sob story though. It feels like ages since we have seen her properly for lunch. I do miss having her round every other week."

"I know what you mean darling. The children have missed her too." As they hear me talk both Sophie and James jump up and rush over.

"Mummy is Melia coming over today?" cries Sophie.

"Not today sweetheart. But soon. I'm sure." My daughter wears her disappointment on her face as it crumples into tears. Reaching down, I envelop her in a cuddle as James clings to my leg.

"I miss Melia, Mummy." James doesn't want to be missed out of the conversation.

My lap is soon full of both children as I stroke James's hair and kiss Sophie on the cheek. "Your big sister has just been really busy recently my lovelies. But she will be round again soon. You know how much she loves you both."

CHAPTER THIRTY-FOUR

It's late when the door of the bedroom opens, creaking to break the silence.

Despite the hour I am still awake and reading a book. Charles could see the bedroom light on and knows he doesn't need to creep about. Ever considerate, he has crept up the stairs trying to avoid disturbing the children and Jessica.

He looks shattered. He's not used to late night distractions and would have much rather met Amelia at the weekend. Unfortunately, tonight was the only night she was free this week, so Charles had agreed to take her for dinner after work. I don't think he had anticipated the length of time they would be talking.

I hadn't either.

Charles had texted me at 9pm to tell me they were going back to Amelia's flat. He had said that he would get one of the pool drivers to bring him home. Will he want to talk tonight? I decided earlier this evening that I wouldn't probe him the minute he gets through the door. Well, that was then. This is now.

"So how did it go?"

Charles is pulling at his tie with a weary look on his face. I jump out of bed to help him undress. I have a secret purpose. I want to know the whole sorry tale. Whilst he finishes removing his suit, I sit on the edge of the bed cross-legged in anticipation.

"Oh darling. It was a long night." Charles sighs as he flops down beside me. "She is totally smitten with Peter. Over dinner she just kept going on and on about everything they are doing together. He is clearly paying her an awful lot of attention."

"Did she open up about anything negative about him?"

I'm trying not to push too hard. I need to keep my emotions in check. I must play the part of the concerned stepmother. As far as my husband knows, I have no idea about this guy. Other than what Amelia has told us, of course. Well, that's what Charles thinks.

"When we got back to her flat, she did start to talk about a few things. It was so hard to get her to be blunt about it. The conversation kept going round in circles."

"How so?"

"Well, it was almost like she was trying to get a man's view on their relationship without telling me the whole story." Charles groaned as he stroked his bald pate. "I'm not the best person with all this relationship stuff, Madeline. Perhaps it would have been better if she had spoken to you."

"Oh darling. You know that wouldn't work. I have talked to her, but all I got out of her was how fantastic everything was. And how brilliant an older man was. She tried to relate her relationship with Peter with our age gap."

"I understand. But this is so different to when we got together. I do think Catherine may be right. Reading between the lines, something is just not right."

Charles lay back on the bed with arm raised. Without needing to say a word I snuggled into his shoulder. "There is something not quite right. She was trying to imply that you like me being in charge and making all the decisions. She knows that's not how we operate. Doesn't she?"

"That is weird. She knows fully well how our relationship works and I certainly don't think she has ever seen you impose your decisions on me or Catherine."

"Exactly. I can't put my finger on it but there is definitely a change in her. And a change I don't like."

"What do you propose doing?"

It was clear Charles would not let this one go. It was far too important to him. The welfare of his elder daughter was at stake.

Charles took his time before he answered. "I'm going to pick up with

Catherine tomorrow and update her. The trouble is we will need to be careful. I got the feeling that as soon as I started to ask questions she didn't want to answer, then she just moved the conversation on. That is just not Amelia either. Avoidance tactics. She's never been like that with me before."

"We must all keep an eye on Amelia. At least once you and Catherine have shared your views then we can join forces to keep a watch on her. The trouble is that she won't thank us for interfering. You know how independent she is."

"I know. It's so hard watching your daughter behave troubled and not be able to do anything about it." Charles gently kissed me on the forehead. "Now sleep, my darling. Everything will feel better in the morning."

As I listened to Charles drop into a deep sleep, I thought about what he had told me. I don't think things will feel better any time soon. Dave is manipulating Amelia to get at me. I'm sure he will know that his actions are getting to me. I cannot see that he has any intention to just walk away and leave me and my family at peace.

Even as I tried to imagine the troubles ahead, I seriously had no idea how bad it would get.

Dave Roberts is determined to destroy me. To make me pay for my mistakes. How he will do this is anyone's guess, but I know that's his purpose. Deep down.

In all seriousness, I am not making this situation all about me. His motives appear to be driven by a desire to hurt me, deeply. To make me pay for rejecting him. To make me pay for falling for him. To make me pay for everything.

CHAPTER THIRTY-FIVE

The buzz of numerous conversations swarmed around the room like the buzz of honeybees.

Charles and Jessica have organised a birthday party for me. It was a surprise. I am quite staggered at how they managed to keep it secret from me. How this family has discovered the art of secrets. Amelia had taken me out shopping earlier in the day whilst the rest of them had worked hard to prepare. Decorations doubled up to celebrate St. George who shares my special anniversary. The décor certainly looks like the most patriotic party ever.

As we had struggled through the front door, laden down with shopping bags, I was overwhelmed with the noise and enthusiasm of my closet friends and family calling out birthday wishes. James and Sophie had almost pushed me over as they ran at me, jumping up and down with excitement. Champagne corks exploded in the kitchen. My darling husband had presented me with the first glass. The sweet, cold nectar soothed my throat and settled my initial nerves at being surrounded by people.

I had been looking forward to a quiet night in with a film.

One can't complain though.

Can I?

It was so special of Charles and Jessica to organise the party. Fortunately, they had the foresight to employ caterers to prepare vast trays of delicious morsels to feast on. A team of immaculately dressed young men and women circulated the rooms, offering an array of goodies to our guests. They had organised themselves so that at no point would a guest be out of reach of a scrumptious delight. Just reach out a hand and help yourself to what's on offer.

In the dining room, the table was covered with a number of different deserts including cheesecakes, pastries, and individual Crème Brûlée, my favourite guilty pleasure. At one end of the table stood an impressive birthday cake. It was chocolate of course. The artwork on top of the ganache was beautiful. The detail, which the designer had employed, was outstanding. I felt humbled to see the lengths my darling husband had employed to make my day so special.

During the course of the evening, I had the chance to circulate, spending time with each of my dearest friends. My throat felt sore from the chatting, but again I cannot complain. It had been so lovely to spend time catching up with old colleagues and some of my oldest friends from university days. Catherine and Roger are with us, along with Amelia.

The only downside of the evening is the presence of Dave. I have done my best to keep out of his way. As I wander from room to room, my first thought is to scan the space for his smarmy face. Once spotted, I have quickly become adept at weaving in another direction without making it too obvious.

Conversations are interrupted suddenly by the sound of our dinner gong. Charles is motioning me over to join him in our lounge as the rest of our guests squeeze into that space.

"Ladies and Gentlemen, I hope you will indulge me for a moment." Charles is in his element. He is an excellent public speaker and is certainly not put off by the number of guests we have in our home. "I would like to say a few words about my beautiful wife Madeline. The day Madeline walked into my life she changed it for ever. I was fast approaching middle age and she revived me."

Laughter resounds around the room as Roger pretends to apply CPR to a dying Charles. They are quite the double act. Catherine watches on with a sardonic smile.

"No, but seriously, I consider myself the luckiest of men to have found Madeline. Not only has she brought expert experience to my business, but she has done me the honour of being my wife for the last seven years. She has given me two wonderful children and made my world complete. I don't know what I would do without her."

"Oh darling," I cried as I kiss his cheek. "Stop it. You are making me blush."

"Before I get even more emotional, I would like to propose a toast. To my darling wife, Madeline. Happy birthday, darling."

"Happy birthday, Madeline." Voices chorused in celebration. Glasses were raised in salute.

My eyes scan the room acknowledging the best wishes. Suddenly my gaze lights upon Dave and his evil face. He raises his glass towards me fixing me with his stare. The salute is mocking and sends a shiver down my spine.

He smiles and winks, seeming to share a secret.

I turn my back in disgust. He is the proverbial fly in the ointment of my pleasure. How do I ever get rid of him from our life?

CHAPTER THIRTY-SIX

The party is drawing to a close.

Most of our guests have departed. Catherine and Roger are staying the night, so we have settled in the snug with a brandy. Amelia and Peter are still with us. Thankfully, they will be going home tonight. I seriously could not entertain the thought of them sleeping together in our home. That would just be wrong on so many levels.

There is a satisfying silence surrounding us. After the hubbub of activity, it feels lovely to kick back and relax. Well, relax as much as I can with the threatening presence of that man in my home.

"Mum, Dad, it's good to have you both together. We wanted to have a chat." Amelia looks nervous as she makes eye contact with her father. Peter is sat back with his arm placed casually across the back of the sofa behind Amelia. He looks far too at home in my domain.

"Yes, Catherine, Charles, it is opportune to have both your company," continues Peter. "We have news. Gosh, your speech earlier was lovely Charles. All good practise for your father of the bride speech."

You could cut the atmosphere with a knife. Catherine's face reads panic, Roger perks up and my darling husband looks shell-shocked. The colour has drained from his face. I dread to think what my face looks like.

"Sorry, are you saying what I think you are saying?" Charles breaks the awkward silence.

"We are getting married," replies Amelia. She has a beaming smile on her face now that the news has broken.

"Darling, that's quick," says Catherine. It's clear she is struggling with how to get the balance right. I can tell she is fuming by the news, but at the same time doesn't want to upset her daughter. "You have only known each other five minutes. Are you sure?"

Amelia's face drops. She seems crushed by her family's reactions. It's clear she simply has not picked up on the reservations of both of her parents. I know it is not my place to speak so I remain silent, observing the play of emotions flying around the room. I'm a coward really. I wouldn't know what to say. You honestly could not make this situation up.

What a bloody nightmare.

"I guess when you know it's right then why delay?" answers Peter. He has not moved from his relaxed stance with his arm laid across the back of the sofa. Amelia meanwhile has edged forward on the seat, arms crossed in defiance.

Charles clears his throat theatrically as he plays for time. "Amelia darling, you know that your mother and I will support you in whatever you decide. You are our world and we only want what is best for you. We just want to be sure that this is the right thing for you just now." Charles reaches across the divide to hold his daughter's hands in his.

"I know, Daddy. I do understand that you are concerned but I am so happy. Mummy, please be happy for me."

Amelia fixes a firm stare on Catherine as she finishes. That stare speaks volumes. It says please Mum, don't embarrass me in front of my new man; please Mum just be happy for me.

Catherine does look uncomfortable. Her instincts are obviously telling her one thing. Her daughter's pleading face pulls at her heart, overriding her instincts. "We are happy for you, darling. Peter, congratulations. Roger and I wish you every happiness for the future."

Charles takes my hand as he prepares to respond to his ex-wife's declaration. He can't be the only one not to congratulate the happy couple. It's not the way he operates. I know that for sure.

I feel sick.

Seriously, this cannot be happening.

What next from this monster who is determined to ruin my life and my family?

"Amelia. Peter. I honestly don't want to burst your bubble of happiness. We are just a bit shocked at the speed your relationship is moving at. If you are both in agreement, then of course Madeline and I will support your wishes wholeheartedly." Charles stands and takes his daughter in his arms. "I love you so much my beautiful girl and all I want is for you to be happy." He kisses her cheeks.

Peter gets to his feet and reaches out his hand. Charles grabs hold and shakes his hand with enthusiasm.

All eyes lead to me.

I know what is expected of me. Can I pull off an act that is convincing?

"Congratulations, darling." I pull Amelia into my embrace and kiss her gently on the cheek. In her ear I whisper, "I hope he treats you well, my dearest and you know I will support you whatever happens."

Amelia looks puzzled at my remarks but doesn't mention anything. Peter, or Dave, looks for a similar embrace. He can think again. Bastard. I let go of Amelia and return to my seat without making any eye contact with Peter.

There remains an atmosphere despite the pretence of happiness shown by both parents. It doesn't take long for Peter to realise that it's time to leave now. Let the parents have time alone to absorb the news. And reflect on my spoilt birthday celebrations. He and Amelia make their excuses and leave soon after the bombshell had settled into the room.

Charles refreshes our glasses as we wait for someone to break the silence.

My mind is a turmoil of emotions. Deep down I know that Dave does not love my stepdaughter. This is all part of his sick plan to punish me and hurt my family. But why has he decided to take this horror show to a whole other level? Could he seriously be interested in Charles's money or patronage? Is that sufficient motive to tie himself to a woman he doesn't love? Or perhaps he has grown to love Amelia. Perhaps his initial plan to hurt me has backfired and he has lost his heart to our daughter.

Catherine is the first to share her thoughts. "Charles, this cannot happen. She has only known him a few months. I'm just not convinced that she knows what she's doing. We have to stop this now."

"Catherine, how do we stop our daughter from doing what she wants? She is 26 you know. Not six. When was the last time we told her what to do? And more importantly, when did she do it?"

Roger is shaking his head slowly as he listens into the exchange. "Catherine, Charles. I do understand how you are both feeling. It's a shock. Our role, as parents, is to be there to catch our children when they fall. We cannot stop them from climbing." As usual his words hit the mark. We are all stunned as we absorb his message. "I know I am only Amelia's stepfather and I don't have children of my own, so you may think I'm talking out of my arse, but we must all be there for Amelia as she takes this new path."

I love Roger. He is a steady presence. He adores Amelia like a daughter and with that I can empathise. He also has the ability to step back from the emotion and try and strike a balance between our views and Amelia's. Who are we to judge her feelings?

"You are right, Roger," continues Catherine. "I am just so worried that it's all too fast. Amelia appears to be very taken with this guy but I am worried that he has some form of hold over her. Trouble is, if we push it, she will hate us for it."

"We need to be there for her," said Charles rubbing his hand over his forehead. I know that sign. It means my husband is wrestling with a problem he really doesn't want to face. "We may not like the speed this relationship is taking. As Roger said, we cannot stop Amelia spreading her wings and flying. I just hope she is not following Icarus and flying too close to the sun. I would hate her to get burned."

As before my silence is purposeful. How can I share my views about this disastrous decision? I want to scream out my fears but doing so will expose me.

Am I being totally selfish? Shouldn't I be putting the welfare of Amelia ahead of my own shame?

Unfortunately, over the last year I have made some dreadful decisions because of my own selfish behaviour. This is another such example. I will hold my counsel when I could put a stop to it all now if I had the courage.

Again, I think of myself and not my family.

A decision I will live to regret.

CHAPTER THIRTY-SEVEN

The entrance hall to the apartment building is dimly lit.

It feels uncomfortable as I wait for the lift to arrive. My mind is racing, thinking about what I'm about to do. But I still make a mental note to speak to Amelia about the lighting. I certainly don't like the idea of her arriving home late at night to this gloom and I'm sure her father would agree. Speaking of Charles, Amelia is out tonight with her father. It had been arranged for a few days now. It's Charles's attempt to recover the situation since my birthday. He has felt rotten that he didn't greet her engagement with his usual aplomb.

My conscience is compelling me to make one last attempt to convince Dave to stop this fiasco.

With a bit of luck he will be at home and my trip across town will not have been a waste of time. The lift arrives and I step inside pressing floor five. I haven't warned Dave of my impending arrival. Not that I have any contact with him outside of what is forced on me by my naive stepdaughter.

Hopefully, it's going to be an uncomfortable surprise for him.

All too soon I make it to the door of the apartment he shares with Amelia. My stepdaughter had moved in with her boyfriend a month ago, leaving her previous flat share. Charles doesn't realise that I know he is still paying the rent on her old place. It's his attempt to provide a fail-safe for his daughter, if and when it all goes wrong. My husband is as confident as I am with the future of this fated relationship.

Ringing the doorbell, I wait. Butterflies are jumping around my stomach with hobnail boots on. I am seriously scared now I'm here. What possessed me to do this? I have not been alone with that snake since we ended our relationship.

The door opens wide. Dave stands there dressed in tracksuit bottoms and a tight t-shirt. His hair is tousled and he has nothing on his feet, all signs that he has wound down from a day at work.

"Maddy, how lovely. Is Amelia expecting you?" His smile grates on me as he ushers me into the lounge.

"She isn't. It's you I came to see, Dave."

Expecting it will annoy him, I insist on using his actual name. Or, well, the name I think is his. I have never got to the bottom of his true identity.

"I knew you couldn't stay away from me Maddy. We were so bloody good together, weren't we?"

The sneer on his face is crying out for a slap. It takes all my self-discipline to keep my hands down by my side. The bloody cheek of the guy.

"Look Dave. Let's forget the pleasantries. I won't keep you long. Just tell Amelia it's all over and the wedding is off. Then we can all go back to normal. She will be upset but she will get over you." I pause for dramatic effect. "Quickly."

There is no way I am holding back on my fury. I really don't care if I hurt him. He deserves it after what he has put my family and me through.

"Oh, come on Maddy. Let's face it, you are just jealous. You don't want Amelia having what you lost. We could have made a go of it if you hadn't suddenly developed a guilty conscience."

"You bastard. You set me up and used me. For money. Don't you remember?"

Seriously where does this guy get off? He has spun his own version of the truth in his sick mind.

"You were the one who decided it was over, Maddy. Don't you remember? I was enjoying myself so much and you put an end to it. That's why you had to pay for it. You dropped me like a stone."

"How can you stand there and talk such bullshit? You had no feelings for me. You used me. You hurt me for your own pleasure." My voice betrayed me as it wobbled with emotion.

"I loved you Maddy."

"Stop it. You didn't care for me."

My bloody voice is getting worse as I try to conceal a sob. Come on. Get a grip woman, I think to myself. Do not let him get the upper hand. You came here to sort things out so don't let him control the situation. He is far too good at that.

The great manipulator.

"I did love you, Maddy. You have to believe me. I still love you. I still want you." As he whispered those last words, he gently touched my face, circling my cheeks with his fingers.

My stomach is now performing handstands as it churns with conflicting emotions. I hate this man. So much.

But at the same time, I want him.

Too much.

Dave pulls me into his arms forcefully. There is no turning back. Tipping my head back he kisses me. Deep kisses. His tongue explores my mouth. Without thinking my arms are around his shoulders pulling him into a deeper kiss. I moan with passion as my mouth is filled with his probing.

He pulls at my dress, lifting it over my head. I yank his t-shirt off and put my hands down his joggers reaching for his penis. It is hard and throbbing for me.

Dave's hands are snapping off my bra and pushing down my panties. Within moments we are naked in front of each other. We don't stop kissing as he lifts me up and onto him. I scream out as he fills me up, panting with excitement. He thrusts into me, faster and faster as we topple back onto the sofa.

Dave is an amazing lover. He brings me to heights before allowing himself to peak. As he comes down from the high, he holds me close. My face snuggles into his chest, enjoying the feeling of skin on skin.

My body has betrayed me again.

Why?

Why?

The come down is hard.

It smacks me in the face with a harsh dose of reality. What the hell have I done?

Dave is sat back on the sofa gazing at my body. His smile is turning to a sneer. "You are still a good fuck, Maddy. Too easy though. I like my women with a bit more self- respect."

Bile builds in my throat.

Grabbing my underwear and dress, I dash to the bathroom just in time before the contents of my stomach hit the toilet pan. Shaking, I fumble to put on my bra. Pulling my dress on I hear a tear. Shit, that is one of my favourite dresses ruined. The least of my troubles but it helps distract me from the shame of my stupidity. What in God's name drove me to have sex with this man? Again. Will I never learn?

As I leave the bathroom, I can see that Dave is dressed and is pouring a large glass of whiskey. Just the one glass. Nothing for me. In fact, he doesn't turn as I make my way to the door.

"Goodnight, Maddy. Thanks for the fuck. Anytime you want a repeat performance you know where I am."

"You bastard," I scream, losing control.

"Grow up, Maddy," Dave shouts back at me. "You are such a selfish bitch. You think you can play with my emotions. You have no morals but you stand there trying to take the moral high ground."

I don't know why I'm still standing here listening to his wicked diatribe.

"You lost, Maddy. I have moved on and Amelia is my choice. You chose Charles, so get on with it. You made your bed, so fucking lie in it. But of course, if you miss me then I am happy to oblige as long as Amelia doesn't find out. Wouldn't want to wreck my plans now, would I?"

I'm shaking with rage as I grab at the door handle. Dave gets there first and grabs at my wrist.

"Don't mess with me, Maddy. You wouldn't like me when I'm angry." His face pushes against me in a threatening fashion. "Off you go then."

Slapping my arse, he guides me out of the room.

The door shuts and my heart breaks one more time.

What a stupid fool.

Why the hell did I come here tonight?

Was I subconsciously wanting sex with him? I daren't ask myself that question.

I'm too ashamed of the answer.

CHAPTER THIRTY-EIGHT

My bed is my sanctuary.

Charles isn't home yet so I'm curled up under the duvet in a foetal position. Cold chills my bones. I shiver with both the temperature and my shock at what just happened. My stomach is still churning, with acid rising up my throat. I honestly don't know how I carried off a performance of normality on my way home. Surely the watching bystanders must have been able to see the disgust and self-hatred oozing from my pores.

Once I got home and relieved Jessica of babysitting duties, I had rushed to our bathroom. Ripping off my clothes and throwing them in the laundry basket, I jumped in the shower. Running the water as hot as bearable, I scrubbed until my body was red and sore. My crutch took an extra focus. Still raw from his sex, I trembled as I touched myself. With guilt running through my blood, I could still feel his hands over my body, bringing me to life.

I am ashamed that my touch excited me.

My body ignores the personal turmoil rushing through my thoughts. It betrays me in its desire.

Why has that man got such a hold over me? I thought I had conquered my feelings for him. Washed him out of my life. But no. He's still there under my skin. I still desire him even though he is a bastard to me. There must be something wrong with me. What woman would throw themselves at the man who has tried to destroy their life? What woman would throw themselves at the guy who is marrying her stepdaughter? Out of spite.

Me of course.

Stupid cow.

I went to see him tonight to try and stop this marriage farce. How the hell had it ended up with us ripping our clothes off and having sex? You could not call it making love as that emotion is certainly not present. He used me for sex.

But to be honest I was using him too.

We are both as bad as each other, using sex as a weapon to hurt each other. I don't believe he is as hard as he makes out. Reflecting on what happened when we ended our affair, I must have hurt his feelings. Why else would he go to such lengths to remain in my life and torment me. They say a woman scorned is a dreadful thing.

What about a man's fury?

Was I the reason he was doing what he was doing to destroy my family? Was it all my fault? Am I reaping the rewards of my selfish behaviours?

My actions tonight have set things back months. If he was getting over me then I have just reminded him of how good we are together. I have betrayed my husband yet again and if this was ever to come to light, I will be responsible for breaking up my stepdaughter's engagement.

What the fuck is wrong with me?

I'm like a dog on heat.

I can't control myself when alone with that man.

Tears start to fall as shame hits me one more time. This man is destroying my life and I'm an active participant in the destruction.

I always thought I was a good person. I care deeply for those I love. I value loyalty and respect. My ethos has always been to treat others as I wished to be treated.

The shame of my behaviour envelops me in a mist of rage. I have let myself down. I have let my family down. I have betrayed those I love for a moment of pleasure.

I really don't like the person I have become.

Suddenly I hear the door of our room opening quietly. Charles tiptoes into the room desperate not to wake me. I feign sleep. I cannot face my husband tonight. He will see the guilt on my face.

It's a shame I have to bear alone.

CHAPTER THIRTY-NINE

It had been a month since my latest disgrace.

The last few weeks had been manic at work. Charles had a new sales promotion running which had all the heads of department in a spin. The competition between them was frantic as each team tried to impress with their sales performance. Charles had been working long hours and seemed to be permanently exhausted. He rolls in late each evening, grabs some food and is asleep before I join him in the bedroom. Which has been a blessing.

There has been no need to pretend.

The sales drive had a knock on impact on my work stack. As night follows day, sales drives lead to HR issues. A case of bullying had hit my desk early on which had resulted in me pulling together a set of guidelines and a training course to support line managers. Despite the negative catalyst, I thrive on training and developing our team. Throwing myself into a module and imparting my knowledge with our staff has kept my mind occupied.

I haven't had a chance to think about that snake.

My evenings have been fully focused on home. The children have been my distraction. Sometimes it takes a shock or a sense of shame to realise you have been neglecting the most important people in your life. My obsession with Dave Roberts and his relationship with Amelia has been an unnecessary distraction. I have spent far too much time concerned with their engagement. My resolution now is to leave them to it. They are both old enough to make their own mistakes.

I should know. I've made enough of them myself where Dave is concerned. Amelia is just going to have to get on with it and live with the consequences of falling for the wrong guy.

Well, that's my resolution.

I just need to find a way of sticking to it. My previous track record in that department has not been great, let's face it.

Charles hasn't spoken much about his evening out with his daughter. Reading between the lines on his face, the conversation didn't go well. Amelia is a very confident young lady and she certainly won't change course just because Daddy says so. She adores Charles and respects his opinion, but even the emotional strength of their relationship does not appear to give her father the status to advise on her future marriage. The defeat seems to have hit Charles hard.

I guess that's why he hasn't really opened up to me. He doesn't want to admit defeat. He had been quite bullish before they met up. He'd been verbose as he prepared to talk some sense into his daughter. His words not mine.

I guess he doesn't want to share the reality of his defeat.

Today we are lunching with Catherine and Roger at their place. It's the first time I have seen Catherine since my birthday. We have been in touch a few times over the phone. Snatched conversations driven by Catherine's need for a progress update from Charles and to bemoan the fact that her daughter is avoiding her.

I understand Amelia's approach. When Catherine has a bee in her bonnet, she is relentless. Her efforts to stop the engagement, or at least slow things down, are simply driving Amelia to speed up the whole affair. Even as adults, our children have the capacity to do the opposite to what their parents suggest. It's part of growing up and spreading your wings from the familial nest.

The lunch today is a chance for Charles and Catherine to discuss the plans for the forthcoming nuptials. Amelia is determined for an autumn wedding and has secured a booking for the second weekend in September, much to the surprise of both sets of parents. Amelia has set her heart on the local church, near to her mother's home, and has persuaded Roger somehow that the reception can be hosted on their pristine lawn. A vast marquee will be covering the garden. Roger appears to be keeping his counsel in the face of his formidable stepdaughter. His garden is his pride and joy, but he will do anything for his wife and, by default, Amelia.

Today, Catherine has hosted a bountiful spread of roast beef with the traditional trimmings. The children have finished and, breaking all my normal rules, we have ensconced them in the snug with the Cartoon Network so the adults can talk without little ears tuning in. Sophie is definitely old enough to understand and loves to follow a conversation. She is certainly a cute child. She would probably spill the beans to her big sister, given half a chance. Her parents, as a team of four, are keen not to ostracize Amelia. We may not agree with the speed at which she is planning her wedding or even the suitability of the groom, but the last thing we all want is to drive a wedge within the family.

As I have mentioned before, Roger is a man I really respect. He is a gentle soul with a strong understanding of human nature. He totally gets the impossible situation his wife is struggling with. At the same time, he knows better than all of us how fragile Catherine can be when faced with emotional issues and he will do all he can to protect his beloved wife. What is abundantly clear is that he wants to be blunt with his views without hurting either Catherine or Charles.

It's Roger that kicks off the discussion.

"Look, I know we have gone round the houses on the subject, but will you indulge me please?" Roger has everyone's attention. "Whilst I totally empathise with your views, Catherine and Charles, I think you need to change approach."

"Change approach?" Charles looks up as he takes a sip of wine.

Roger has our attention as he glances at Charles and then pointedly fixes his eyes on Catherine. "I think we all agree that Amelia is rushing things. She has only been with this chap for five minutes. We don't know enough about him. I totally understand all the concerns we are harbouring. But."

Catherine interrupts. "Roger, darling. Your point?"

"Please, darling, let me finish." Roger reaches across the table to touch Catherine's arm. "My point is that we need to change tack. Trying to persuade Amelia that she is making the wrong decision is not working. If anything, it will drive her away from us. Please let's all think what it must feel like from her perspective. It's going to be the biggest day of her life and what are her parents doing? Challenging her feelings and virtually pissing on her bonfire. Excuse my language."

Silence fills the room. We are all lost in our thoughts.

"Look, Catherine, Charles, we have this all wrong. We need to accept that Amelia is in love with Peter. She wants to marry him and she wants us to be happy for her. It's not our place to judge her decision but celebrate her happiness."

Catherine looks shocked at her husband. She remains silent for too long. Slowly a tear escapes from her eye and rolls gently down her cheek.

No-one speaks.

Embarrassment seems to overtake the birth parents.

Catherine wipes the tear away and places both hands down firmly on the tabletop. You can almost sense her pulling herself together, mentally.

"Roger darling. You are right. I'm so sorry that you needed to remind me that this is about Amelia. Not me."

"Darling, I didn't want to make it sound so callous. I'm sorry."

"No, no. I'm not offended. I think I needed that. The last few weeks I have been obsessed by how I feel. I haven't stopped to think about how Amelia must be feeling. I have been a selfish cow." Catherine stands and moves over to her husband's side. She places a hand on his shoulder in a gesture that speaks volumes about their relationship.

Throughout this exchange I have been an observer. I don't really think I have any right to express an opinion. I watch Catherine and Roger sharing a moment of togetherness. My attention moves to my husband who has remained stoical during Roger's pitch. Charles looks uncomfortable. His fingers work at his collar, seemingly in an attempt to release pressure around his throat. He coughs nervously, again very unlike my confident husband.

"Roger, as much as it pains me to admit it, you are right. I have been derelict in my duty as a father and I am somewhat ashamed that you have had to point this out to me."

"Charles, old chap. That certainly wasn't my intention. I have the luxury of being able to step back from the situation. I can only imagine how challenging it is for both you and Catherine. I am Amelia's stepfather and I love her so much. My intention was to bring her voice to the conversation. And please believe me, I haven't spoken to Amelia about any of this." Roger looks uncomfortable.

"Roger, I respect your views and I needed to be told. We need to club together now and support our little girl on her big day. I, for one, will be the proudest dad walking her down that aisle. I certainly don't want my concerns about the speed or suitability of her future husband to taint her special day."

Oh My God.

Thank you, Roger.

In the space of one conversation, he has changed the whole debacle into a love story.

Now I cannot share any negative views on the wedding of the year.

I will have to keep my counsel.

Within moments the discussions move onto wedding plans. It feels like a light switch has been flicked. The energy within the room transforms from negative to positive vibes within seconds. Catherine is animated as she gushes at the spectacle they will perform across their garden. Marquee, flowers, and catering requirements are being picked over.

I sit there in shock.

How did the mood change so drastically? It feels totally false. Roger has pricked their consciousnesses'. Both Charles and Catherine are like mannequins, dancing to a new tune. Am I the only one who sees this crazy performance? Both parents were dead against this wedding. Now they are obsessed with which colour wedding flowers would complement the garden. A long debate about place settings and whether a band would disturb the neighbours too much is now underway.

No-one notices as I leave the table and wander out into the garden.

Roger has done such a good job on the lawn. There isn't a weed present as I curl my toes into its velvety carpet. Strolling down to the end of the garden I find a love seat. Crazy day. I sip my wine as I listen to the silence surrounding me.

My fight is over.

Now that Charles and Catherine have had their prejudices challenged and been found wanting, they will mobilise their efforts to make Amelia's wedding one to remember. I will need to keep my own counsel now. Charles will need my support as he prepares to give his daughter away to my ex-lover. Catherine, being Catherine, will share the responsibilities of mother of the bride with me. That's her nature. She is generous with her daughter. She understands how much I love her too and will be at pains to ensure I don't feel left out.

But I deserve to be left out.

I have slept with Amelia's future husband. Forget about the original shame of my affair with Dave. The treachery of my marriage was bad enough. But to top it all, I slept with him again. Trying to persuade him to break it off with Amelia.

Was I? Or was it just another excuse to go back to him. He is like a rash. The more I scratch at it, the more embedded he is under my skin.

How the hell am I going to get through this?

It is going to be a nightmare. But one of my own making.

Please no sympathy for me.

I don't deserve it.

The whole debacle is of my own making. It will play out its mind-blowing scene and I will carry on the role of understanding stepmother despite being the villain of the piece.

CHAPTER FORTY

The pop of the champagne cork bursts through the chatter.

We are relaxing on deep, velvet sofas waiting for our host to hand out the bubbles. The boutique is gorgeously decorated in lace fabrics. Lace covers the carpets, adding to the sumptuous feeling. A huge bouquet of white roses rests on the coffee table, along with scented candles. Away to the back of the room hang the dresses, like a series of brides waiting for their big day. Glass roof panels provide the scene with light and reflect against the floor-to-ceiling mirrors sparkling with a wondrous glimmer.

Amelia is in a heightened state of excitement. This is her big day. The chance to try on numerous beautiful dresses which will make her big day complete. With her are the two bridesmaids, Victoria and Marilyn, school friends who have been by her side since they were toddlers. Catherine sits with me and glances adoringly at her daughter.

Today is a special day.

Jilly comes to join the group, passing out long, slim glasses of champagne, each with a delicate dried rosebud bobbing in the liquid. Jilly has the huge responsibility of finding the perfect outfit for Amelia. She has an even bigger challenge than that today. Not only must she find the dress of Amelia's dreams, but she must also find complementary bridesmaids' dresses. As the wedding is only weeks away, there is a huge pressure to create both the image for the day and make sure any adjustments to size can be completed. Money is no object.

Charles will be covering the cost, of course. Anything for his darling daughter.

Honestly, I'm not being sarcastic.

Much.

We have taken over most of the boutique for the morning. At least that will mean that Amelia will be given the VIP treatment. It's the least we can all do after our initial tepid reaction to her news.

All too soon the bride is standing in thong and nothing else, bar a smile, as a serious of gowns are passed by her, each lovingly carried by a member of staff. The first gown she tries is a shift type silk number which barely covers her modesty. Tiny straps hold the dress above her nipples and a split up the front shows a great deal of leg. The train is the most beautiful part of the dress, in my opinion. It is magnificent and shows off her back and bottom at its best. I think that's why she chose this one to start.

Funnily, we are all quiet as Amelia stands before us. Catherine is blushing. I can see she hates it and doesn't know how to break her daughter's heart. Amelia breaks the silence.

"No, I hate this one. I look like a tart. Come on guys. I want your honest opinion so please don't hold back."

I laugh. "You are not wrong darling. You look a right tart in that one. The back is gorgeous but the front just does nothing for you. Unless you want to walk down the aisle backwards."

That breaks the awkwardness. Trust me to make everyone else feel at ease when my own stomach is churning, despite the calming effect of the bubbles.

The next dress has an overcover of lace which spreads out into a small train. Cut close to her hips with off-the-shoulder lace sleeves. It is so much classier than the first dress and Amelia looks like a princess as she twirls in front of the mirror. The detail of the lace is stunning and seems to glisten as she moves.

"Now that one really suits you," I cry as I wipe a tear from the corner of my eye. She looks so beautiful and more importantly so happy.

Catherine dissolves at each dress. She is a mess. Amelia has tried on about ten dresses now and champagne is warming us all up. The excitement in the room is electric as Amelia narrows down her choices.

The final dress comes out draped over Jilly's arms.

This one is far more modest with a sweetheart neckline in satin with a delicate pearlescent lace overlayer covering her chest area, long lace sleeves and dropping to the floor, pooling into a round train. The back is cut away and buttons dance down her bottom, hugging the material to emphasise her rear. Jilly arranges the fishtail train in a circle, giving the impression of an elegant champagne glass.

Catherine doesn't cry. No-one says a word. We just gaze at the wonder of this dress.

"This is the one," gasps Amelia. "I love it."

We all squeal with delight.

Amelia is reluctant to take the dress off now she has found the one. Jilly is fussing over her, working out where a small number of nip and tuck adjustments will need to be made. Thankfully, they will be few as the dress just seems to hug her figure in all the right places.

I look across at Catherine and we make eye contact. She is beaming with pride. I raise my glass in salute as she blows me a kiss.

The next hour is given over to Victoria and Marilyn. Both girls are dark-haired with great skin tones, so choosing a dress which both suits their colouring and their body shape is easier than expected. In a nod to a late summer and early autumn wedding, Amelia has chosen deep purple colours for her table settings and flowers. The girls finally agree on a maxi dress in a dark purple colour. The design flares out from the waist, draping elegantly to the floor. Again, Jilly takes measurements to arrange the adjustments before the dresses are shed and the girls go to the dressing room to change.

As her friends wriggle into their jeans, I grab some alone time with my stepdaughter. Charles is paying for the dresses so we meet up with Jilly in the office to settle the bill. Once completed she leaves us to grab a print of the receipt. I reach my hand across the divide between our seats and take her hand.

"You looked so lovely in that dress, darling. Your dad will be so proud when he walks you down the aisle. He might even cry," I say.

"Oh God. I hope he doesn't cry Madeline. He will have me in tears too. I'm so happy I think I will burst."

"Well enjoy every moment, sweetheart. It will be such a beautiful day and it will fly past, so remember to savour every moment."

I was thinking of my own nuptials with Charles. It was quite different to the plans laid out for his daughter. We married in a small, select ceremony at Dartmouth House. Amelia had been my bridesmaid. We had been surrounded by our closest friends, including Charles's ex-wife. I had loved every second of the day. I was marrying my soul mate, the man who had plucked me out of nowhere and made me the centre of his world.

How could I have betrayed that trust?

Amelia interrupted my troublesome thoughts. "Thank you so much, Madeline. I know you played a part in winning mum and dad over to Peter. I am truly grateful."

"I don't know what you mean darling." My confusion is evident.

"Peter told me."

I gasped. "Told you what?" I am trying to stay cool despite hearing the beating of my heart, which seemed to be trying to burst right out of my chest.

"He told me that you had a word with Mum and Dad. Winning them over to the idea of our marriage. I know Mum thinks it's too soon so I really appreciate you persuading her that this is true love. I won't forget it." Amelia pulls me in for a hug.

"That's OK darling," I whisper into her hair as I rest my cheek against hers.

That bastard is even manipulating my thoughts about their wedding. He must know that I would be the one most against these nuptials so he has used me again without my knowledge.

What depths he will sink to in his need to hurt me.

"I want you to be happy, my darling. I will do everything in my power to make that happen."

CHAPTER FORTY-ONE

The wedding is only a week away.

Against my better judgement we have Amelia and Peter (aka Dave) with us this weekend. Charles decided it would be a good idea. He wanted to spend a final weekend with his beloved daughter prior to handing her over to her future husband. It has been incredibly difficult having that man in my house and the thought of him sleeping across the corridor from us is making my skin crawl. Needless to say, I haven't slept a wink. Listening out for his step on the landing. The reality of that happening is unlikely but my mind is certainly not playing the rationale game.

The last few months have been manic as we balance work commitments with preparations for the big event. Catherine called in my support early on and we have worked tirelessly to ensure the plans, which Amelia had in her head, are brought to life. Interestingly Amelia has floated through the arrangements like a swan gliding across a river. Catherine and I are the feet underneath the surface paddling frantically as we struggle to keep up with her ideas.

To say Amelia has been an absolute diva would not be far wrong. I know it's her big day but it would be good if she could step back and see the chaos she had created by constantly changing her mind. Catherine is far too accommodating. But Catherine doesn't have to work. I have been rushing back from the office each night to a list of actions I need to crack on with.

Personally, I will glad when this is all over.

I am past caring that her future husband is a cheat and a liar.

She's welcome to him.

Does that make me a real bitch?

Probably.

It's Saturday evening and we have just finished a lovely Indian meal which Amelia helped me to pull together. Charles had to go out this evening to meet a client, who needed to discuss a forthcoming deal. It is rare for Charles to work at the weekend and because Amelia is staying, he had arranged it late on a Saturday so that he had the bulk of the day with the happy couple.

Amelia had offered to put the children to bed. Sophie and James have been over-excited to have their big sister for a sleepover. I can hear the noise from upstairs as she tries to manage the bathtime routine without causing a tidal wave. Jessica has the weekend off which means I am likely to be up late tonight clearing up after them. I smile to myself thinking of the relationship between the three siblings. They adore each other. Sophie is so excited to be a flower girl at next week's wedding and has been practising walking down the aisle, scattering petals. She is determined to get it right for Amelia. James is too young for a part in the day, which is a relief as I think I will have my hands full enough with my daughter's excitement.

The washing up awaits so I leave Dave in the snug and make my way to the kitchen. I really don't want to be in the same room as him, so even household chores are a blessing in disguise. The kitchen will be my sanctuary until the children are safely tucked up in bed. It's been such a difficult day for me and my face aches from the false smile which has been plastered on it all day.

No-one would suspect anything. A brilliant actress, putting on a performance for my family. The secret must be maintained. This situation must play its way out.

I don't know what the outcome of this crazy mess will be but, as far as I am concerned, that is no longer my problem to solve. I have tried and tried without success.

I just don't care anymore.

The dishwasher is finally full and I reach into the cupboard next to it for a washing tablet. As I press the buttons to set the machine off, my attention is drawn to Dave. He has slipped quietly into the room and is facing me across the island. He has a beer in his hand and sips it slowly as he watches me.

"Dinner was excellent, Maddy. Thank you." He tips his glass in my direction in a form of salute.

"You are welcome," I respond. My voice lacks any emotion. I honestly don't care about his lousy opinion. I am just so over this now.

I really don't want a conversation with him. Oh yes, there are so many things I could say to him. But if I start, I'm not sure how it would finish. The last thing I want is for Amelia to pick up on any tension between us. Let's just keep things civil for now. My current role is future mother-in-law, not angry and discarded lover.

"Are you looking forward to the big day next week, Maddy?"

The smile looks more like a leer. Just stop talking to me, I scream inside.

"Amelia is looking forward to her wedding so much. Charles and I will do everything we can to make her day special." A necessary swerve to avoid sharing my own feelings.

Dave settles his frame onto a bar stool as he watches me. His eyes follow me around the room as I gather the rest of the dishes which need washing. The sink is starting to fill and the noise of the water pouring gives me time to regain control of my feelings.

My heart is pounding. I'm not sure I can cope with his proximity. It makes me feel trapped being in the same room with him; alone. Why did Charles have to go out and leave me with him? Why did I let Amelia manage the children's bedtime and leave me with him?

It's not safe for me. I cannot be trusted.

I glance over my shoulder to look at him. For a change he's not looking my way but is checking out the rest of the kitchen. It gives me the chance to look at this man who has obsessed me for the last year. He is a beautiful man. It cannot be denied. Amelia is one lucky girl to be spending the rest of her life with him. If he can behave himself and make her happy, she will be content.

If.

A thought pops into my mind and, as much as I don't really want to ask the question, I am compelled to do so.

"Dave, what is your real name?"

The legality of next week had been troubling me for some time.

Silence stretches between us as we both think of the enormity of my question. Could he really marry Amelia under the wrong name? How will he explain that? All my previous investigations had shown his actual name was Dave Roberts. He had signed a non-disclosure agreement with my solicitor in that name. It's not a trivial matter, especially as marriage is a legal ceremony.

"What do you mean?" he growled. It seems I have hit a nerve.

"Well, you told me your name is Dave Roberts but your future wife thinks you are Peter McKay. So, who is she marrying?"

Dave stands and walks around the island to stand behind me. His face is a picture. He looks really pissed off with the change of atmosphere in the room. Things have gone up a notch. He was up for a bit of flirting whilst Amelia and Charles were out of the way. A forensic examination of his genealogy was not top of his agenda.

Obviously.

"Don't you worry your pretty head over the details, Maddy." His fingers reach up to my hair and gently caresses it behind my ear. His attempt to regain control are obvious in the extreme. "Everything will be legal before the wedding. There is no way I am going to make the mistake of leaving an exit route for your daughter. I want to get my hands on Daddy's money. So, no mistakes, my darling."

"What the hell are you on about?" I cried as I slapped his hand away from my face. "Daddy's money? What's that got to do with anything?"

Dave pulls me towards him and grips both my arms, tethering them to my sides. The movement is not seductive like his previous gesture was.

The atmosphere has changed at an alarming speed. An air of menace hangs around him like a bad smell. There is no longer any pretence of friendliness.

Dave is angry. He doesn't like being challenged. And he certainly doesn't like it when he's not in control.

Sarcasm drips from his mouth as he launches into an explanation of his twisted plans. "Oh, come on, Maddy. Did you really think I was marrying Amelia for love? I'm not the marrying type. Once it's all legal next week I can put things into action. Your darling husband will pay big money to protect his daughter from the scandal."

Dave moves closer to me, pinning me against the sink. His face gets closer to mine as his icy glare pierces into me. The grip he has on my arms is pinching into my skin. His crutch is thrust up against me and I can feel his excitement rising.

His face is saying one thing, hate. His body another, desire.

I'm frightened. This man is unstable and I have just stoked his fire, unnecessarily.

"Dave, stop it please."

He ignores me and continues to push his crutch at me. His breath is coming in slow waves of desire. He rubs himself against me. In different circumstances his attention would be welcome. But not now and not here in my own house. Where does this guy get off? He's like a dog on heat. If he doesn't get his own way this could all turn nasty.

Dave is strutting with pride, boasting of the ingenuity of his crazy plan.

"Daddy Saville will pay good money to stop the scandal hitting the press. Won't he? There's no way he will want all his posh friends and business partners finding out that his son-in-law is fucking his wife. And I will still be fucking his wife. Marrying Amelia will not stop us, darling Maddy. You are mine and you know it."

"You are sick. You bastard. We are over. We were over when I paid you off. You seriously are mad if you think I want you anymore." I struggle in his arms as I try to pull away from his grip.

"Oh Maddy, stop lying to yourself. You still want me. I can tell. Under your hard exterior you are gagging for me. Amelia cannot hold a torch to you, darling. You are the best fuck ever. Don't you remember coming round mine and practically begging me for sex?"

The shame of my guilt hits me again. "That was a mistake." I cry out as I try to push him away. He is not giving ground. "I came round yours to try and stop this whole fiasco. I wanted you to let down Amelia gently before you broke her heart. I should never have slept with you again. It was stupid and I regretted as soon as it happened."

Seriously where does this guy get off. He believes his own PR. He played me that night. It won't happen again.

I manage to pull my right arm out of his grip and push him away from me. "Get the fuck of me, you bastard. I suggest you leave this house now and piss right off out of our lives. The wedding is off. I will make sure of that. There is no way you are getting away with it."

My anger has taken over. I'm no longer thinking about the pain and destruction this will bring to my family. I need to protect Amelia from this man. He will not ruin her life because of me.

"I'm going to tell Amelia everything. And Charles. I will live with the consequences. But you will not play me any longer, you nasty little man." I shouted the last few words in his face.

"Not so fast, bitch."

Before I know what's happening, Dave grabs my face in his hands and slams my head down onto the worktop. The pain shoots up my jaw as my face squashes against the wood. My nose is pushed up against the surface as I struggle to breath. Flailing around I try to grab hold of his hand to release myself. My eyes notice my Chef's knife lying on the draining board. My fingers ache as I try to reach for it but it's just too far out of range.

At that point he knees me in the stomach.

The air is sucked out of my lungs as I double up in pain. The shock of what is happening hits me with the force of his knee. My worst fears are materialising. He is out of control.

His laughter taunts me as I gasp with pain. He is enjoying my humiliation and is getting off on my fear.

"Oh, Maddy. You are going to pay. Have no doubt about that."

Suddenly he releases my face from the work top and I start to slip to the ground. Every part of me hurts. I have lost control of my feet; they cannot hold me up anymore. I don't have the strength to stand. His knee meets my face, as I hit the ground, crunching into my jaw.

He laughs. A harsh cynical laugh.

Blood rushes from my nose as the pain pierces my brain, shooting upwards. I cough. Blood spurts from my mouth and streams down my face. The pain is overwhelming. My ribs scream with every breath. Rolling into a ball on the floor I try to protect myself from the kicks which are raining down on my bruised and battered body.

I am terrified. He won't stop until he kills me.

I don't have the strength to escape. Even knowing that he could kill me. I lie there thinking of Charles and the children. What will happen to them? Will he turn on them next?

The thought of my children galvanises me into action. I grab hold of the cupboard door handle, using it to pull myself further away from his swinging foot. The next kick connects with the cabinet and misses me. One more step. One more and I can be free from him.

Every ounce of energy is working now to escape. He will not kill me. I have to survive.

I cannot see a thing as blood covers my face but can hear him behind me. He swears as his foot connects with the cupboard but he doesn't give up. The next stride brings him behind me and he stamps on my reaching hand.

Another searing pain shoots up my arm. The bones in my fingers crack under the force of his weight.

I scream.

My screams will probably rouse the rest of the house, but I don't care anymore. I need help.

He is going to kill me.

The kicking has stopped.

Why?

Suddenly I hear a strange gagging noise coming from his mouth then his body falls across me. Blood pools around us spreading across the kitchen floor. As I push myself out from underneath him the first thing I see is the knife. Wedged between his shoulders. Blood pours from the wound and from his mouth. He is choking from his own blood pooling in his lungs.

Suddenly it's all quiet.

He's gone.

The bastard is dead.

I collapse on the floor as our blood mixes. I watch the pool growing and covering the pristine tiles. My mind tries to figure out how I am ever going to get the blood out of the grooves in my slate tiles. Weird what you can think about at such a time.

Gradually I become aware of another presence in the room. Amelia stands above me staring down at her fiancé's body. Her hands are shaking and she is crying hysterically.

She looks at me with big, scared eyes.

"I killed him."

The words hang there between us.

Amelia has saved my life.

Oh God, I owe her my life.

What happens next will determine both of our futures.

CHAPTER FORTY-TWO

After the extreme violence there is silence.

Amelia is rocking back and forth on her heels as she cries uncontrollably. Snot runs down her face as she sobs. I watch her as I lie in the pool of blood, trying to establish any part of me that's not hurting. My face is covered with blood, some of it mine and some his.

My jaw feels broken and I'm sure one of my teeth is hanging out. My fingers throb and I am pretty sure I have broken a number of bones. The pain in my side is worrying. It feels like I'm on fire as the pain washes over me in waves. As I look at his dead body, I heave. Swallowing down the bile in my throat, I know I need to check on Dave.

He is dead. I'm sure.

I place my fingers on his neck seeking a pulse, but there's nothing there at all. The amount of blood coming from his mouth has dried to a trickle. His evil eyes are glassy. There is no life left in them. I noticed a wet patch on his trousers. In his shock and pain he must have wet himself. Inexplicably, I pull the tea towel hanging from the drawer, placing it to cover his modesty.

The smell of death lingers and I can't help throwing up. Luckily, I have enough warning to direct the vomit away from his corpse. The shaking of my hands makes it impossible for me to clean up my mess. Wiping my arm across my face will have to do. At last, I can see properly as I wipe the drying blood and vomit on my new shirt.

Strangely, my first thought is that the material is totally ruined. A man lies dead and I'm thinking of my clothes. Shock is playing with my brain. A natural defence to the enormity of what has just happened. Wiping my face has made my nose bleed again and I spit out the blood which is flowing down the back of my throat.

The crying seems to have stopped. It's gone quiet.

Amelia moves away from his body and grabs a glass. Reaching for the brandy on the top shelf she pours a stiff measure, glugs it down in one and gasps as the hard liquor hits the back of her throat. She pours another measure and hands to me.

The warmth of the brandy has a healing effect on me. Slowly I pull myself up to stand. The shock of the pain in my stomach makes me gasp as I down a further measure of brandy. It has a numbing impact which is just what I need with what comes next.

"I heard you talking," Amelia drops those words into the silence between us. "Why didn't you tell me, Madeline? Why did you let this happen? I killed him. Because of you."

"Amelia, I don't know what to say. I am so sorry." I tried to reach out to her, but she shrugged me off.

"Don't. Don't touch me."

She's crying again. It's calmer. but heartbreaking to listen to.

In the space of a few minutes, she has found out the harsh reality of deception. Her stepmother has been having an affair with her fiancé. Her fiancé is not who she thinks he is. The marriage is a scam. The shame of my part in this whole episode is more than I can bear.

"Amelia, I did try and stop this. Sorry isn't enough. I know. But you have to believe me; I never wanted you to get hurt."

I try to reach her again but she moves away, shaking her head furiously.

"You didn't want me to get hurt? Well, you did so much more than that, didn't you? You made me kill him. How could you do this, Madeline? You are like a mother to me." Amelia is shouting now as her fear turns to anger.

"I'm so sorry, Amelia. I made a mistake. A bloody dreadful mistake. It got so out of hand. I never wanted this to happen. The guy is a monster. It's all his fault."

"No," Amelia shouted directly in my face. "It's all your fault. You cheated on Dad and then cheated on me. I will never forgive me. You are dead to me."

Amelia walks over to the window seat and curls into a ball. In one hand she has the brandy bottle and looks intent on finishing it. There is no way I am continuing this conversation whilst she is so angry. Later I will explain it all to her and beg her forgiveness.

I have a bigger problem to face now.

Soon Charles will be home and I will have to break his heart too.

Oh shit. Charles will be home soon. There is no way he can know what his beloved daughter has done. That will kill him.

Without thinking things through or even understanding what the consequences will be, I know I must act.

It took every bit of courage I possess to take hold of the knife and pull. It slides out of Dave's back. Rubbing blood from the wound around the handle I press my fingers into the grip. Once satisfied that my prints are all over the knife, I throw it to the ground.

Amelia is watching me. Shock then realisation plays across her face. "Madeline, what are you doing?" she screams at me.

"I'm doing what I have to do to keep you and the children safe. You say nothing. Just back up everything I say. Can you do that, Amelia?" I have grabbed hold of her shoulders as I look deeply into her eyes. "This is so important, darling. Promise me you will do exactly what I say now."

She nods slowly. I can see the relief in her eyes. Just at this moment I am not thinking about Charles or my darling children asleep upstairs.

I must protect Amelia. She has her whole life ahead of her. She's right. None of this is her fault. It's my responsibility and I must stand up and face the consequences.

Like a sleepwalker, I pick up the phone and dial 999. It doesn't take long for a voice to ask which service I require.

"Police please. I have killed someone."

Those four words will change everything for me and my family.

And so it starts.

The nightmare which will be the rest of my life.

As a convicted murderer.

CHAPTER FORTY-THREE

The clock on the interview room wall indicates it's 11am.

God, it's been a horrendously long night. One of many more to come.

It started when the police arrived, shortly before Charles got home.

I will never forget the look on his face. He walked into the kitchen to see his future son-in-law dead on the floor. Charles had rushed to my side as I sat with my head in my hands, shaking with the delayed shock. There was no need for me to pretend for the police. I was a mess. Not only did I hurt all over my body, but the enormity of what I had decided to do for Amelia had sunk in. Meanwhile, Amelia was sat on the window seat with a female officer who was trying her hardest to calm down my stepdaughter's hysteria.

Thankfully, Sophie and James had not stirred. After I phoned the police, I rang Jessica and asked her to come home immediately. God knows how I had managed all those phone conversations in such a calm way. I just think the shock hadn't kicked in yet.

Jessica was up on the landing watching over my babies. Her natural curiosity meant that, of course, she had an ear to what was happening in the kitchen. What must she be thinking? She definitely didn't sign up to this chaos.

The police didn't ask me many questions immediately. As soon as they had arrived, I admitted my guilt to the detective first on the scene. He had been very understanding and almost gentle with me. A confessed murderer being shown a level of human kindness I probably didn't deserve. I guess there are protocols about what they can and can't say to me at the scene of the crime so were obviously keen to continue any formal questioning down at the station.

Charles was horrified at the state of me.

It hadn't occurred to me to try and clean the blood from my nose and lips. The feel of a huge swelling under my eyelid was closing my eye up rapidly.

Charles took control at that point and insisted that I was taken to hospital first before any questioning took place at the police station. All he kept saying, over and over, was that this must be some sort of horrible mistake.

The worst horrible mistake of my life.

And it all started when I chose to be unfaithful to this kind man standing in front of me and caring for my wellbeing. I wish I could go back to that fateful train journey. Oh, I would do things so differently. Knowing what I know now.

But life isn't a dress rehearsal.

You don't get second chances.

You cannot turn back time.

The hospital had patched me up. Two broken ribs, my left hand had two broken fingers, a broken nose and severe bruising. My fingers were strapped together and a sling employed to ease the pain. I have been scanned and x-rayed to ensure I am in a fit state to leave hospital. I guess if I wasn't under arrest I would have been kept in for the rest of the night. My admission of guilt wasn't enough to give me time to recover. There were no life-threatening injuries so discharge was possible.

All my wounds were photographed and documented with a police officer present. My injuries will form part of my future defence. It's all I have left. My solicitor will no doubt strive to prove that I killed Dave in self-defence. But that's for later. There are far more twists and turns for me to get through before a court case.

Once we had arrived at the police station I was booked in and taken to a cell for the rest of the night.

Sleep was impossible.

The bed was a hard concrete shelf with a thin mattress placed over it. A flat pillow and a scratchy blanket were all I had to keep the chill off. My normal duck feather pillows and luxurious bedding seemed a long way off. It's a shock to the system, but a shock I guess I need to get used to. The thought of using the toilet, which gave off waves of urine stench, was repulsing me. Would there be CCTV within the cell? Would someone be watching me use the toilet? The thought of that was enough to clench hold of my bladder and will it to stay strong. Lying on the hard bed was the perfect recipe for an overactive brain.

Sleep was impossible.

I lay there listening to the noises coming from the other cells in the custody suite. Drunks screamed as they were manhandled into their accommodation for the night. Curses and obscenities were shouted out. Feet kicked against the steel doors. Is this my future? My mind runs through the possibility of prison and how I would cope with all that entailed. Could I cope? For the last few years, I have got used to a pampered life; having everything I want. Freedom is precious. Why was I giving up without a fight?

Sleep was impossible.

My conscience kept me awake. I had to face my husband and tell him of my guilt. I don't mean the murder of that bastard, Dave, but my behaviour over the last year which had led to this dreadful night. I owe it to him to hear the painful truth from me. The truth, I had jumped through hoops to avoid all this time, had led to a far worse outcome than if I had just confessed and faced his wrath months ago. If I had done that, poor Amelia would have been spared her heartbreak. Oh, how I wished I could start over and make it right. How I wish I could turn back time to that first fateful night together. If I had known how it would end up, that would have been the perfect passion killer.

Sleep was impossible.

Before I knew it, the grey swirls of light crept through the high window of the cell. The room seemed even more shabby in daylight. Crawling from the bed, I faced the embarrassment of using the toilet. My bladder was screaming at me so being coy was not an option. My night of restlessness had done nothing to help me prepare for the day ahead. Hopefully, the interview would be short. I'm going to confess so what more is there for them to ask me?

How naive am I?

A COSTLY AFFAIR

The detective, I think his name was DCI Marshall but I really wasn't with it, came for me at 9am. For the last two hours I have faced the full force of their questioning. Charles has sent his solicitor, Dennis White, along to represent me. My shame is complete as I have to talk about my affair in front of one of my husband's best friends. Dennis knows me so well. He's been in our house and played games with my children. He's had supper with us and now he is subjected to my shame. Poor Dennis fidgets uncomfortably at my side. He has been adjusting his tie continuously for the last hour. Another reason that I need to speak to Charles as soon as possible. Having Dennis share the sordid details will be mortifying for both of us. It's my sorry tale to tell.

I think we are getting to the end now. The DCI is pulling papers together and clears his throat as he looks at me.

"Right Mrs Saville. I think we have everything we need now. Let me just summarise what you have told us before I share the statement with you. I will then ask you to sign that. Is that OK?"

I nod.

"For the tape Mrs Saville."

"Sorry, yes I understand."

"Mr Roberts was staying at your home ahead of his wedding to your stepdaughter Amelia Saville. An argument ensued between you and Mr Roberts. Your husband and Amelia were not present during the argument. Mr Roberts got violent and hit you, kneed you in the stomach and kicked you in both the face and stomach. You have told us that the argument happened because you threatened to tell Amelia Saville that Mr Roberts was purporting to be her fiancé, Peter McKay. He had duped Miss Saville into a relationship in an act of revenge for the end of an affair you had with Mr Roberts back in March of last year."

He paused allowing me time to correct him, I guess. It's a story he will share with his mates in the pub, I bet. An unbelievable story. But that has been my life for the last year. An unbelievable nightmare. As far as I am concerned the least amount of information I have to share the better. Just listening to him makes me shiver with the absurdity of what's happening.

"Whilst Mr Roberts was attacking you, you reached for a knife on the draining board and stabbed him in the back. I do have my concerns about how you managed to reach his back with the right amount of force to embed the knife as deeply as you did. But our forensic team will be looking at your statement in that respect. However, you have admitted to the offence and you confirm there was no one else in the room when the incident occurred. Amelia Saville found you in the kitchen with Mr Roberts, who was dead at this point. She will be interviewed formally later today, but her initial statement confirms that you admitted to her that you stabbed Mr Roberts resulting in his death. OK, so do you have anything more you want to tell me at this point."

Dennis looks questioningly at me. I honestly don't have a clue what I want to say. Inside, my head is screaming that I didn't do it. I was beaten up by that bastard and, to my shame, I am over the moon that he is out of my life now.

But I didn't do it.

There is no way I am letting Amelia carry the can. I have wronged her so deeply.

It is my crime to bear, whatever the consequences. It will destroy my marriage and no doubt I will lose my children. But could I really allow Amelia to go to prison for murder when it's all my fault?

A moment's decision will change the rest of my life.

Both of our lives.

All of our lives will change, including my darling children's. But I can't go back on my promise. I owe it to her to shoulder the blame. Her father will hate me. But he would hate me so much more if I wasn't doing this. Amelia has everything ahead of her, a good job and hopefully the chance to find a decent man who will love her. If I am going to lose everything anyway it sort of makes sense that I do this one last thing for her.

"No, I have nothing further to add." My voice trembles with the enormity of what I am confessing to.

Murder.

"OK, Madeline Saville, I am charging you with the murder of David Roberts. The charge sheet here outlines the full details of the crime. As you have willingly confessed to the crime and we do not consider you to be a flight risk, I am prepared to release you on police bail. The conditions of your bail include that you remain at your home address, that you submit your passport to the police station here and you will report to us weekly until your case comes to court. We may need to question you further once the outcome of our forensic examination is complete. Do you understand the charge?"

"Yes, I do, officer."

My heart is racing at the thought of going home. That had been the furthest thing from my mind. I will have to face Charles today. I'm not sure I'm ready for it.

"OK. If you can wait here for a few minutes while I process the charge sheet and then I can release you into the hands of your solicitor who will make sure you get home safely." DCI Marshall stands with his colleague and leaves Dennis and me alone in the room.

Dennis looks even more uncomfortable now we are alone. He clears his throat as he tidies his papers. Slowly he places his hand over mine and squeezes it gently. No words are spoken. Neither of us has any desire to talk.

"Let's get you home, Madeline."

His kindness opens the flood gates as I dissolve into tears.

CHAPTER FORTY-FOUR

"Mummy, mummy."

I longed to hear the cries of Sophie and James as I turned the lock in the front door. Unfortunately, silence greets me. Staggering in, I drop my bag and kick off my shoes. Charles must have heard the door and slips out of the snug. Within moments I am in his arms. He holds me as I weep quietly. Gently he rubs my back. His touch consumes me with grief. Selfishly, I savour the moment. Once I start to explain everything to Charles there will be no more kindness. Coldness will replace comfort.

I cannot bear the thought of hurting this wonderful man. Will he ever forgive me for the wrong I have done him? Let alone the chaos and destruction I have brought to his door.

"Charles, where are the children?"

I break the silence. The need to hug my children is tugging at my heartstrings. I can see the answer in his face before he says the words. I know I'm about to be devastated.

"Jessica took them out for the day. Sorry darling. I just thought it was best they were out of the way. They are confused enough as it is." Charles tucks my hair behind my ear, caressing my cheek. The affection is so welcomed but so undeserved. "I didn't know what to tell them. The police were here most of the night and I had only just managed to clear up the kitchen before they woke."

The disappointment is written across my face. Charles has done the right thing, the only thing in the circumstances, but I want my babies with me. The need to hold them is all consuming. If I hug my children perhaps it will all go away. Foolish, I know. It's a primeval need in me.

"Amelia is upstairs," Charles continues. "The doctor gave her a sedative. She's been out most of the day. I think it's best to let her sleep. Helps to ease the pain. She was in a right state last night."

Anger wells up as I think about what I am doing for Amelia.

All the focus will be on her. Her poor, dead fiancé. Her wedding called off. I didn't think this through at all. All the negative focus will be on me. A court case; potentially a prison sentence; a marriage break down; loss of custody of my children.

It's too late now. I can't change the decisions made; the promises made to Amelia. However much this hurts me, I deserve it. I deserve the shame and humiliation. It's a just punishment for the wrongs I have done.

"We need to talk, Madeline. I couldn't get any sense out of Amelia and the police wouldn't tell me anything. Please talk to me about what happened, darling." Charles is holding me tight, clinging to me as if his grip will make it all go away and we can go back to normal.

"Soon, Charles. I need to shower and get out of these clothes first. I'll be quick and then I promise we will talk."

Wriggling out of his embrace, I make my way wearily to our bedroom. The sight of our bed is beckoning me into its soft folds. As much as I would love to curl up and sleep, the important task now is to bare my soul to Charles. The longer I wait, the harder it will be.

Dropping my clothes on the floor I head for the shower. The warm water splashes my body. I wince in pain as my ribs cry out with the feel of water. I struggle to wash with my strapped up fingers. I have a few futile attempts to clean myself and settle for standing under the powerful jet of water. Washing the blood from my hair, I wonder if that was Dave's. It is probably a combination of both of our blood. There was so much. I grimace as I think about washing that bastard out of my life.

Finally.

He cannot hurt me anymore. The hurt will be dished out by me now to my family. They honestly don't deserve it.

I don't feel any regret for his death. That must sound so callous, but he deserved it. He got under my skin and paid the price for his actions. I had wanted him desperately, but hated him at the same time. But I didn't deserve how it played out. Never saw that coming. Why had he turned on me like that? Like the flick of a light switch, he went from normal to evil within seconds. He showed his true colours. The man was a monster.

Now a dead monster.

Cleaning my teeth was a luxury which I savoured. Morning breath on top of blood residue stained into my gums. I felt filthy. The taste of my breath was rancid. God knows how Charles had kissed me without retching.

A towelling lounge suit was my best option to ease the pain of my bruises. My whole body aches. It cries out for rest but there is a quite different pain ahead of me. The thought of talking to Charles is gut-wrenching but it must happen.

Charles is sat in the snug with a glass of whiskey. He has poured me a glass and despite the fact that my stomach is grumbling with the need for food, the warm liquid is all I need at this stage. I choose to sit across from my husband and spend a few moments gathering my thoughts. If I'm honest with myself, I am playing for time.

Time I just don't have. Charles is clearly waiting for me. Ever thoughtful, he is not pushing me to start. I really do not deserve this man. He really doesn't deserve to be hurt with my revelations. But I cannot protect him from the truth any longer.

I owe it to him to hear the truth from me and no-one else.

"Charles, before I start, I need you to know that I love you with all my heart. You have made me the happiest woman in the world and I am so deeply sorry that I have betrayed your trust." I pause as I watch my husband's face. He is confused. Taking another sip of whiskey, he smiles weakly at me, encouraging me to continue.

"I have been a fool, darling. I am so deeply sorry. I really don't know where to start." My stomach is now churning and I can feel my fingers shaking. Putting my glass down, I clasp my fingers together trying to prevent the visible tremble.

"Madeline, you are worrying me now. Please just tell me what is going on. I have been racking my brains all night trying to figure out why Peter would attack you. It just doesn't make sense. I can't ask Amelia. She was in such a mess last night, there was no way I was getting any sense out of her. So, you need to tell me what's going on." Charles shifts forward in his seat and fixes his stare on my face.

"Peter McKay is not who he said he was. His real name is Dave Roberts." I drop the bombshell at my husband's feet. The shock on his face is clear. "I met Dave at a conference over 18 months ago. I'm so sorry darling but I was a fool and an idiot. We had an affair."

Charles breathes out a huge gasp and his head falls into his hands. As I watch, it is clear that he is crying. His shoulders shake. That was not the reaction I was expecting. I really thought he would be angry; would shout or would give me the cold shoulder.

But not this.

I have never seen Charles cry before. Even when Sophie was born, which was the most emotional moment of our marriage so far. He's not the emotional type. He is from that generation which sees emotion as a weakness. Sharing this reaction with me now only goes to show how wrong I have been, jeopardising my relationship with this man.

It feels inappropriate to continue so we sit in silence for some moments.

"Why Madeline? Was I not enough for you?" I can hear the tremor in his voice.

His eyes meet mine and shame hits me once more. How could I have done this to my wonderful husband? What a bitch, he does not deserve this.

"Charles, I love you so much and I have never stopped loving you. I cannot explain why I slept with Dave. It was a moment of madness. He entrapped me. I didn't realise it at the time, but he targeted me and I was stupid enough to fall for it. My biggest regret is that I have hurt you."

"How long?"

"Please. Don't ask for the details, Charles."

"How long?" His voice shows a change in tone. There is less sadness and more anger.

"A few months. Months of madness when I just didn't know what I was doing and why."

"So, it wasn't just a one-off then. You slept with another man and then did it again and again. Without any thought for me or your two children. How fucking selfish, Madeline? Did you not think about us while you were screwing around?"

The tears start to roll down my cheeks as I watch my marriage implode.

"I am deeply ashamed of my behaviour. I am not going to try and bullshit you with excuses. I made a mistake. A huge mistake and I am just so very sorry for betraying you."

"I don't know you anymore, Madeline. I thought you were my soul mate. My best friend. And you do this to me? What about our beautiful children? If you couldn't be faithful to me then could you not be faithful to Sophie and James?" Charles was hurting and he knew how to turn the knife in my wound.

My body is heaving with sobs now. I cannot stop the tears from falling and I wipe my hands across my eyes. I catch my swollen nose and almost welcome the pain of reopening the scabs across my nostrils. Blood seeps out and I let it flow.

"I didn't think of the children. If I had, this would never have happened. Charles, I cannot explain my actions. I was stupid and selfish and I am paying the price."

"You are paying the price? Don't make me laugh. You had all the fun you stupid woman. It's me and the kids who are paying the price for your wanton behaviour."

Only my husband could use the word wanton in this way. If the conversation wasn't so highly charged, I could have laughed. When he is angry, Charles can be so pompous. Not that I blame him. I deserve all I am getting here, being on the other end of his disappointment.

"Charles, I cannot change what happened. My shame and disgust at my own behaviour made me end the relationship. The guy was a maniac. He wouldn't let me go and threatened to tell you unless I paid him off." As I spoke, the story of my downfall just felt increasingly unreal.

"He blackmailed you?" Charles looks even more shocked at the surreal story.

"He told me if I didn't pay him fifty thousand pounds he would tell you everything and wreck our marriage. I couldn't let that happen. Stupidly I thought that if I paid him, he would go away. I could forget my stupid mistake and spend the rest of my life making it up to you. I even got him to sign a non-disclosure document. It was all done legally." Taking a glug of whiskey, I reached for a box of tissues to try and clean up the congealing blood on my face.

"Where did you get the money from, Madeline? Did you not think I would notice that sort of cash going missing?"

Charles had known about the inheritance from my parents and had insisted the money had been placed in my name only. He had obviously forgotten about its existence. As I explained the lengths I had taken to hide my treachery, giving up my parents' hard earned cash to pay off my lover, his slow shake of the head confirmed his disgust at my behaviour. The whole conversation was a disaster. Listening to my own explanations just sounded even more unbelievable.

Why hadn't I admitted my disgrace right at the start and taken the punishment then. It definitely couldn't have been as bad as this. The longer you hide a wrong, the worse it gets. It snowballs as it rolls forward, increasing in magnitude with your deceit and lies.

"So, Madeline, how did this man then end up in my daughter's life? I just don't understand where Amelia comes into all this?"

"Because he is one sick bastard. That's why. Well one dead, sick bastard." I took another swig of whiskey. The warm liquid burnt down the back of my throat making me cough. My eyes watered and I rubbed at them aggressively. "I didn't know Dave was Peter until we met in that restaurant in Covent Garden. God knows how you didn't work out there was something wrong. I was as sick as a dog that night with shock. He decided to punish me another way. The NDA ensured that he couldn't talk to you so he decided to use Amelia to get to me. How was I to know that he was some sort of psycho?"

"Madeline, you brought this man into our lives. You let him touch my daughter. Why didn't you stop him?" Charles got out of the chair and started to pace the room. His face exhibited the anger brewing just under the surface. "I will never forgive you for what you have brought to our door, Madeline."

"Charles. I am so very sorry. There was no way I could have known. I tried to warn him off. Both you and Catherine sensed he wasn't the right man for Amelia. I tried so hard. I really did."

Charles stopped pacing and fixed a deathly glare at me. "Madeline, you could have stopped it just like that." He flicked his fingers together in my face. "You could have told me. We could have sorted this out. Then my daughter would not have been hurt. Your selfishness is unbelievable."

Any chance of saving our marriage had gone up in smoke. A line had been crossed. Charles may have forgiven me for the affair. In time. But hurting his precious daughter was a step too far.

"And on top of your betrayal, you bring murder to my door. What will your children think when they find out their mother has killed a man? Especially a man who they thought was in love with their sister. How fucking twisted is that." Charles never swears. "How are we going to explain this when it comes to court? When their mother ends up in prison? I will tell you this now, Madeline. My children will not be visiting you in prison so get that into your thick skull now."

"Charles, you are angry and I deserve it. We have to manage the situation for our children. They are my children too and don't forget that."

The turn of direction is starting to frighten me. I haven't had a chance to think how we are going to work through this as a family. The police have insisted I live here, so leaving is not an option. We will have to maintain some form of pretence for the children as this plays out.

"You should have thought about your children before you decided to sleep around, Madeline. So don't start guilt tripping me. The children's welfare is my only consideration now."

Charles slumped back onto the sofa. Grabbing the whiskey bottle he refilled his glass. He obviously had no intention of offering me any so I took the bottle and replenished my glass.

We sat in silence, drinking.

The atmosphere was charged. We now faced the most difficult part of the discussion. What would we do for the next few months before the court case? The children needed consistency. What about my job? Would Charles keep me in position after all this? Did we have a marriage for me to come back to?

After what seemed like hours, Charles spoke.

"We need to keep up appearances until your case comes to court. I don't want our children exposed to your shocking behaviour. So, you will act as if it was just a freak argument which got out of hand. You will stay on at work. No one in the office must know. You owe me that." I'm nodding. This is far better than I expected. "I will take the spare room for now. I cannot bear the thought of sharing a bed with you. If the sordid details have to come out when this comes to court, then at that point we will part. Anything to protect the future of our children. I will ensure you have support once this is all over but the children stay with me. Non-negotiable."

The tears fall again as my heart slowly breaks. The cost of my betrayal is laid out before me. My marriage is over in all but name.

My children will be lost to me.

Deep down I know that I have no option but to agree to Charles's demands. He holds all the cards now. I have no moral high ground. My morals have brought me to the abyss and somehow I have to live with the consequences.

Perhaps Charles will forgive me over time? Perhaps he will understand my dilemma and try to see why I made the decisions I did. I was trying to avoid hurting my family due to my selfish stupidity. But by doing that I have created a far worse situation where everyone gets hurt.

Including me.

CHAPTER FORTY-FIVE

I approach Amelia's bedroom with trepidation.

Tapping softly on the door, I push it open and crane my neck to see where she is. Amelia is lying on the bed, above the covers in a foetal position. She looks to be asleep so I tiptoe across the dim room. The curtains are drawn and only a small shaft of daylight is flickering across the carpet. If it wasn't for the fact that it was now mid-afternoon, I would have left Amelia to sleep. Perching on the side of the bed, I stroke her hair, gently pushing it away from her face.

She looks so peaceful and untroubled. Looking at her, it is hard to imagine she is a grown woman who was on the cusp of marriage. In repose her face looks childlike. Her eyes are puffy from the tears and her breathing troubled from a blockage to her nose, again from all her crying.

After some moments, my presence must have roused Amelia from her doze. She opens her eyes, blinking to shift the sleep from her gaze. As her eyes adjust to the gloom, she recognises me. I am not sure what to expect. What reaction will I see from the stepdaughter I have wronged? She smiles weakly then holds out her arms.

Without hesitation I collapse into her arms. We both burst into tears and hold each other tightly as we cry. After all the emotion we have both endured since last night, it is surprising there are any more tears to flow. I gently rub Amelia's back, as I would do my own babies, as she sobs. We comfort each other which to the impartial observer could probably seem confusing.

The truth is, we share a secret. A secret which her father must never know. This is the one goodness left in this whole situation. The gift I am giving Amelia is her freedom. Both of us realise the enormity of that gift. Amelia should be full of fury after finding out about me and her fiancé. She has had the time to think about the consequences of her actions and the irrefutable fact that I am taking all the blame on my shoulders.

Eventually we are both cried out. Amelia breaks away from my embrace and sits back on the bed, plumping pillows behind her. I wriggle up the bed to sit beside her and we hold hands. I can feel her fingers tracing circles on my palm as I reach across and kiss her cheek.

"How are you feeling, Amelia darling?" I ask. "Stupid question, I know. But how are you now?"

Amelia grips harder onto my hand as she looks deeply into my eyes. "I feel numb, Madeline. I honestly can't believe what happened last night. I fucking killed a man."

"Darling, you have got to forget that, please. Try and block it out of your mind. I am responsible for this bloody mess. I need you to stick with the story. For your father. For you, darling."

Amelia pulls back her hand and drops her face into both her palms. I can see her shoulders shaking as her sobs start up again. Gently I rub her back, feeling her pain.

"I feel so guilty, Madeline. You are taking the blame for me. That's so wrong. It's going to destroy your life and it's my fault."

Amelia rests her head in my lap as I stroke her hair. What an absolute nightmare this is. No-one is a winner in the debacle. That bastard deserves everything that happened, Dave Roberts and his devious schemes. Dave is dead, Amelia is a killer and I'm now a criminal.

I have a huge responsibility for the part I played in this nightmare. If I hadn't fallen for Dave in the first place, it wouldn't have led to this. That's why I have to do what I have agreed to.

I don't really have a choice.

"Look Amelia, we agreed. You are not taking the blame for this. Dave tricked you into falling in love with Peter McKay. I should have stopped all of this months ago. I should have told your father and faced the consequences. I was selfish and weak. I didn't want Charles to leave me." I shrugged at the futility of my thinking which had led to all of this. "Either way, now I have hurt your father far more than you can ever imagine. There is no way back. But how do you think your father would feel if his precious daughter was blamed for Dave's death? How would he cope if you were charged or sent to prison? He wouldn't. It would destroy him."

I paused as my mind shifted through the conversation I had just had with Charles. "I love your father so much, Amelia. This is the only thing I can do for him now. It's my penance for the hurt I have brought to our door. Now you have to promise me that you will not tell your father the truth. Promise me Amelia. This is just so important." I reached for her hands and held them firmly, staring deeply into her eyes.

"I promise, Madeline. I don't agree with you, but I respect your decision. The thought of going to prison scares the shit out of me." Amelia squeezed my hand. "Thank you, Madeline. I will never forget what you have done for me."

CHAPTER FORTY-SIX

A noise wakes me. My eyes scan the bedroom looking for its source. Having left Amelia to rest, I collapsed on our bed and fell asleep immediately. Sleep had avoided me for over twenty-four hours so I was exhausted. Judging by the light, it was later than I thought. Glancing at the bedside clock I could see it was 6pm.

Suddenly a pair of little hands crept up from the floor. I could hear the giggles before I saw Sophie. My darling daughter clambered onto the bed and threw herself at me. I winced with the pain in my ribs and held in my gasp.

"Mummy, where you been? I missed you, Mummy." Sophie snuggled into my chest and sucked furiously on her thumb. As she sucked, her fingers twirled her hair; a sure sign she was tired.

"Hello my beautiful girl. Have you had a lovely day with Jessica?" I drank in the smell of her hair like an alcoholic smells wine. These moments with my children will be so precious over the coming months. They cannot understand how important these moments will be for me. Making memories which will have to give me comfort over the years of solitude ahead.

"We went to the cinema, Mummy. Jessica took us to see Frozen. It was brilliant. Can I have an Elsa doll? Please, Mummy." It's amazing how children can forget bad stuff, like the absence of their mother overnight, and just enjoy the simple things in life.

"We'll see, darling. Where's James?"

I searched the room looking for my youngest. I spotted him in the corner staring at me. James has always been the more sensitive of my children. He seems to sense tension and picks up on my emotions. Beckoning him over to the bed, I reached down and pull him into my arms.

"Mumma, love you. I missed you, Mumma, where were you?" His little sticky fingers grabbed at my cheeks trying to monopolise my gaze.

"I'm sorry, darlings. Mummy had to go and do some important stuff this weekend. But I'm home now and all yours."

I enfolded my children into my arms, holding back the tears. How can I leave my babies behind? It is going to break my heart. My head tells me they will be cared for, but my heart resents that it won't be me who will care for them.

They will have their father. I know Charles will shower them with love and protect them from gossip. Jessica is such a godsend for me. She will love my children like her own. She will give them security and stability and, alongside Charles, will try and keep their lives as normal as possible.

In the coming months I must put my children first. Work will take more of a backseat and I will spend long weekends taking Sophie and James on great adventures. I will create the most amazing memories for all of us. They won't notice the coldness between me and Charles. They won't question the absence of Daddy in Mummy's bed.

Between us we will cocoon them with love and affection.

We will have to explain why Amelia is not getting married and where Peter has disappeared to. For the first time, we will lie to our children so they don't know the real reason for Peter's absence. Amelia will move back in with her father and me. She will join us in protecting Sophie and James from the outside world and the harsh reality of recent events.

At some point I will have to explain what is happening to me.

But not yet.

Let me enjoy my last few months of freedom.

Let me enjoy my darling children.

CHAPTER FORTY-SEVEN

It's the night before the court case.

The children are asleep and Amelia has gone out with a friend. There is no excuse for Charles to avoid me tonight.

We have eaten dinner together and shared a bottle of wine. Our conversation has been stilted, as most of our interaction has been over the last months. We have got used to putting on a show for the family and our friends. I have savoured the food tonight, appreciating the meal as a convict enjoys their last supper.

After dinner we settle in the snug and Charles cracks open a bottle of whiskey. Again, this will be the last drink I will have over the lonely years ahead so I sip slowly, rolling the nectar across my tongue; enjoying the flavours and the warmness which creeps down my throat.

"Madeline, are you ready for tomorrow?" Charles puts into words the thought I have been trying to avoid for so long.

"My affairs are in order, if that's what you mean?" I look across at Charles trying to judge his mood.

"I was thinking about the case. What are you going to say? Being selfish really but I would like to know what I am facing."

Charles has not spoken about my plea or the approach I was going to take in court. Not sure I have made my own mind up yet. Many scenarios have been playing around in my head for weeks. I think I have settled on an approach then fear takes over and I grasp at another. I think I know what to do, but haven't put that into words. I hadn't shared my feelings with anyone.

"My defence counsel wants me to plead not guilty on the grounds of self-defence."

Charles nods his head slowly. The realisation of what that will mean is weighing heavily on his shoulders. "Just one plea from me, Madeline. Keep the sordid details to a minimum. I don't want the shame of your behaviour staining my family name. I know people will find out what you did, but I really don't want our dirty linen washed for all to see."

There is no empathy in his voice. I suppose I shouldn't expect his support, but the coldness of his words burns into my heart. This was the man I had loved so deeply who is now only concerned with saving his face.

"Don't worry, Charles. I won't do anything to hurt you anymore than I have to. You will still be able to hold your head up high at the office." Sarcasm drips from my mouth.

"Madeline, don't forget none of this is my problem. I have done nothing wrong. It's your behaviour which is on trial and it's your behaviour which could destroy my family."

I'm seething now. "It is my family too, Charles. And don't you ever forget that. They are my children. Oh, you may have the upper hand now but remember, my children will grow up and they will judge their father. You think you can keep me away from the kids after this but you can't. They love me and always will. If you drop poison in their minds, they will never forgive you."

I think I may have pushed it too far as I can see the redness in Charles's cheeks as he stands and walks towards the drinks cabinet. He's playing for time.

"Give me some credit, Madeline. I love my children more than life itself and I will never put their happiness at risk. Unlike you. It's very easy to spout about your love for your children. But where was that when you were jumping into bed with Dave Roberts?"

That hurts. Oh, he knows how to turn the knife. "Thank you," I respond sarcastically. "Look Charles. I really don't want to talk anymore. We may both say things we will regret. You have my word that I will do everything in my power to keep you and the children out of this."

I stand and turn to walk out of the room. "I'm going to bed. I will see you in the morning. After tomorrow, you will no doubt have me out of your life for good."

As I walk away, I don't see the look on his face. Charles watches me go and I do not see the tears which are making their slow route down his face.

This conversation has helped me to decide.

I know what I have to do for Charles and the children.

CHAPTER FORTY-EIGHT

The day of the court case has finally arrived.

The last few weeks have been fraught with worry as I try to put my affairs in order. Other than last night, Charles and I have tiptoed around each other, making polite conversation, and keeping up appearances for friends and family. He is hurting so badly. Sometimes I catch him looking at me and that look cuts me to the bone. He still loves me; I'm sure of that, but his pride will not allow him to forgive me. As promised, he has slept in the spare room since my confession. I have missed his presence in our bed.

It's incredibly lonely without him.

At work we have remained totally professional. No-one could know what's going on behind our closed door. Except for Stacey of course. My best friend and PA knows everything. Well almost everything. She has been my rock in the workplace. If any gossip rears its ugly head, she will be the first to tell me and to squash it. The official line which Saville's is promoting was that a drink-fuelled family argument got out of hand. Peter had gone crazy and attacked me and during the scuffle, he was stabbed.

It was all a dreadful accident.

With typical efficiency, Charles has already lined up my replacement, who joined the week before the court case to ensure a handover. Many of my closest work colleagues were heard muttering "innocent until proven guilty." Unfortunately, that one act alone has painted my husband in a poor light with many of the top team. But they won't tell him to his face. None of his colleagues are brave enough to express their true feelings over this situation. It's just all too sensitive.

Catherine and Roger have been incredibly supportive. Charles must have told Catherine about my deceit; well of course he would. They share most things. The first few times I saw her, the coldness was evident. Seeing the way Charles and I have conducted ourselves in the build up to the court case has perhaps softened her anger. She even admitted to me last night that she was glad Amelia and Peter were never married. She knew he was a wrong one all along.

We had so many missed opportunities to put a stop to events which unfolded.

Unfortunately for me, we missed them all.

If we hadn't, then I wouldn't be facing a bleak future without my family around me.

Roger has been here throughout as a shoulder for me to lean on. He hasn't judged me or shown any animosity to me. On his many visits, he has just sat and held my hand in an avuncular fashion. A rock of stability in the disaster which my life has become. With Charles withdrawing his emotional support, it has been good to use Roger as my sounding board. His advice has been outstanding, especially as we prepare for my court case.

Early on, the CPS agreed the charge should be reduced from murder to manslaughter. My wounds, evidence of the beating Dave subjected me to, were taken into consideration. The police investigation into Dave Roberts revealed a history of threatening behaviour. I wasn't the first to fall for his coercive charms, but I was the last. He suffered from a complex psychological order which severely impacted on his character, especially when a relationship came to an end. He couldn't rationalise rejection. He needed to have control over the course of a relationship and without control, he had tipped over the edge and was unable to moderate his actions. That had explained the way he had suddenly resorted to violence that night when I had threatened his plan. He had lost control of the situation and took that out on me.

Roger had worked hard with my solicitor to understand the benefits of me pleading guilty and my chances of a not guilty decision. We had spent hours ensconced in the study discussing my approach. I believe Roger is the one person who has an idea what I plan to do. We haven't verbalised it, but with the odd look and glance, our minds have reached synergy.

Amelia has been living with us all this time. Our relationship has built in strength with our shared secret. I have forbidden any further discussion about what I'm doing for her. She wasn't happy with that, but she knew she had to agree to my wishes. Trying to forget the court case ahead, we have enjoyed each other's company. She has joined me on the numerous trips out, at the weekend, with Sophie and James. I am thankful that my darlings will have their older sister alongside them in the years ahead.

On one particularly drunken night together, we had spliced our fingers and mingled blood, vowing to care for each other for the rest of our lives. Despite the pain and hurt I had inflicted on her father and herself, we have found a place where we can operate as equals. She has become the sister I never had. Amelia swears to me that she will visit me in prison. I won't hold her to that. The passing of time and the pace of life will no doubt lead her to break her promise.

I will understand when that happens.

Part of my preparation for what lies ahead has been to build an emotional wall around me. I have gradually stepped back from my family over the last week. I want them to remember the good times and I don't want my children to be traumatised by my departure.

Jessica and I have talked through my wishes for Sophie and James. She has clear instructions on how she will address their questions around my absence. Between Charles, Amelia and Jessica, I have confidence that they will do everything in their power to nurture my babies.

I will be the one alone and yearning for those I love. I'm not sure how I will bear that. As much as I am mentally preparing for the months and years ahead, I am quite sure I will break down when it comes to pass.

For appearance's sake, Charles has accompanied me to the Isleworth Crown Court for my hearing. Amelia wanted to come but I insisted she didn't. Today is going to be so hard and selfishly, I really don't want to see the distress on my loved ones' faces. Charles rarely shows any emotion to me at the moment so his sternness is probably all I need to get through this.

I am resolved to fix my eyes on him during the proceedings. His coldness is what I need to get through the day. His distaste will remind me of the hurt I inflicted on him. If I waver and try to defend my conduct, I only need to look at him and realise I deserve whatever punishment is inflicted on me.

Once we arrive at the court building, I am ushered into a side room to meet with my defence team. They have been preparing my case over recent weeks and believe that I should fight the charge, even though it has been downgraded to manslaughter. My expensive barrister seems to feel he is confident of a win, especially once the jury knows the background to my case and the sordid details of my affair. Dave clearly set out to bring me down, in their esteemed opinion.

It's this particular stance which has been tormenting me for weeks.

If I defend myself then the world will know about my affair; about the blackmail; about the fact that I allowed this monster to get to the point where he nearly married my stepdaughter. All this information is mitigation to my 'crime of passion.' If I take this course of action, I may get off but it's still a big if. But if it doesn't lead to a not guilty decision, I will have dragged my family through the dirt for nothing. There is one option left open to me which I tried to talk to my barrister about with little success. Their confidence in the ability to defend me makes any other options not open for discussion.

Hey, I'm only the defendant! I guess my opinion doesn't matter.

Whilst my legal team discuss process, I sit in silence. My mind is made up. I think I've known what the right thing to do has been for weeks. My behaviour over the last few days has been an indication of my mindset; strange that my family and friends haven't picked up on the warning signs. I think Charles is bracing himself for the embarrassment of the coming days. His warnings from last night resonate in my decision making. I owe it to him and the children. It's my penance.

I'm invisible to my legal team. They are talking between themselves but no-one asks for my opinion. Oh well, if they don't ask me then they really can't be surprised when I enter my plea.

My case is called before lunch.

Thankfully, I am spared the humiliation of entering the defendant's box in handcuffs. My co-operation throughout the police investigation allows me the dignity of walking in and taking my position facing the judge's seat.

As I would prepare for an important meeting at work, my appearance has been well planned. I'm wearing a shift dress in navy with matching jacket, dark tights and elegant heels. Power dressing gives me the confidence to withstand the rows of eyes watching me, analysing me, judging me.

We all rise as the judge enters. It's a woman. Not sure if that makes me feel better or worse. Perhaps a woman may go easier on me.

What the hell? I am definitely grasping at straws now. It really doesn't matter who the judge is now. Does it?

The clerk of the court rises and starts to speak. He calls the case as Crown v Madeline Saville and the charge of manslaughter. At this point he addresses me. "Madeline Saville, you are charged with the manslaughter of David Roberts on 2nd September 2014. How do you plead? Guilty or Not Guilty?"

All eyes switched towards me. Drawing on all my inner strength, I cleared my throat.

"Guilty."

The words came out as a whisper and I could see the clerk straining to hear me. Raising my voice a notch I repeated.

"Guilty, sir."

My barrister shot round in his seat, staring at me. I kept my eyes fixed ahead, trying my best to ignore his frantic signals. Before I knew what was happening, he approached the bench and asked the judge for the ability to speak to his client.

Noting the confusion, the judge called an hour's recess.

Within moments I was bundled into a side room with my barrister, who was near to exploding with rage. Perhaps if he or his team had cared to listen to me then he would have been better prepared.

"Madeline, what are you doing?" he shouted once we were alone.

"Look I know you said I should fight this, but you didn't really listen to me. I am not having my private affairs discussed in court. It's my decision. So please respect that."

I had definitely pissed off my barrister. "Why didn't you talk to me about this before we went in there? You have made me look a complete idiot."

Typical, my barrister is more concerned about his own reputation than the welfare of his client.

"Look, Mr Wilkins, I'm sorry if you feel I have embarrassed you, but I have tried to talk to you and you have not been listening. I have had concerns for weeks now and tried to talk to you and your team. No-one listens to me. You have just bamboozled me into following what you want to do. If you had listened to me, you would have understood my nervousness." I pause as I watch my barrister finally start to take on board what I'm saying. "If I plead not guilty, my marriage will be examined in detail. I cannot do that to my husband and children. I'm sorry but I have made my mind up."

Eric Wilkins breathes out deeply, slowly shaking his head. He takes some time to answer, using that silence to jot down notes on the pad in front of him. "OK, Madeline. Here's what we do. I am going to push for clemency. Hopefully Her Right Honourable Lady will take into consideration your confession and the injuries inflicted on you by Mr Roberts. It's now about damage limitation. I have to point out that this is not my legal advice, but I will try and mitigate the position you have put yourself in."

He is really getting on my nerves now. Who is paying his ridiculous salary anyway? And now he is lecturing me like a naughty schoolkid. "I understand, Mr Wilkins. I have made my decision and I trust you to see what you can do to keep my sentence as low as you can. Thank you."

I am not apologising to him. The arrogance of this man has grated on me for weeks now. It is really his own fault. He wouldn't give me the time to explain how I was feeling or take me seriously. I sat in silence as he prepared his notes. The silence was extremely awkward.

Actually, I was pleased to get back into court and face the outcome.

As I took my seat, I looked across at Charles. I can see the shock on his face. He looks confused and fiddles with his tie which I know is a sign of stress. The realisation of what I have done is written across his face. I can sense that he knows our life will no longer be under public scrutiny. All his fears are washing away. Following that realisation, the consequences for me obviously hit him. Charles looks at me as if he is trying to give me some subliminal message.

Too late, my darling. I have made my mind up and nothing can stop this now. It's my penance for the wrong I did you, my husband.

Suddenly I am drawn back to proceedings as my barrister starts to address the court.

"My Lady. My client has pleaded guilty to the charge of the manslaughter of Mr David Roberts. In the circumstances I would ask for the early admission of guilt to be taken into consideration when sentencing. I would also ask My Lady to take into consideration that Mrs Saville was subjected to a beating by Mr Roberts prior to his death. My client was acting in self-defence, and whilst she is pleading guilty to the charge, she was provoked into action. Details of my client's injuries have been previously submitted to the court and are available for review."

"Thank you, Mr Wilkins." The Honourable Lady Griffiths responded. "I have had the opportunity to review those papers during the recess and I will agree to take both of your requests into consideration when sentencing. Mr James, does the prosecution have any concerns with that?"

The slick-suited young man scrambled to his feet, agreeing with his defence colleague.

"Right then. Madeline Saville, will you stand please." The judge looked directly at me. "You have pleaded guilty to the manslaughter of David Roberts. I accept your counsel's plea that you were being attacked at the time of Mr Roberts's death. Notwithstanding that, I do have to recognise that you took this man's life. That is a serious crime, whether provoked or not. Taking everything into consideration, I sentence you to eight years in prison."

She paused as the reality of the sentence hit home.

"Take her down."

With those words, my liberty was over.

As the court guard moved to my side to direct me away, I caught Charles's eye. He stared at me in complete shock, shaking his head slowly.

"I'm sorry." I mouthed a final message as I left the court.

PART THREE- FORGIVENESS

FOUR YEARS LATER

CHAPTER FORTY-NINE

The rattle of keys broke the silence.

The door of my cell flew open and Ruth strode into the space. Ruth had been the warden on my floor for the whole of my stay in Holloway. I guess you could say I am lucky to have her. Ruth is renowned as the kindest prison officer on our wing. She's a big girl whom I have seen crush a woman, with ease, under her armpit in a head lock. Ruth is barrel-shaped, short, dumpy with the most magnificent chest. Her face is shaped like a moon, with her hair scraped back into a ponytail. But she has the most beautiful smile.

If she likes you.

We hit it off immediately. She could see I wasn't a career criminal. The officers know our crimes and must have a good idea which girls will cause them grief and those who will be easy. I wasn't going to give her any trouble. In fact, when I arrived, I was a mess. So scared of the years ahead of me. Rabbit in the headlights was Ruth's first assessment of me. She wasn't far wrong. I think my first few weeks I jumped at my own shadow. This was an alien world for me and I wasn't tough at all. In business I thought I was a confident player, but that all went out the window once the cell door shut on me for the first time. Hysterical sobs had been my comfort that first night.

She has been a good friend to me during my stay; protecting me as much as possible from the bitchiness. The choice of roommate had probably been vetted by her too. She has made sure I haven't been paired with anyone violent despite that fact I'm in there for manslaughter. She didn't have to care like that. I can see the kindness in her that others don't see, maybe because I have taken the time to get to know the woman behind the uniform.

We have talked so much over the years. She knows my back story. Well not all of it. I couldn't tell her the truth about Dave's death. Those first few months I would have made some disastrous mistakes without her quiet words helping me to navigate my way through the informal rules and regulations within Holloway. I soon found out who to avoid, who to befriend and what to do to protect myself from unnecessary attention.

"OK Maddy. Visiting time. You ready?" Ruth holds her arm out as if to usher me from the room. "Is it your lovely friend Stacey?"

Ruth has a bit of a crush on Stacey. It's blatantly obvious. Luckily, Stacey has no idea, probably as she has no interest in the fairer sex. Ruth just admires from a distance and shares far too much of her fantasies with me. Another reason why we seem to get on so well. My friendly guard is more than happy to share her secrets with me and she trusts me to keep her counsel.

"Actually, it's not Stacey today," I reply. "It's my stepdaughter Amelia."

"Wow, she hasn't been for years. What's up? Guilty conscience as your release date is looming?"

Another thing I love about Ruth. She says it as it is. She's not a cruel person, despite the last remark. She just doesn't sugar-coat it.

"I know. I was pretty shocked when I got her visit request. I don't think she's been since the end of my first year. I'm intrigued to know what's up."

Ruth had never probed me as to why my ex-husband never visited. My divorce papers arrived within six months of my trial. Charles must have been working on them before I was sent away. Ever efficient, my Charles. It hurt big time. He hadn't even discussed it with me. Just cracked on and legally separated us.

He has been generous, financially. When I'm released, he has bought me a new home in Teddington, not too far from the family home. He's been renting it out for the last few years and putting the money aside for me. I will have enough money to keep me in a decent state, especially as finding a job will be hard with a criminal record.

Charles has legal custody of Sophie and James for now. He has promised that when I get out, we can talk about joint custody. It's going to be bloody hard for a start. Sophie will be eight and James seven when my release date comes through. I have spent half their life apart from them. They won't remember me so it's going to be so hard for them.

And me.

Stacey keeps me updated on their development. She meets up with Jessica on a monthly basis, who shares stories, pictures and messages from my darling children. I honestly don't know how I could have got through these years without the support of Stacey and Jessica.

The man who I devoted my life to has punished me to the extreme. I know I hurt him and deceived him, but the way he acted after the truth came out has shown me a different side to the man I loved. They talk about a woman spurned and the damage they can wreak, well I know a man can be just as vengeful. His coldness has shocked me deeply. There is no hint of forgiveness. No healing with time. It's like he's just washed his hands of me.

The visitor's room is filling up as Ruth guides me towards my allocated table. Once all the prisoners are seated, they allow the visitors in. I spot Amelia as soon as she enters the room. She stands out. Her clothes speak of money. She hasn't made any attempt to tone it down. Tailored trousers with a cashmere jumper. Jimmy Choo's and an Yves St Laurent handbag are testament to the rich girl impression. I can already see the faces of some of my fellow prisoners, checking her out.

She looks well. Her hair has the most amazing glossy sheen and she carries herself with such confidence. I feel so proud as I watch her strut across the room to me. She doesn't look away but keeps her eyes fixed on me. I've seen this behaviour so often with Stacey; not wanting to make eye contact with any of my fellow inmates.

We go through the normal awkwardness of not being able to hug and sit facing each other. We are both silent at first, mentally checking each other out; observing the changes in our faces and bodies. Mine certainly has not improved over time. My hair has lost its style and sheen and my dress code in here does nothing to flatter. Oh god, I seriously cannot wait to have my hair coloured and professionally cut. It will be one of my first tasks, even before seeing the children. I don't want their first impression of their mother to be this old hag.

"Oh Madeline, it's so good to see you. How are you? You look well." Amelia gushes out words as she blushes with embarrassment. Bless her, she lies well. No-one would describe me as looking well. I look drained.

"I'm OK Amelia darling. It's been a while. You actually do look amazing. So lovely to see you looking so happy." I'm not being sarcastic. She seriously looks good. I would have hated it if I had sacrificed so much, only to see her fade away.

"I'm so sorry I haven't been for so long, Madeline. I feel so guilty." She looks down at her hands placed neatly in her lap.

"Don't be. You have a life to live. Stacey comes most months and she does update me loads on you and the children. How's your father?" Stacey rarely tells me anything about Charles. I think she is still angry with him and, despite them working together, her loyalty is with me.

"He's OK. He misses you. He just isn't the same without you."

"You don't have to say that to please me, darling. I know your father has moved on. He doesn't want me in his life. It's OK. I understand." I reach across the table and touch Amelia's hand gently, quickly checking around to see whether the guard has noticed.

"Madeline, I'm not just saying it. He rushed to distance himself from you when this all first happened. He was angry and reacted. I know my dad, and even though he wouldn't admit it to me, he made a mistake. He should never have divorced you while he was angry and hurt. I'm sorry Madeline, you may not want to hear this but he is still in love with you and misses you like mad." Amelia fixes her eyes on me intently as if she wants to believe her words.

To say I am shocked is an understatement. "Did he ask you to come and see me? Did he tell you to say that?" I'm confused. This certainly wasn't what I was expecting.

"Oh my god, no. He would do his nut if he knew I was talking to you like this. You know what dad is like. He doesn't do emotion. He doesn't even know I'm here today. But Madeline, I have been living with him for the last four years. I've seen how he has been on a rollercoaster of emotions about you. We've spoken loads too. I honestly wouldn't be telling you this if I wasn't confident he loves you and wishes he hadn't been so impetuous."

I laughed. "Impetuous! Oh, come on Amelia. Your dad divorced me within months and I haven't heard a word from him since. He doesn't even send me a birthday card. He can't even console me with any updates on James and Sophie. If it wasn't for Stacey, I would have been kept in the dark all this time." I'm feeling angry now. "So please, don't come here telling me the man who cut me off like a diseased limb, feels anything for me. And also, you are making a big presumption that I don't hate the man for the way he has treated me since then."

Amelia looks shocked at my outburst. We sit in silence for a few moments, each mulling over the conversation. Amelia breaks the awkwardness.

"Sorry, Madeline. I shouldn't have said anything. It's not my place to interfere. That's not even why I came to see you today."

"I'm sorry too, Amelia. I don't want to fall out with you. So, what's up? Tell me your news?"

"Well, I'm getting married." It's at that moment I notice the huge rock on her finger.

"Wow. That's brilliant news, darling. Tell me more. What's his name? What does he do? Picture?"

Amelia wafts her ring in front of us, admiring the stone. "His name is Will. William Sullivan and he works for Sotheby's. He is the most amazing man ever."

She pulls her smartphone out of her handbag and clicks on a photo. He does look a lovely guy. Tall, dark and handsome comes to mind. The photo is of both of them. They look well suited and very much in love.

One of the prison guards walks over and warns Amelia to put her phone away. She complies and shoots the most engaging smile at the bored-looking official. An awkward moment is diffused by her childlike grin.

"I'm so happy for you, Amelia. Congratulations. When is the big day?" I am genuinely delighted for her. After that whole drama with Peter or Dave, she deserves to find happiness at last.

"In August, in under five months. I am so excited, Madeline. We are going to move out to Guildford after the wedding and we will commute into London for work. Will has a house in Guildford. It's beautiful. I think his Mum and Dad lived there for years, but it's been empty since they both died a couple of years ago. Plane crash when they were on holiday in Africa." Amelia pauses. "Will was an only child so we are planning a small do. Just close family and friends. Say you will be there, Madeline? Please come."

The thought of witnessing my stepdaughter's nuptials fills me with mixed emotions. Whilst I will be so enormously proud to watch her walk down the aisle, the thought of facing the whole Saville family fills me with dread. Delay tactics may be my best option.

"Let's see, Amelia darling. I need to get out of here first. I know I have an indicative date but until I walk out those doors, I am not getting complacent. But please pass on my best wishes to your lovely fiancé."

"That's the other thing I need to talk to you about, Madeline." The atmosphere has suddenly changed to be a bit more serious. "I am going to tell Will the truth. I cannot marry him and not tell him. You have got to understand that, Madeline."

Her eyes are pleading with me to understand her emotional quandary. Oh God, I can see why she feels like this. Would you really want to go into a long term relationship with a secret between you? But what a secret. Huge. What if he walks away when he finds out his future wife has killed a man? And what if he tells the authorities about my perjury?

"Shit that is a right nightmare. How do you think Will might take it? If he takes it badly, we are both up shit creek without a paddle, you know that don't you? We both lied. To the police. To our family."

With a sigh I drop my head into my hands. Having spent four years of my life in this place to protect the woman I wronged, I cannot imagine what would happen if this all gets out. The police would definitely arrest Amelia and charge her for the crime and hell, what would happen to me? Seriously I am so relieved that my time here is nearly up. I just cannot afford anything getting in the way of it.

"Madeline, calm down." Amelia can sense my panic. "This is the right thing to do. You must realise that. I love William so much and I will not keep secrets from him. He is a good man and I am confident that he will understand and forgive me."

"I know. I'm being selfish." Reaching across the table I grab her hand. I really don't care if the guards see me. "I'm just so close to getting out of this place. I can imagine holding Sophie and James in my arms. Smelling their freshly washed hair. I don't think I could bear it if they turned down my early release date."

"Madeline, I do understand. I promise you it won't come to that. Trust me. I know the man and I wouldn't be doing this if I didn't trust him with my life. I know my track record isn't the best." She smiled at her own joke. "I have learnt some tough lessons myself in the last four years and one of them is how to spot a decent man. Not a lying, cheating bastard." Amelia laughed awkwardly to dispel the atmosphere.

"OK, I will just have to trust you. Or should I say, I will have to trust Will." My heart is in turmoil. I totally get why Amelia needs to do this. I'm just so scared it will backfire and everything I have put up with for the last few years will be in vain.

"OK ladies, visiting time over." Ruth projects her powerful voice so that we all hear her words.

"Good luck, Amelia. Hopefully, I will see you in a few weeks. Thank you for telling me and for coming to see me. I really appreciate it."

Amelia is on her feet and gathering her belongings together. "I love you,

Madeline. Dad does too and don't ever forget that. See you on the outside."

I watch her walk away and I wish with all my heart I was going with her.

Please God don't let things get out of hand, especially now I am so close to getting my freedom. It's in touching distance. I don't think I will cope if my early release gets blocked.

CHAPTER FIFTY

My last night in here has arrived.

Lying on the bottom bunk bed, I watch the hands of my alarm clock creep slowly towards morning. Sleep has been impossible tonight. My heart is spinning with the events ahead of me. Fear and excitement wash over me in waves as I lie here contemplating the day ahead.

Before lights out, I had a last, long conversation with Lisa my roommate. We have bunked up together for three years now and I honestly could not have asked for a better person to share this narrow room with. Lisa is from Newcastle. She has a terrible addiction to Class A drugs which had been her roadmap to prison. Petty crime then prostitution had taken her away from her childhood home and dumped her on the streets of London, which were certainly not paved in gold for her. One dark, cold night she decided enough was enough. Her pimp was accustomed to beating her up on a fairly regular basis. He pushed it one step too far.

Lisa had snapped and cut his throat. She's doing life and doesn't expect to be out until she's middle aged.

When I first heard her story, I was shocked at the callous way she told me how she enjoyed drawing the knife across his throat. Like some sort of badge of honour. How he had fallen to his knees in front of her as his life blood seeped from his neck. She revelled in the look of surprise on his face as he died slowly, slumping to the floor. How she had searched his pockets for hard cash and drugs before leaving him in an alleyway to be found the next day. She had wanted to know how I felt when I had stabbed Dave. Did I get a thrill?

Of course, I had to make some story up to satisfy her.

But when you get to know the person Lisa, you understand. Here was a kid who had been abused by her own father at the age of 14. A kid who had run away from home to live in a bedsit in Newcastle city centre. Still a child, she was fresh meat for the local pimps and drug dealers. Before she reached 20, she had tried to commit suicide once and had been in hospital twice with drug overdoses. Things had got even rougher for Lisa so she fled to London. Her family had no idea where she was or even if she was alive.

Coming from a caring childhood and privileged marriage, it was impossible for me to understand how wretched Lisa's short life had been. Underneath the hard exterior she is actually a beautiful soul. We have spoken often about our hopes for the future and she does have hope. Something that really surprised me. Knowing the length of her sentence, I just assumed that she would not be making plans. Not Lisa, she has been using her time effectively. She is studying A levels at the moment. She left school with no education, limiting her chances in life. Hopefully by the time she gets out of here, she will have the qualifications to lead her onto a different path.

I have made a promise to keep in touch with Lisa and it's a commitment I know I will keep. At some point in the future, she will need a support structure around her to help her avoid a further yo-yo back into crime. It's the least I can do for her. Alongside Ruth, she has helped to navigate my route through prison life as smoothly as possible.

I owe her everything and when the time comes, I will repay.

Tomorrow is the big day.

I'm feeling so nervous. Stacey has promised to pick me up. She has the keys to my new home and promised me that she will be plying me with wine and a wonderful dinner for my first night out of here. She's offered to stay the night too, which is really generous of her, but deep down I know I will want some time alone. When you spend so much time alone or just with another person in a prison cell, the thought of other people around can be overwhelming.

The thought of seeing my children again in the next few days is scary. I am so desperate to see them; to hold them; to smell them; to kiss them. But what will they think of me? Will they even remember me? It's going to be difficult and I must remember to think about them and how it must feel to be faced with the stranger their mother has become. They will be confused and I need to manage that first meeting carefully.

My gut feel was to try and see them the minute I got home. Lisa had been a great verbal punchbag this evening. She listened to me ranting on about my needs and what I wanted. Once I had spilled my heart out, she just looked at me and called me a selfish bitch.

That hurt.

But once she explained her reasoning, it became glaringly clear. Sophie and James are not toys to be put down and picked up again when you can. They are small, human beings with minds which are developing at a pace. The mistakes I could make over the coming days could shape our relationship for ever.

So, less haste.

I need to take it step by step and gently introduce myself to my children again. Like a frightened kitten, I need to regain their trust. Love for their mother will follow unless I balls it up, focusing on my needs.

Thank the lord for the wise words of an ex-addict who knows all there is to know about crap parents.

Tomorrow is now today. Just stay calm and count down the minutes until I breathe the fresh air of freedom. Hopefully at last my nightmare is coming to an end.

I have paid for my behaviour twice over.

Now I will begin my life again. Not everyone gets a second chance to make up for their stupid mistakes. This is mine. And I will not mess it up.

I promise.

CHAPTER FIFTY-ONE

I feel sick.

The children are due to arrive any minute. Jessica is bringing them over for their first visit to mine. I have cleaned the house from top to bottom, despite only being there for a week; it has hardly got messy in that time. I am just so desperate to make a good first impression. I really do need to calm down or I will make such a mess of this.

And breathe.

The last week has been strange to say the least. The noise and bustle of the outside has blown my mind. I know I was only locked up for four years, but it's hard to understand how different it feels when you don't hear the noises of cars and buses. Night-time has felt so weird too. Not hearing the shouts of other women; not hearing Lisa snore all night. The comfort of a soft mattress and sweet-smelling bedding has been a luxury I had really missed. The joy of spreading out across my double bed like a starfish has been beautiful.

My transformation from prison inmate to mother is complete. An early trip to my hair salon led to a new, fresh colour and an exciting bob style. It's very different to my old hairdo but seems to fit with the new me. Most of my clothes had been in storage while I've been away, and I spent some interesting hours sorting through to find out what fits. I've dropped a dress size in prison, a combination of lack of decent food and no wine, along with a personal exercise routine. God, I missed the wine. Anyway, it is so much easier to exercise when you have nothing else to do.

It helped me keep sane on those long days of nothing to do. And no wine.

I have salvaged enough from my old wardrobe for now. It may not have the variety from before but there is enough to make me look presentable. My confidence levels aren't yet strong enough to venture out alone. The thought of clothes shopping scares me. Stacey came to the hairdressers with me, coaxing me out of the house. It was like encouraging a small, frightened deer out into the open. And like the jittery deer, I bolted back inside as soon as I could.

It is a strange feeling being free again. But a nice feeling.

Having the choice to do things when you want rather than when you are told to. Even so, I don't feel ready to meet old friends, even by chance. Think I will need to build up to that gradually. Other than a welcome home card, I haven't spoken to Charles. Amelia has rung a few times but I let it go to answerphone. Texting her back, I reassured her I am fine and will catch up with her soon. I want to get the big milestone of seeing the kids out of the way first. I have been so stressed about the simple chance of seeing my babies that I cannot focus on the rest of the family just yet.

A car pulls up onto the drive.

I can feel my stomach doing somersaults as I peer out behind the curtains. Jessica steps out of the car and releases the children from the back seat. My children. Oh, they are so grown up. I have missed them so much. I gasp with shock and shake my head, trying to clear my thoughts and focus on them; not me. I can feel the tears pushing at my eyeballs, trying to escape. I brush them away with a sleeve.

This is not about me, remember. It is all about my beautiful children.

Jessica flings herself into my arms in a gesture she would never have made before. We always maintained a level of professional distance in the past. I kiss her soundly on each cheek, noticing the tears which are falling down her cheeks. With my fingers I push them away into her hair to hide the evidence from her charges. Meanwhile, Sophie stands hesitantly behind her nanny. James clutches his sister's hand. My little babies look lost as they stare at this woman in front of them, their mother. My heart rips looking at their little faces; confused and weary.

"Come in, come in," I stammer over my words.

I lead them into the lounge where Jessica fusses over coats and shoes while I just gaze at my beautiful children. Sophie has lost the chubby baby face and is already blossoming into an exceptionally attractive young girl. Her long blond hair is tied back into two long plaits which she twirls as she stands and stares at me. She has a summer Joules dress on and matching cardy. James continues to hold Sophie's hand and is twirling his finger around his soft brown curls. He is dressed in jeans and a sweatshirt with the most adorable trainers.

The hair twirling of both children confirms their nerves. In a strange way it is reassuring to know it's not just me who is worried about today. These children have been through so much in their short lives. Being separated from me has to have impacted on their developing personalities. It's so easy for me and Charles to worry about our relationship, but we are adults and have made life choices. For our children, these choices have been thrust upon them, whether they like it or not.

"Here we go Sophie, James, I have put out some juice for you. And biscuits. Help yourselves."

Gingerly they edge over to the coffee table, watching me as they go. Jessica had suggested, when we spoke last night, that we ignore them initially and let them settle with a drink while we chat. Best not to bombard them with questions and conversation and let them come to me when ready.

The children must dictate the pace.

Jessica and I speak softly to each other. I cannot tell you what we talked about as I was really not paying any attention. I'm trying my hardest not to look at Sophie or James, which is killing me. I want to drink them in with my eyes, but the last thing I want is to freak them out. Jessica smiles at me and nods her head, drawing my eyes towards my side. Suddenly I feel little fingers probing my hand, trying to hold it. Taking a grip, James pulls himself up onto my lap and snuggles his head into my breasts. My heart is literally breaking with joy and I stifle a cry. My eyes are welling up with tears, but I hold them back.

"Mummy, I missed you," whispered James. His thumb finds its way into his mouth.

"Oh James, I missed you too. Mummy's back now. I promise." My voice cracks with emotion. Jessica is clearly crying now and turns away from the children.

Not to be left out, Sophie walks over to join us. She wriggles her bottom onto the sofa next to me and reaches out for my other hand.

"Why did you go away, Mummy?" Children's questions are normally frank. They don't employ strategies to soften their way around a difficult subject.

The elephant has trumpeted its way into the room.

I have spent four years preparing for this conversation. Even with that preparation it is the most difficult subject to face. "Mummy did a very naughty thing, darling. Mummy is very sorry for what happened but I had to go away for a while to show how sorry I was. But it's all OK now and I won't leave you again. I promise."

I don't think Sophie is totally convinced. "But why haven't you come home to stay with Daddy, James and me."

"Well, I let Daddy down and I upset him. Me and Daddy think it is best that we live in different houses for now. You and James can come and stay with me whenever you want, darlings."

Sophie's little face is working out whether she will let me off with that. Clearly not. "But, Mummy, I want you to come home to our house. I don't want to stay here. I want my room, with my toys."

My heart is breaking with the joy of seeing my darlings, tempered with the sadness that I cannot give them everything they want. "Sophie darling, Mummy needs to stay here for now. I have missed you and James so much sweetie. Maybe in the next couple of days we can have a day out together and a sleep over here. We can have pizza and watch a movie. What do you think?"

James is wriggling against my chest and I can tell he is nodding his head. Sophie takes a bit more effort but I can see the promise of pizza is winning her over. I know it's shocking that I'm using bribes to win over their support but needs must.

It doesn't take long for Sophie to decide having two bedrooms may be a great option. Suddenly she kneels up on the sofa and wraps her arms around my neck. "I love you Mummy." She whispers in my hair.

"I love you too sweetheart" I whisper back.

It will take baby steps to build up my relationship with my children. I must remember to focus totally on their needs and push the selfish bitch part of my nature into the past. It will be difficult. I'm not kidding myself on the challenge ahead. But families survive breakdowns and mine will too.

In the months and years ahead, things must get easier. I have to believe that. It's what has got me through the last four years.

CHAPTER FIFTY-TWO

I had literally just eased my body down into the bathwater when the doorbell went.

"Oh shit."

I'm not expecting anyone. Especially not at this time. It's 10pm. Who comes calling at this time of day?

The doorbell chimes again breaking my much awaited peace and quiet. I had been looking forward to a lazy bath surrounded by candles. A huge glass of wine is winking at me, tempting me into its red mist. It's a treat I have missed so much over the last few years. You honestly don't realise how much the simple pleasures are missed when they are denied you.

Many a night I lay on the uncomfortable bunk bed dreaming of a hot soak. The smells of luxury bubble bath enveloping me in memories. Bath time in prison consists of a quick shower in front of other inmates. I have never been one for 'all girls together.' That was a real challenge for me to adjust to a total lack of privacy. Other women staring at your body as you have a quick sluice was something I never got used to.

Easing my body out of the warm bubbles, I grab a towel and vigorously dry as much as I can. My towelling bathrobe is hanging on the bathroom door so I struggle into it as I make my way downstairs. The doorbell goes again and I shout out to confirm I'm on my way. Whoever my late night visitor is, they are persistent.

Putting the chain across, I peer out of the crack. "Charles. What are you doing here?"

My ex is standing in the porch with a look of thunder on his face. What the hell have I done now?

"Let me in, Madeline."

His tone is matter-of-fact, cold, with very little emotion. This is the first time I have seen Charles since my release. It is the first time I have seen him since my day in court. Even though it's been three whole weeks since my release, I haven't had a peep from him. All interactions with Sophie and James have been via Jessica. I have seen Amelia a few times but not a word from Charles. I guess I shouldn't have expected to see him. I thought he was just giving me space to adjust before he started discussing formal stuff.

Charles doesn't seem to notice my state of undress as he strides into the lounge. He makes himself at home, dropping onto my sofa.

He's changed.

We all have. It's been four years; what can I expect. The years haven't been kind to either of us. Charles has aged. Bags under his eyes give him a hangdog expression. He has lost weight too. It doesn't sit well on his frame. His shirt hangs rather than the snug fit of old. I'm shocked to see the changes in the man I had loved with all my heart.

Suddenly I have an overwhelming desire to hold him; or for him to hold me. Totally inappropriate looking at the sternness of his face.

Shaking myself out of my contemplations, I decide on action. "Drink?"

I wander over to the cabinet where I have a decent scotch, Charles's tipple. I honestly don't know why I bought it as I hardly ever touch the stuff. It reminds me of those dreadful hours after Dave's murder. Old habits, I guess. I pour Charles a slug and retrieve my opened bottle of red, along with a fresh glass. I perch on the chair opposite him, rearranging my bathrobe in an attempt to cover my modesty. I can feel tendrils of hair starting to drop out of my hair tie so break the stillness by fiddling with that.

"Honestly, Madeline. I really don't know where to start." Charles stares straight at me.

"Well, why don't you give me a clue, Charles? I haven't heard from you for four years and all of a sudden you turn up on my doorstep with a face like a bulldog chewing a wasp. What's up?" I smile trying to break the mood.

"Why didn't you fucking tell me?"

Charles very rarely swears so now I am worried. What the hell have I done now? And why is my current default position to believe I have done something wrong?

"Tell you what, Charles? I honestly don't know what this is about so please just tell me. What have I done?"

"It's what you didn't do that's bothering me." Charles leaves a dramatic pause. "You didn't kill Dave Roberts. Did you? Why didn't you and Amelia tell me the truth?" Charles takes a deep slug of whiskey.

Oh no, Amelia. Why didn't she warn me? Glancing down, I notice my mobile on the coffee table and can see missed calls from my stepdaughter. Damn. Oh well, here goes. Now is the time to come clean to Charles after all these years of deception.

"So, I guess Amelia has talked to you. I didn't want her to, Charles. You have to believe me. She told me she was going to tell William as she didn't want to go into a marriage with secrets." My words peter out as I watch Charles looking at me. The sadness in his eyes is evident.

"Oh Madeline, why? Why did you take the blame? Why did you let me believe it was all your fault?" He looks broken. His face has gone from anger to sadness.

I'm really not sure how to handle this. So perhaps the truth is the best policy.

"Charles, how could I let Amelia take the blame? She stabbed him to save me. She reacted instinctively. He was kicking me in the head and stomach. It was horrible and Amelia walked in on the attack. She must have been so frightened and reacted. She saved my life. What else could I do?" Charles is listening intently. "It was my fault all this happened in the first place. If I hadn't been such a fool and had an affair with that bastard, none of this would have happened. I hurt everyone that mattered to me. There was no way I was going to let Amelia's life be ruined."

Charles groaned.

"I really had no choice, Charles. Once we agreed that I would say it was me, there was no going back. The police didn't believe me at first. The state Amelia was in, it helped. They didn't suspect her at all."

"But why didn't you tell me? I could have helped. We could have figured something out between us surely?" Charles is wringing his hands together; his scotch forgotten.

"How could I? It would have destroyed you. I could not have you thinking Amelia had killed someone. Even if it wasn't really her fault. She's your little baby. How could I do that to you? I had hurt you enough Charles." My eyes are willing him to believe me. "I had made such a mess of everything. This was the least I could do to stop Amelia paying the price for my stupidity."

"Oh, Madeline. I'm so sorry. I have been such a fool." Charles drops his head into his hands. "I was so angry with you. I should have known something wasn't right. I turned my back on you when you needed me the most. You sacrificed yourself for my daughter; and I treated you like shit."

Shifting from my seat, I move over to where Charles is sitting and kneel at his feet. I reach out and touch his arm trying to get his attention. He slowly raises his gaze towards me.

"I did you wrong, Charles. I am so desperately sorry that I hurt you. If I could go back and do it all again, I would do it so differently. Except I would still cover for Amelia. It was the right thing to do and I honestly will never ask for your forgiveness for that." I squeezed his arm gently. "The last four years have been so hard. I missed the children every day. But that was my penance for the wrong I did you and the family."

"I missed you, Madeline. So much. My stupid pride got in the way and I let you down just when you needed me most. I never stopped loving you." Charles's eyes pierce into mine. He is willing me to believe him. "I still love you."

I wasn't expecting that. After everything that has passed between us. There is still love. I know deep down that I feel the same. Oh yes, I have been so angry with Charles for his coldness; for punishing me by withdrawing his heart. That anger helped me get through the hard days without losing my head completely. But there is a fine line between love and hate. It's a line

I'm about to cross.

"I love you too, Charles." And I mean it, deeply.

Reaching forward I kiss his lips.

He grabs hold of my head, pulling me into him. I gasp with the need building in me. Suddenly his fingers reach inside my bathrobe and gently caress my breast. We are both panting with a built-up need and desire.

Rising, I take his hand and lead him upstairs to my bed.

That was not the way I expected my evening to go.

But what a perfect way to forgive each other.

CHAPTER FIFTY-THREE

The door closed gently behind me.

These days I do everything with a little less noise. I guess I have got used to silence. I value its silky tone. The adjustment to normal family life is going to be tough. But a tough pleasure, I embrace with enthusiasm. The boisterous chatter of the children is a welcome change from the clunk of cell doors and the grinding clink of keys shutting me away for the night.

Sophie and James stand at the other end of the hallway holding Jessica's hands. She smiles, encouraging me forward. Charles, noticing my trepidation, gently places his arm under mine and guides me across the floor. The house looks similar but different at the same time. My stamp is missing from the place I called home, but it will come back.

In time.

Sensing the children's lack of patience with my cautious approach, I nod my head and Jessica releases her charges. Both children are in my arms within seconds. I smell their hair, overwhelmed by their scents. I have missed that so much over the last four years. It's the little things in life which become so valuable when you lose them. You adjust to the lack of comfortable clothes, luxury bedding and quality food. I have never adjusted to missing four years of my children's lives. That was the final twist of that bastard's knife. He took my children away from me.

May he rot in hell.

Sophie dances from foot to foot with excitement. Her relief was obvious when Charles and I spoke to her about me moving back home. She had not bought into the idea of sharing time separately with both parents. After all the change in her short life, she is determined to keep me close. James is that bit younger and at the age where he accepts what's happening with little complaint. I realise that both my children have been damaged mentally because of my mistakes. I will do all I can to give them the stability they need now to grow.

I will repair my family.

I will not let the legacy of Dave Roberts damage this family any longer. We will heal and grow together as a unit without the stain of his actions creeping into our thoughts. He is dead. And will remain dead in my head. Despite the ghosts of memories which overwhelm me as I enter my home.

All too soon the children are off. Their attention is easily distracted. Their mother is home. Children have an uncanny knack of adjusting to changed situations. They are far more resilient than us adults. I think it's all about trust. Children trust the adult in the room to do the right thing for them. They are secure in that knowledge. Perhaps Sophie and James will take time to get used to my presence back in the house, but I think the bigger adjustment will be for me.

Charles is hanging back as I wander through the rooms of our home, reintroducing myself to the familiar surroundings. I smile at various pieces of furniture I have missed and gently wipe my fingers across the oak table, enjoying the sensual feeling of the luxurious wood.

Finally, I reach the kitchen. It's the room I have been dreading.

Surprisingly the kitchen looks the same. I had expected changes considering the carnage which took place there. I thought Charles and Amelia would have stripped out the units and tried something new. To escape the dreadful memories, especially for Amelia. Surely looking at the site of her future husband's murder would have driven her mad.

But no, everything is the same. I walk around the island touching the familiar cupboards and work surfaces. I stare at the floor tiles and, in my head, I can see the blood seeping across the surface as the life was sucked out of Dave.

Then it becomes clear to me. Amelia didn't want to hide from the events of that dreadful night. It was her way of coping with the enormity of what happened and the decisions we both made that night, which had huge consequences for our family. It wasn't some ghoulish need to be reminded of the bloodshed, but a nod to what happened and a need to move on together and face the consequences together.

Charles senses my troubled thoughts and comes to stand beside me. His fingers entwine with mine and he squeezes gently as we acknowledge the challenges ahead. We have found our way back to each other. Forgiveness can be a difficult path, but it's a journey we have committed to travelling together.

Because the truth is, Dave Roberts can no longer hurt us. He is dead. He has gone from our lives completely.

CHAPTER FIFTY-FOUR

We are awaiting the arrival of the bride with anticipation.

Sitting with me on the front pew are James, Jessica and Bella. Keeping James still is a nightmare. He literally has ants in his pants. James is excited to see his big sisters walking down the aisle. Amelia had asked James to be a page boy, but he really didn't want to be the centre of attention. In contrast, Sophie squealed with delight when she found out she was to be a flower girl. She hasn't come down since.

I gaze around the congregation. Further along our pew, nearer the aisle, sit Catherine and Roger. Catherine looks amazing in a pale blue dress and the most enormous hat ever. It suits her though. It adds an air of mystery to the mother of the bride. Roger is relaxed as he doesn't have any responsibilities today. Charles was a nervous wreck at breakfast this morning. He is so used to being at the centre of business negotiations, but the thought of walking his precious daughter down the aisle has freaked him out.

He is determined that today will be special.

For all of us.

It's a fresh start.

Catherine and Roger have taken me back into their hearts; delighted at our family reunion. We haven't really spoken about what happened that dreadful night. I understand Amelia has talked to Catherine and told her the full story. The only gesture of awareness was when Catherine saw me for the first time after I moved back into Charles's bed. She enfolded me in her arms and kissed my forehead, whispering the words "bless you darling."

Since that day, we have not mentioned it again. A very British behaviour, but a sensible one. No need to go over the past forensically. Amelia shared her secret with William and, like the gentleman he is, he took the news with stoicism and understanding. He has kept her secret from his friends. His view was that there was no need for wider knowledge. The fact that he has no immediate family obviously helps. It will remain a closely guarded secret within the extended Saville family.

Sophie and James were delighted when I moved back in. It took some time for us all to get used to the family dynamics. My fear of crowds has started to dissipate, but I still find it hard sometimes when the children are at their most excited and the noise levels hit the roof. At those times you will find me sneaking off to a quiet space for a bit of 'me time'. Charles understands and will divert the children for an hour or so until my nerves are calm.

I have missed so much of the children's lives due to my incarceration.

I have had to relearn their likes and dislikes. Knowing how to interact with my daughter as she grows has been an interesting experience. Sophie is very demanding and has a tendency to act like a spoilt brat. Carefully, I am negotiating my way back into mother mode. Setting her boundaries and taking over disciplinary strategies from her father has been important.

Charles showered both Sophie and James with love during my absence. Understandable, but his behaviour has made it hard to change the focus without seeming to be the evil parent. Sophie and I have had a few humdingers when I have tried to lay down the law. It cut to the bone when she shouted at me that she hated me and wished I was still in prison. The argument was soon forgotten, but it hurt just the same.

James is a sweetheart. He is such a gentle soul who permanently seems to be happy. He has adjusted to the change in family dynamic better than his sister. If anything, he has become more clingy with me and I can see his eyes following me around a room. It's as if he thinks I'm going to disappear if his back is turned.

Having the consistency of Jessica in their lives during my absence has been so important to them. I raise a silent prayer for finding Jessica. She is not just a fantastic au pair, but a loyal friend and part of our family. Her relationship with Bella is going from strength to strength. Bella proposed last summer when they were on holiday in New York.

So, another wedding to come in the near future.

Since our reunion, I have made some big decisions about the future. I had plenty of time to think during my time at Her Majesty's Pleasure. Working together and living together is not going to work for us going forward. Charles has been really supportive and isn't putting any pressure on me to work. Getting a new job will be hard with a criminal record, so I am currently exploring the idea of setting up my own consultancy company.

My relationship with Charles is beautiful.

We delight in spending time together. Charles has become even more attentive, checking in on me during the day whilst he's at work. It's not an intrusive checking up on me; it's quite endearing. Our love life is strong. We hold each other a little bit tighter and love each other a little bit harder every day. It will take time for Charles to trust me completely and I am determined to spend the rest of my days justifying his love and care for me.

The church organ springs into life booming out the opening cords to the Wedding March. As the congregation stands, I get to see my wonderful husband gently guiding his beloved daughter down the aisle. Ahead of them walks Sophie looking picture-perfect. Her blushing pink dress is designed like a milkmaid of old, with ruffled skirts held up in drapes decorated with rosebuds. Her hair is festooned with flowers and her ringlets halo her face like an angel. She holds a basket of rose petals, which she is liberally spreading on the flagstones ahead of the beautiful bride.

Charles is beaming with pride. He looks amazing in his top hat and tails. I feel a stirring as I watch him enjoying the sensation of all his family and friends watching his big day. He is the best thing that ever happened to me.

How did I ever put that at risk?

But today is about the future, not the past.

Amelia is smiling as she walks beside her father. Her dress is simple. A figure-hugging lace gown which bears no resemblance to her previous one. She floats gracefully down the aisle, acknowledging her friends as she passes. As she draws level with me, our eyes meet.

She mouths the words, "Thank you, Madeline."

We both understand what she means.

Our lives are interlinked and will be so for ever.

We both have our happy ever afters ahead of us.

CAROLINE REBISZ

The End

ABOUT THE AUTHOR

Caroline Rebisz enjoyed over 30 years working in the Financial Services sector. After taking early retirement she was determined to fulfil her passion for writing. As a child she wrote stories but the business of working and raising a family put that passion on the backburner.

 Her first book, A Mother's Loss, is published via Amazon Books. A Costly Affair is the author's second novel. A Mother's Deceit published in early 2022 is a prequel to A Mother's Loss.

Caroline lives in Wiltshire with her husband and their cat Elsie.

Printed in Great Britain
by Amazon